The Case of the Lady in the Luggage

A Cruise Ship Cozy Mystery

Cheri Baker

Published by Adventurous Ink, Seattle

First edition. November 20, 2020.

978-1-952200-08-3

Book design by Patrick Baker
Cover art by Cheri Baker

6BF5261DFE

Chapter One

ELLIE TAPPET BOUNDED OUT OF bed with a song in her heart. Who needed an alarm on such a beautiful morning? She turned on the television that hung alongside her twin bed like a digital window. The sunny skies of Miami flooded her tiny stateroom, and the live feed of the starboard view confirmed the forecast she'd read in *Cruise News You Can Use*. It would be eighty-eight degrees in Miami without so much as a cloud in the sky. She hummed a cheerful tune as she showered, dressed, and applied her favorite rose colored lipstick. After putting on her necklace and sliding the tiny golden cross into the center, above her heart, she checked her appearance in the mirror hanging on her stateroom door. Satisfied, she put her crew badge in her shorts pocket, turned off the screen, and headed toward the captain's stateroom.

Living and working aboard the *Adventurous Spirit* had taught her to carve out moments where her life was fully her own. Ben was always busy with work, and so was she! But they'd found one hour per day where they could be together, no matter what. And if their hour happened to be at six in the morning, so be it. Ellie had always been an early bird, and Ben was the same way. In the early morning, her mind felt like a clean sheet of paper, ready for whatever came next. By dinner time her mental scratch pad would be full of scribbles. As the ship's social coordinator, she lived and worked in *The Lofts*, the ship's area for solo travelers, and there was always someone that needed her help. Sometimes they wanted to know what excursions to take at port, and sometimes they needed advice on a personal matter. She loved every bit of it. Most of the time, she felt like a productive honeybee in the center of a massive hive. The days went by in a blink and the months sped by even faster.

She smiled to herself and thought, *Really, I don't know how they survived so long without me.*

The quiet melody in her heart played louder as she ran up the wide-beamed, blue-carpeted stairs and turned left on the upper platform. Ben was waiting for her with a room service breakfast. Some days, like today, she imagined she could feel his anticipation as strongly she felt her own. It was as if they were two strong magnets, and every morning they flew through the ship toward one another. Her steps were becoming hops, and she was halfway to a jog! Smiling, she forced herself to slow down. Victor Vasquez, the Hotel Director, took a dim view of running in the halls. The mental image of his dour expression amused her. She was running in the halls? Rushing off to see her boyfriend? Sometimes she felt like twirling around on one foot at the mere sound of his name: Benjamin Spark. How strange it was to be a teenager again in her sixties! Ellie's excitement propelled her forward through the ship, past the servers delivering room service breakfasts on their white-sheeted carts, past the darkened storefronts, already closed for turnover day, and through the long winding line of guests at *Cuppa*, the ship's tiny Italian-style cafe.

In about an hour, their guests would begin to disembark. The ship would be reprovisioned at the dock, and the cleaning crew would scrub the *Spirit* from top to bottom, mopping, cleaning, and tossing fresh white linens over more than a thousand stripped-down beds. There would be a brief pause after the ship emptied out, like the stillness between two deep breaths, but before long a new group of guests would stampede aboard feeling ready to party, rest, and play. Turnover day was old hat now. She'd been through it dozens of times, and it formed a regular part of the rhythm of life at sea.

She reached the forward stairwell and pressed her badge against the black plastic pad until it beeped. Then she descended the stairs all the way down to the crew level. When she reached a nondescript door labeled 101, she tugged her shirt down, smoothed her silver hair, and knocked softly. The door opened a scant inch. Ben's blue eye looked her up and down from beneath the dark slash of his eyebrow. "Yes? May I help you?"

She stood on tiptoe to put her eye level with his, resting her hands lightly against the wall and the door to keep balance. "I'd like a word with the captain," she said primly. "I have a complaint about the service."

Ben sighed with mock-weariness and opened the door wider. "If you insist." As soon as she stepped inside, he pressed the door shut behind her and gently pushed her against it, kissing her with enough passion to make her forget where she was or what she'd been thinking about earlier. After a moment (or was it longer?) he stepped back, cleared his throat, and made an apologetic gesture. "Ahem. Sorry, ma'am. You said you had a complaint?"

She looked up at him. "Well, I was going to say that I missed you. But you took care of that, didn't you?"

"So, you don't miss me anymore?" He sounded faintly disappointed.

"I'll miss you next week. Plenty."

After several delays, including the shocking murder of Morgan Picklewick, half-owner of the cruise line, she was finally taking a proper vacation. It had been far too long since she'd been home! She couldn't wait to see her boys and Marcie, to hug her granddaughter, and to check in on the house she'd left behind. Her regular video calls with the family were a gift, to be sure, but they were a poor replacement for hugs and kisses and breathing the same air.

Junior was an officer with the Gainesville police department, just like his father had been before him. He was married to Marcie, a good-hearted woman with an unfortunate tendency to treat Ellie like she was older than Moses. Their daughter, two-year-old Clara, was a brilliant little girl, full of attitude and sweetness in equal measure. And Ellie's youngest son Cole worked as a special needs instructor at the same school district where Ellie had once taught. She missed them so much that it felt like she'd ripped out a piece of her heart and left it onshore.

She followed Ben toward the small table where he'd set out their breakfast. "How was the docking? Any problems?" The *Spirit* had arrived at port in the wee hours of the morning, while she and most of the guests were still sleeping.

Ben sat down and poured her a cup of tea from a silver carafe. "No problems. Granted, we're in and out of PortMiami so often that this feels like my personal driveway. I could pilot us in with my eyes closed." He grinned. "Not that I would."

"I don't even like driving my son's pickup truck," Ellie admitted. "I can't imagine parking a ship this big."

Ben patted the wall of his stateroom with a fond expression. "Ah, she's not so big. 848 feet long, 123.4 feet wide at the max beam, and shy of eighty thousand tons. She's a dainty little thing, really. And quite the beauty." He looked over at her in the way that always made her heart melt.

"Enough of that," she said, smiling at him. "I'm starving and if we don't eat, I won't get a bite until lunch." She picked up her fork. "I do wish we had more time together."

Ben looked pleased. "Well, I'm not going anywhere, El." Always the gentleman, he waited until she'd taken a bite before digging into his own breakfast. "Besides, you've definitely earned a break. You've been missing your family for too long, and you've been doing Roberta's job as well as your own. That's a lot for one person."

As a reward for catching Morgan Picklewick's killer, the owners of *Adventurous Cruises* had given her a five percent stake in the cruise line. And as soon as the ink was dry on the paperwork, Roberta Crowley had announced it was time for her annual trip to New York. She'd handed over her keys and her emergency radio, and she'd said 'don't let the business sink' before rushing off, her butler Stuart on one arm, and a cadre of porters hauling a mountain of suitcases behind her.

Ellie settled her napkin in her lap. "I'm happy to fill in for Roberta, but I don't like the way the crew looks at me now."

"What do you mean?"

She thought back to some of her recent interactions with the crew. "They stand up straighter when I walk by. Their mouths snap shut like mousetraps when they see me. And they work even harder, like they're trying to prove something. It's like they think I'm the boss of them, and I'm going to get them in trouble."

Ben nodded. "The same thing happened when I became captain. It comes with the job, El. People want to make a good impression with the boss."

"But I'm *not* the boss," Ellie insisted. "I'm just the social coordinator for *The Lofts*, and I don't manage anyone! Some words on a piece of paper shouldn't matter so much."

"Well, being an owner comes with some perks, at least. Did you take Roberta up on her offer to get you a nicer stateroom?" Ben asked, pausing with his fork in the air.

"No. I wouldn't be able to do my job half so well if I didn't live in *The Lofts.* And besides, I see no reason to move out of my room until..."

"Until what?"

Her face felt warm. Ben understood that her faith was important to her. Did he view her as hopelessly old-fashioned? If her caution bothered him, he'd never said anything. "Until I have a *very good* reason to," she said, leaving it at that, sipping her tea to cover her awkwardness. She nudged the big wooden chest below the tabletop with one toe. The table was acrylic, and the chest served as the base. It looked like a pirate chest out of a movie and it had a big bronze keyhole on the front. "I've been meaning to ask you. Where did you get this?"

If he noticed the abrupt change of subject, he didn't show it. "Oh! You'll like this story. Madame Tiffany gave it to me the first time I met her."

Madame Tiffany was the name of a shopkeeper and psychic on the tiny Caribbean island of St. John in the US Virgin Islands. Not that Ellie believed in psychics. Still,

Madame Tiffany was a kind woman, and her store held many unique treasures. "You bought it at her shop?" Ellie asked.

"No, I mean she literally gave it to me. I had a few hours of shore leave one day — it wasn't too long before you came aboard, actually — and I was headed to Honeymoon Beach."

"I love that place! We should go there sometime."

"Well, I stopped because I needed sunscreen, and—"

"Wait. You went to a fortune teller to get *sunscreen*?"

"You know how tourist towns are. They always have things like sunscreen and cheap sunglasses in a bin by the register. Anyway, we got to talking, and Tiff said—"

"You call her Tiff?"

"What can I say?" Ben grinned. "We're kindred spirits. We were talking about something — I don't remember what — and she didn't have any sunscreen. So I was looking for something to buy. She had some hand-sewn leather journals, and I had my eye on one with a sailboat on it. And she said, 'I have something even better for you.' Then she goes into the back and drags this big chest out and says, 'You're meant to have this.' She wouldn't take no for an answer, and she refused to let me pay for it. But she did loan me a dolly to wheel it back to the ship." He shrugged. "I never did make it to Honeymoon Beach."

"What did she mean by you were 'meant to have it'?" Ellie ran her toe along the front of the wooden chest. It was made of dark wood planks and while they appeared tightly fitted the chest had seen better days. There was a long slash along one side, scuff marks in several places, and it was wrapped with a pair of wide metal bands that were discolored with age.

"Who knows? But when I managed to get the thing into my room — it took three of us to do it, by the way — and I cracked it open, it was empty and clean inside. So I use it to store my books." He nudged it experimentally with one foot and grunted in satisfaction when it did not budge.

"You and your ships," she teased. "You work on a ship, and you read about spaceships in your spare time. You're a man obsessed." She ran her toe along the rough-textured wood. "It was nice of her to give you a present. But also, kind of weird."

"Maybe it was taking up too much space in the back?" Ben waved his hands in the air. "I have seen your future! And it involves clearing unwanted merchandise from my storage room!"

They both laughed. "Well, I might not approve of fortune telling; I think it's rather presumptuous to claim you know the future," Ellie said, "but she's a lovely person. She told me that the pen I chose mattered a great deal to my writing."

"Was she right?" he asked.

"I suppose she was. I finally finished my romance novel. I'm calling it *The Captain's Kiss*, and I let Roberta take it with her to New York to read."

"Roberta?" Ben's eyebrows shot up. "I didn't know she liked romances. She strikes me as more of a Vogue magazine and Machiavelli type." Ben buttered a slice of toast and bit into it. A moment later, he added. "Wait. Why did you let Roberta read it, but not me?"

"Well, Roberta doesn't mince words, as you know. And I'm new at this so I could use someone who will tell me the truth." She reached under Ben's arm to tickle him lightly in the ribs. "Besides, if I let you read *The Captain's Kiss* you'll just flip forward to the smoochy parts."

"I might. I do like the smoochy parts." He leaned forward to prove himself. When he pulled away, he asked, "And the book *is* about me, right?"

"Sure," she said, laughing a little. "You're a spitting image of the hero in the story. Right down to the sword and the fabulous hat."

"Hey, I could pull off a fabulous hat!" He pretended to glare at her, and she laughed. When spending time with Ben, laughter always came easily, and no matter how happy she felt upon her arrival, she felt even better after seeing him. *You are my joy*, she thought, too shy to say the words aloud. *And I hope that I can become yours.*

After their breakfast was gone, she reluctantly checked her watch. "I should say goodbye to my guests." She stacked empty plates on the breakfast tray. "These last few cruises have gone so *fast*! I can't believe I'm heading home next week. I haven't even thought about what to pack."

"Well, you have all week to figure it out. But while we're on the subject of you heading home, there's something I've been meaning to ask you."

"Yes?" Her heart skipped a beat.

"What do Junior and Cole think about their Mom dating someone? I didn't want to pry, but I'm curious."

She averted her eyes and loaded up her fork with a stray bite of freshly cut fruit. "Oh, the kids are fine." As she said the words, her gut twisted. She hadn't exactly *told* the kids about Ben. Well, she'd mentioned him, twice. And she'd said he was a good friend. But as for the rest of her news, it could wait until the family was together in person. It was bound to be a shock to the kids, she thought. After all, she'd left home a grieving wife and mother and she'd be returning home in a different state of mind. The whole thing felt too awkward to discuss over the phone.

And it was hard to know how the kids would react to her dating someone. Junior might take it especially hard. He'd idolized Ronnie enough to follow him right into the police force. Hopefully, the kids would understand that she didn't want to be alone for the rest of her life. Ronnie had given her his blessing before he'd passed, and even though those words had been so hard to hear back then, even though they'd *infuriated* her at the time, she'd come to see them as a gift.

She touched the little cross at her neck. *You're always with me*, she thought with a familiar tenderness. She caught Ben watching and dropped her hand to her side.

Ben glanced down at his heavy silver watch. The interior was dark blue and crammed with dials. Sometimes she imagined his mind working like that wristwatch, always on the move, always full of information. This was her Ben, the man who liked to navigate by the stars and who read big books at night 'to relax.' There was a keen mind in that head of his, and she'd only scratched the surface of getting to know him.

"Well, I need to go call the port agent," Ben said, getting up to his feet. "Devon keeps getting shorted on bananas and he made me pinky swear that he'll never be bananaless again. Oh, and before I forget, Billy wants you to stop by the photography desk around noon today. Something about signing off on new flyers for *The Lofts*? He said there's a deadline for the printer, and he'll be waiting for you at twelve."

"Sure. I can do that." She stepped close to Ben and wrapped her arms around his waist, leaning her head against his shoulder. They rested there for one perfect moment. She looked up with a sigh. "The day awaits. Shall we?"

He held her hand and walked her all the way to the door. "I'll see you tomorrow, El."

Chapter Two

SEVERAL HOURS LATER, ELLIE LOOKED around *The Lofts* with a happy sigh. Her guests were on their way home now, piling into cars and taxis, tossing suitcases into trunks, and preparing to return to their regular lives. In just a few hours, in the afternoon, the *Spirit* would embark on another loop around their popular Eastern Caribbean itinerary. At first, every cruise had felt like a brand-new adventure, but now that the itineraries were repeating, it felt more like a routine. But that wasn't a bad thing. There was a comfort to having a routine. Most mornings, after eating with Ben, she sat at *The Lofts*'s kitchen counter with complimentary maps, drinking tea and giving advice on the best places to play, relax, and shop. In the end, working on a cruise ship wasn't all that different than teaching or being a parent. Kindness, active listening and genuine enthusiasm for the subject matter went a long way.

She went to the big U-shaped couch and plumped up the pillows until the space looked as inviting as possible. Housekeeping would do a final sweep before embarkation, but many hands made for light work. The big digital display on the wall had already flipped to the *welcome aboard message.* It showed the evening's itinerary and a photo of pink flip flops resting on a beautiful beach. Two hallways led back to the staterooms for solo travelers, including her own small living space. Once the lounge was in tip-top shape she pushed her way through the glass double doors that separated *The Lofts* from the rest of the ship and went upstairs in search of Billy, the ship's head photographer.

Next week, the ship would leave port without her. How strange, to have your home push off into the ocean without you! Still, she had her house in Florida to consider. Sometimes she missed it. It had pretty French doors on the lower level and an enormous flowering dogwood tree out front. Her girlfriends back home were still meeting for brunch every other week, and they were looking forward to seeing her. Junior and Marcie were living in the family home, and they'd kept all her stuff, in boxes. Still, the life she'd left behind was starting to feel like a dream. After decades living the blessed life of a wife, mother, and homeowner, her belongings now fit into three big suitcases. She had a new man in her life, a new career, and new responsibilities. She touched the small portable radio clipped to the waistband of her shorts. Occasionally she heard the officers exchanging messages, but usually all was quiet.

If the crew of the *Spirit* felt like family, did that mean she'd left her real family behind? It felt like the kids were a million miles away, and not just physically. But by the time she'd noticed the change, it had become too difficult to talk about. How do you have a heart-to-heart conversation on a five-inch screen? It wasn't that they hadn't tried, exactly. It was almost as if the words floated away and lost their meaning, dissolved in the ether of a wobbly internet connection.

The center of the ship was mostly empty now. A porter jogged by carrying a piece of forgotten luggage. One of the housekeepers ducked into a nearby hallway with a stack of clean towels in her arms. Ellie thought about all the clothing she'd left back home. Maybe she'd go through and donate what she didn't need. The kids were renting the family home, at a reduced rate, of course, and they needed the space more than she did. But chores could wait. All she wanted to do was hug her boys and never let go. She wanted to wrap her arms around all of them at once and squeeze as hard as she could, as if by giving the world's biggest, longest, and most loving hug imaginable, she could make up for her long absence.

Junior loved her famous lasagna, so she'd make the family a big home-cooked meal. And she'd make the carrot cake that Marcie liked, and pick up Cole's favorite ice cream from the corner store. And finally, once they were all stuffed full of good food and hugged within an inch of their lives, she'd do the thing she'd been putting off for too long. She'd tell them about Ben. And if the thought of doing so made her stomach fill with butterflies, well, she'd just have to get over it. Back when Junior and Cole had been little, Cole had needled his older brother by calling him a chicken and making 'bok bok' noises while they ran through the house. And now *she* was the chicken!

A tiny voice spoke up in the back of her mind. *If you tell them about Ben, that makes it real. If you tell the kids that you're moving forward, it means you've moved past... Well, it means you've let Ronnie go.*

Her life in Florida was frozen in time like a relic in amber. And her new life was blooming like a late summer rose. What would happen when those two lives came careening into one another? Could either one survive unscathed? She pushed the question away with an uneasy sigh. She had a whole week left before the kids picked her up in Miami. Why borrow worry before she needed to?

The photography desk was empty. The long counter held a cash register covered in a black drape and a stack of brochures had toppled over nearby. The opposite wall usually held souvenir photos. It was bare except for the plastic strips that held the photos in place. Everything was ready for new arrivals.

Billy had set up a large backdrop perpendicular to the exterior door, and it showed an image of the cruise ship. Nearby, a big black camera rested atop a tripod with spindly legs that looked too delicate to support the camera's weight. She went over to the counter, tidied the stack of brochures, and rang the service bell once. It gave off a loud, metallic chime. "Billy, are you back there?"

She heard a faint thunk, and Billy's head poked around the wall that separated the service desk from his office in the back. He looked happy to see her. "Ellie! You're exactly the person I was looking for."

"Ben – I mean, the captain said that you needed me to look at something."

"I do. But will you give me a hand, first? Go stand over by the backdrop, please. My new camera arrived, and the settings are fiddly. I need to calibrate it real quick." He pointed at a spot on the carpet between the backdrop and camera.

"Sure." She went over to stand in the appointed spot. A familiar figure approached the counter. Violet Wolfe was in her standard cruise director uniform. She'd had the skirt fitted along the sides, so it accentuated her hourglass shape. Her shiny black hair reflected the overhead lights, and her scarlet lipstick was picture-perfect, as usual. She smiled when she saw Ellie waiting. "Hey! Are you taking a new crew photo?" She stood behind the tripod and tried to peer through the viewfinder. Her face screwed up in distaste, and she stepped back. "Billy, I think your camera is messed up."

"I know.; I know." Billy came over and turned the lens with one hand while peering through the viewfinder with the other. "Ellie, look right into the lens. Good. Take half a step forward. One more step please. Keep your chin pointed at me. Now, hold that position. Perfect, just like that."

Violet had a weird look on her face. She was smiling, but her smile was frozen as if she too were standing still for a photograph.

"Okay, I think we're all set." Billy took a step backward. He was grinning like he'd just won a prize. Violet looked quite pleased with herself too.

"Why are you guys being so weir—"

"Hey Mom," Junior said. "How have you been?"

Ellie spun around. Her arms reached out like heat seeking missiles. She saw Junior's pale brown eyes first, and then the softly curling hair on his forehead. She saw his toothy smile, and the small, familiar scar on his chin, and the next thing she knew he was crushing her in a hug and spinning her around. Tears ran down her face, wet and warm. She hugged him, hard, and felt the familiar shape of him. Her eldest son. He fit into her arms like a piece snapped into the center of a puzzle.

He set her down carefully. "Ma. You look really good!" He sounded happy, and that made her want to cry even harder.

She wiped her eyes, laughing a little. "Why are you here? I'm not due home for a week."

Over his shoulder, she saw Marcie watching the proceedings with an amused expression. And she was carrying a little girl in her arms, and the girl's blonde hair lay in ringlets on her mother's shoulder. It was Clara. But it couldn't be Clara! Because she was enormous. Not so much a baby anymore. Her little pink shoe had a strap across the foot, and she looked big and strong and ready to run around under her own power. "Gamma!" she called, her voice sweet, her smile lighting up the room like the sun.

Her heart overfull, Ellie burst into tears again and covered her face. Marcie stepped forward to give her a hug, and Clara's arms waved eagerly in the air. Junior came up on her other side. All the while Billy's camera shutter was going crazy: *click — click – click.*

Chapter Three

"HOW? WHO? WHEN?" IT WAS hard to form coherent sentences. But Junior looked pleased with himself, little Clara was reaching out with her chubby arms, and Marcy was laughing with happiness. For once, having answers didn't seem all that important. After more hugs and exclamations, she settled Clara onto her hip (so heavy!) and tickled her gently behind the knee. Over the little girl's shoulder, she caught a glimpse of Violet whispering to Billy.

"You did this, didn't you?" Ellie called over. As she spoke, Clara kicked, landing a sharp blow right below her ribs.

"Gamma!" Clara shouted directly into her ear. "I meesed you!" She grinned and grabbed a fist full of Ellie's hair.

"I missed you too, darling." She reached up and gently untangled her hair from the little girl's fist. At two and a half years old, Clara was a bit old for hair-pulling, but she seemed more enthusiastic than anything.

"Actually, we got a call from your business partner," Junior said.

"My who?"

"Roberta Crowley," Marcie said. "She said you've been filling in for her with the board of directors." Marcie shot her an amused look, "She wanted to say thanks, so she offered us a free cruise. And she suggested that we surprise you."

"And speaking of surprises, Ma," Junior said dryly, "when were you going to mention that you *own* part of the cruise line?" He shook his head, chiding her. "You'd think that news might make it into the weekly phone call. Don't you think?"

Ellie winced inwardly. "Yeah, I know. I figured we could talk about... things when I got home. In person."

Junior chuckled. And he sounded so much like Ronnie that Ellie felt an involuntary jolt of tenderness beneath her breastbone. She looked up at him. How had she forgotten the way his blonde hair curled softly over his forehead? Or the way he carried Ronnie's smile? Or how he seemed as tall as a mountain standing beside her? "Well, we have a lot to catch up on," Junior said. "Roberta was genuinely nice, and she suggested we join you for a week before you come home with us. And we weren't about to turn down a free cruise!"

When Junior smiled again, she caught a hint of weariness in his expression. He was probably tired after the long drive. "Is Cole coming too?" she asked.

Marcie shook her head. "Roberta invited the whole family, but Cole couldn't get the week off on such late notice. But he sends his love and he's picking us all up when we get back."

Ellie smiled up at Junior. "And you got leave from the precinct? That's wonderful. I know you've been short-staffed."

Junior glanced at Clara. "It wasn't a problem. And I needed some time off, for sure."

Marcie shot her husband an anxious look. He noticed it but pretended not to see. "So, can we get a tour?" she asked in a too-bright voice.

Clara was kicking again, and Marcie looked like she was about to come over and grab her feet. Ellie looked Clara in her big blue eyes and said, "Sweetie, please don't kick. You're hurting Grandma."

The kicks stopped, and Clara nodded solemnly. Marcie looked surprised that she'd listened, and Ellie felt a flutter of amusement. Kids liked to push boundaries with their parents because they knew they were unconditionally loved. It was a normal stage of development, and Grandma was unfamiliar enough now that Clara wasn't sure how to behave. "Absolutely," she said. "Let's—"

Someone touched her on the back, and she jumped! Turning her head swiftly to the right she saw Ben's bright smile beaming down on her. "I see the Tappets have arrived! I'm so sorry I'm late. I wanted to be here when they surprised you, but I got held up on the bridge." He leaned closer, as if he were about to kiss her on the cheek. Ellie released a loud peal of nervous laughter and stepped away. His eyes went wide as she dodged him.

"Hey!" she said, trying to bring her voice back to a normal volume. "Junior, Marcie, I'd like you to meet Captain Benjamin Spark."

Junior held out his hand. "It's a pleasure to meet you, Sir. Mom has told us a lot about the crew. Thanks for taking such good care of her." He shot Ellie a paternal look. "She hates it when we worry about her, but we can't help it. I mean, your mom goes on a vacation and the next thing you know she's run away to live on a cruise ship? We didn't see that coming."

Ben nodded. "Well, I think she takes care of us as much as we take care of her. And she's been talking nonstop about how much she misses you all. Welcome aboard and let us know if there's anything we can do to make your stay more comfortable." His voice was oddly formal, and he wasn't even looking at her now.

Her heart sank two inches. *Smooth, Ellie. Very smooth.*

"Does everyone call you Junior?" Ben asked.

"Oh, you can call me Ron. Mom still calls me Junior, and Marcie calls me that when she's really angry at me—"

Marcie laughed but her cheeks were pink. "Okay, I did that exactly *once*. And the look he gave me convinced me to never do it again."

"Well, it's nice to meet you. I should get back to the bridge. But I hope you'll all join me for dinner sometime soon. Your mother can set that up. If she wants to, that is."

He gave Ellie a friendly nod. Not a look of familiarity or affection, but the same polite regard he gave every passenger aboard the ship.

He's upset, she thought. *And I can't even blame him.* She tore her eyes away from Ben's retreating back and buried her nose in Clara's blonde curls. She squirmed away. "I wanna swim. I'm a mermaid. Mommy, I'm a mermaid!"

Marcie reached for her. "She's tired. And we've been watching mermaid videos all week, haven't we?"

Ellie's mind went to a small shop on the island of Beachcomber Key. They sold mermaid leggings for little girls. The fabric had a metallic shine and there were little fins attached to the hems. She smiled at Clara. "Yes, all mermaids should go to the pool. But first, let's find your swimsuit, shall we?"

"Mermaids swim naked." Clara replied, as if the matter were settled.

Junior smiled wearily. "You won't believe how hard we have to fight to get her in clothes every morning. You'd think we were torturing her."

Ellie looked the kids over again. They were happy to see her, that much was obvious, but something seemed off. Poor Junior's shoulders were slumped, and Marcie's makeup was hiding dark circles under her eyes, circles that hadn't been there the last time they'd been together. Most tellingly, they were talking to her without really talking to one another. Had they been carrying all their burdens alone? If so, that was her fault. Before she'd left for her first cruise aboard the *Spirit*, she'd been Clara's main babysitter. As a sworn officer of the Gainesville police force, Junior was no doubt working long days and nights, just like his father had. Marcie had been working more hours too. Her coworker was receiving cancer treatment and she was pitching in when she could. *Here I was, thinking of my own problems, but the kids need a break. Well, let's make it a good one!*

Ellie turned to Violet. "Do you know where Roberta put them up?" But Violet wasn't paying attention. She'd stepped away from the photo area and into the hallway. Her face was a picture of concentration, and she took a few steps forward, toward the center of the ship and away from the Tappets. As she passed by, Ellie saw her friend's hands were clenched, and her steps were short. "Violet?" Ellie walked over. "Is everything okay?"

Violet's head snapped over toward Ellie. She froze, glanced at the kids, and affixed a stage smile to her face. "Oh! Yes. Everything's fine. I just... I'll see you later, okay?" She took off, walking toward the center of the ship without so much as a backward glance.

Chapter Four

AFTER A SATISFYING LUNCH AT the Seashell buffet, a tour of the ship, and a quick splash in the pool, Clara was ready for a nap and the kids were yawning too. No doubt they'd been up since the wee hours of the morning, and the warmth of the afternoon sun hitting the lido deck was bound to make anyone sleepy after a nice meal and a swim.

She dropped the family off at their stateroom and headed to the Moonlight Lounge. The entertainment staff held a huddle right around this time, and if she got there before they started, she could check in with Violet. Her hand went to the black plastic radio at her waist, but something stilled her. Roberta Crowley liked to bark orders at the officers whenever she wanted something, throwing her weight around without apology, but she didn't want to be like that. Being concerned about her friend wasn't an emergency, nor was it official business. Her hand dropped to her side.

When she arrived at the lounge, Ellie gripped the smooth silver door handle, turned it, and pressed the door open. Inside, perhaps forty crew members were seated in the semi-circular booths waiting for the meeting to start. Up on the low stage, framed by purple curtains, Wynona, the theater manager, adjusted the microphone to the height of her mouth. Ellie walked up the central hallway, through the booths. She waved at Wynona and stepped up onto the stage. "Hey, I need a quick word with Violet, is she here?"

"I'm afraid not, hon." Wynona frowned slightly and blinked her dense black eyelashes. With her mild Texas twang, ample bosom, and sweet demeanor, Wynona reminded her of a brunette Dolly Parton. One of these days, after they'd gotten to know one another better, she'd have to ask if she was a fan. Wynona pointed at the double doors that Ellie had just come through. "She asked me to fill in for her and she left. That-a-way."

"Do she say where she was going?"

"She didn't, and I didn't ask. Is everything okay?"

"Yes," Ellie said. "I just need to ask her a question."

Ellie caught the eye of one of the DJs, a guy in his early twenties with dark curly hair whose name she couldn't remember. He was standing outside the DJ booth adjacent to the stage, making a show of not listening to their conversation. "Excuse me," Ellie said, beckoning him over with one finger. "Do you know where Violet is, young man?"

The quick shake of his head said no, but the way his eyes shifted toward the door said something else entirely. Ellie stepped down off the stage and went over to him. "Hey," she said in a low voice. "I need to find her. Pronto."

His eyes flung wider like she'd just poked him with a stiff finger, and Ellie winced. She tried to come up with something to say, something about how she hadn't meant to boss him around, but he was already talking. "Well, you didn't hear it from *me*, but I'd check the smoking deck. She bummed a cigarette from me half an hour ago."

"Thank you," Ellie said, patting him on the shoulder. Wynona was looking over at them with curiosity in her eyes, so she gave the kid a quick wink and turned toward the stage to call out, "No luck here. Have her come find me if you see her, okay?"

"Will do," Wynona said. Then she tapped on the microphone and asked the crew to take their seats. As Ellie moved toward the exit she heard Wynona introducing the lead performers in the ship's new musical, *The Pirates of Peking.*

A musical would be a nice change. They'd had an acrobatics show, then a variety show, and masked karaoke had been all the rage for a while. Junior and Marcie might enjoy a night at the theater. And maybe Ben would go too?

The thought of Ben's flat expression made her heart ache. She owed him an apology. But one thing at a time. If Violet was out on the smoking deck, that was a bad sign. She'd kicked that habit long ago, and whatever had sent her sprawling back into the diseased arms of Big Tobacco couldn't be good news. Ellie punted her disapproval to one side as she walked. Violet didn't need a lecture right now; she needed a friend.

She descended the stairs to the crew level and pushed through the metal door that led to the smoking deck. Her nose wrinkled when the stink hit her. But a gust of clean sea air blew past like a blessing, taking the smoke away. The view was of the shimmering aquamarine sea. The deck was little more than a long balcony with metal receptacles welded to the railing every few feet. The bulk of the ship threw the balcony into shade, and Ellie rubbed her bare arms. Compared to the sunny lido deck upstairs, it was quite chilly!

Violet was at the far end, leaning on the white metal rail, looking out to sea with a lit cigarette in her hand. A bulkhead provided cover from the worst of the wind, but as she leaned out, the ocean air whipped her black hair around her face. And she looked like she'd been crying. No. That wasn't it. Whatever was bothering her, she was holding it back with effort.

"Hey," Ellie said softly once she'd reached Violet's side. The sea sped by, down below where the water met the ship's bright white hull. Looking forward she saw a thick green line on the horizon. Some distant landmass. Ben would know what it was. The ship had left Port-Miami, and before long Florida would be a thin gray haze on the horizon, its features melting away into the sea. She turned to Violet. "What happened?"

"I'm fine," Violet said evenly. She stubbed the remainder of her cigarette out on the metal receptacle near her right thigh and dropped the butt into the hole.

"Of course you are. First, you ran off before I could introduce you to my kids. Then, you left your new manager in charge of your team meeting. And now you're smoking again? Tell me more about how you're doing *just fine*." Ellie's words came out sharper and more school-marmish than she'd intended, and she felt a twinge of guilt. She'd been feeling bad ever since she'd blown Ben off, and now she was being snappish with Violet for no good reason. She sighed quietly. "I'm sorry. Let me try that again. You seem upset, hon. And I'm worried about you. Is there anything I can do to help?" She glanced over at Violet. Her red lipstick had worn off. And her mouth pulled in on one side, showing a faint web of fine lines.

"Your family is here. You should be with them." Violet sounded tired, and she folded her arms atop the railing. Her head dropped down, like she might take a nap right there.

"They're having a rest before dinner." Ellie stepped close enough to set her elbow next to Violet's on the railing. "And thank you for the surprise. I don't think I've been so happy in... well, ever." She gave Violet's elbow a tiny nudge. "And don't change the subject. What's up? You know I'll get it out of you eventually, so you may as well let me have my way."

Violet flicked an amused look in her direction. It only lasted a second, but it was something! When she spoke again, her voice was dull. "Do you remember when we first met? I told you about my former partner. Melanie."

Ellie thought back. "Yes. You said that she'd left you and that you didn't know why. Later, I tried asking you about her, and..."

"And I blew you off?" Violet smiled bitterly without looking up. "Yeah. I *didn't* want to talk about Melanie. I still don't. But now she's here. On my ship. With a *man*." Violet rolled her eyes.

Ellie hesitated. She had a question, but she wasn't sure how to phrase it without being impolite. Violet was her first gay friend, and Dear Abby had not adequately prepared her for this moment. "Um. Is it... surprising that she's here with a man? I mean — I know *you're* surprised that she's here. On the ship. But her being here with a man, specifically. Is that..." she tried to come up with the politest phrasing, "out of character for her?"

Violet seemed faintly amused at her stammering. "There's no need to dance around it, Ellie. You're asking if Melanie is bi?" She shrugged. "I didn't think so. I mean, she had a boyfriend in college, but that isn't too uncommon for women our age." Violet seemed to be thinking back. "Although, she *did* have a crush on one of the Skarsgårds. The one who played a vampire on HBO?" She sighed and rubbed her eyes with her free hand. "But none of that matters. I don't care that she's here with a guy. I hate that she's here *at all.* This is my ship. This is where I work and live and make my music. And it's not like I show up in the places where *she* hangs out. Why would she take *this* cruise, of all cruises? It's like she wants me to suffer."

"That had to be upsetting, bumping into her like that."

"Oh, that's not even the worst part! I saw her come aboard while Billy was taking your pictures, and I walked up to get a closer look. She was there with that terrible little man. And when I went up to her, intending to be *mature* about the whole thing, she just..." Violet scowled. "Her eyes slid right past me. She pretended not to know who I was! It's like I was nothing to her. Not even worth acknowledging." Violet's hand went to the small pocket in her skirt, but her gaze flicked over to Ellie and she dropped her hand to her side.

"How long ago did you two break up?"

"A year and a half. That is, if you can call walking out on someone 'breaking up'."

Ellie nodded. "I see. And you still have some feelings for her."

"Feelings?" Violet sounded annoyed now. "There are no feelings! No *good* ones, anyway. Why care about someone who ran off without a word? After a seven-year relationship? You'd have to be an idiot to care about someone that cruel." Her green eyes flashed with frustration. "And I'm *not* an idiot."

"I never said you were. But to be clear, I don't think loving someone makes you an idiot. Even if they're not perfect."

"Perfect?" Violet scoffed. "You should have seen the guy she was with. He was short and pudgy and weird, and he had a goatee. A goatee! He was wearing five-hundred-dollar shoes, and he carried a cane." She held up a finger to stave off Ellie's response. "I know what you're going to say. There's nothing wrong with using a cane. But here's the thing. The guy was carrying a *decorative* cane. He was swinging it around like Mr. Peanut and blathering on like the Prime Minister of — I don't know — Peanut land. And she was standing there fawning over him. That freak! Ugh! When I saw them, I could have just..." She made a strangling motion with her hands.

"You could have made some chunky peanut butter?" Ellie quipped.

That got a laugh out of Violet. A small one, but it counted. Ellie smiled. "I'm sorry, hon. That sounds awful. And obviously it was a shock, coming out of nowhere like that. So, let me go back to my first question. What can I do to help? Do you want me to mess with them? I have a list of restaurants to avoid at every port we visit. Maybe if we work hard enough, we can give them food poisoning? Oh, wait! We'll replace her sunblock with hemorrhoid cream. That's the ticket. Act like a you-know-what and we'll treat you like a you-know-what!" She clapped her hands together. "Your ex won't know what hit her."

Violet laughed out loud. "I love it when you pretend to be evil. It's hilarious. Unconvincing, but hilarious." She shook her head. "But no, I don't need you to do anything. I just don't want to be around them. I know that makes me a coward, but..." Her expression darkened. "I hate this! I'm *hiding* from Melanie, and I'm not the one who did anything wrong! I never got any closure, and that was *her* fault. But after today, I don't want closure. I want her off my ship. I'm afraid that if I see her, I'm going to blurt out every mean thing I've been thinking for the last year and a half, and..."

"Yes?"

Violet's chin trembled. "And then I'll burst into tears, like an idiot, in front of everyone."

"Don't be silly. There's nothing wrong with crying if you need to cry. And hey, sometimes blurting can do a person some good! But you don't need to decide anything today. You've had a shock. Give yourself the night to think about it. I bet after a good night's sleep you'll know what you want to do." Ellie tapped her fingers on the round metal railing. "And maybe I can find out what their plans are, so you can zig when they zag. It's only a seven-day cruise, right? They'll be back on land and out of your hair in no time."

"You'd spy on them for me?" Violet sounded skeptical.

"Nothing so devious as that. But I have eyes and ears, don't I? Maybe I can gather some information before you talk to her. That's all I'm saying. People walk around the ship blathering their personal business all the time. And if I just *happen* to overhear their plans, what's wrong with that?"

Violet came over and hugged her. It was a sweet gesture, and Ellie hugged her back, hard. When Violet pulled back, her expression held a flicker of amusement. "So, are we going to talk about the way you blew Ben off in front of your kids?"

"No. We're talking about *your* love life, sweetie. Not mine."

"Ellie! Did you see the look on the man's face? He looked like you'd just kneed him in the junk, but he wasn't allowed to scream."

"Violet!" Ellie scolded, half-laughing. "It wasn't that bad, was it?"

Violet tilted her hand back and forth like a teeter-totter.

Ellie winced. "Well, I *might* not have told the kids that I'm dating someone."

"It's been months!"

"I know! And I was going to tell them. But every time I tried, it was like... I just couldn't. Eventually, it seemed easier to tell them in person."

Violet's green eyes were full of mirth now. "Oh, I see! And we brought your kids here before you'd had a chance to spill. Thus, ruining your master plan of wussing out until the last possible minute."

"It was very rude of you guys to be so considerate." Ellie laughed weakly. "I really hope he forgives me."

"Well, did he *think* you'd told your kids about your relationship?"

She winced. "I may have allowed him to believe that I'd told them."

"Ellie Tappet! How *dare you*. Lying to your boyfriend? Are you a mere mortal like the rest of us?" She tilted her head to one side. "And you know he'll forgive you. But you should definitely apologize. And *tell* your kids about him. Like, right now. They're adults, for crying out loud. They aren't going to fling themselves overboard because their mother is a human being."

Ellie nodded. "I'm headed to see Ben next. And I'll tell the kids. Tonight. I promise."

"Good. You should go. I'll be okay."

"You're sure?"

Violet nodded, and her hand went to her hip pocket again. It rested there, waiting.

"Hold on. You're not getting rid of me so easily. Do you have more cigarettes in your skirt?"

"No." Violet's eyes were wide and too-innocent.

Ellie held out her hand.

Rolling her eyes, Violet pulled a single cigarette out of her pocket and handed it over.

"Is that all of them?"

"Yes." Violet's smile was back, but it was her stage smile, the one she used to charm the guests during the evening Karaoke show.

"I know you wouldn't lie to me, Violet Wolfe. You wouldn't knowingly *deceive* your best friend in the world."

Violet groaned and reached into her pocket one more time. "Your kids are on board for like *five* minutes and you start parenting me."

"If you'll recall, you told me how hard it was to quit last time. So let's not regress just because your ex is here. If you do that, you're letting her win. And do you want her to ruin not only your good mood, and your cruise, but also your *health*?"

"No, Mom," Violet said sarcastically. "And what are *you* going to do, right now?"

"I'm going to apologize to Ben."

Violet looked pleased. "See? Two can play at the Mom game."

"Fair enough." Ellie gave Violet one more hug, then pointed at the portable radio she wore at her waist. "Call me later, okay? Between now and then, I'll see what I can learn about our unwanted guests."

Chapter Five

BEN WASN'T IN HIS OFFICE. Nor was he in his stateroom, the officer's mess, or in the vicinity of the bridge. After her fruitless search she returned to his stateroom and slid a hastily scribbled note under his door. She'd considered asking the bridge officers where he'd gone, but then they might wonder why she was looking, and that could lead to all sorts of unwanted gossip. Keeping your personal business private on board the *Spirit* was like trying to keep a plate of cookies away from a roomful of hungry children. Impossible, once they'd caught the scent.

She stopped by *The Lofts* to see if anyone needed assistance, but the lounge was empty. That wasn't too surprising. It was a beautiful day outside, sunny but not sweltering, and most folks were probably up on the deck enjoying the sunshine, splashing in the pool, or enjoying the daily drink special at the Seabreeze Bar.

With the surprise reunion that morning, she'd missed her chance to introduce herself to the new guests as they'd come on board. But according to the booking office her guests included four middle-aged women on a girls' trip, two brothers in their thirties, a gentleman in his seventies traveling with his extended family, and ten other solo travelers in their forties, fifties, and sixties. She went over to the whiteboard and wrote: *Meet and Greet: 6 p.m. Stop by and Introduce Yourself!*

At the concierge desk she made a dinner reservation for the family, plus one. Hopefully Ben would get her note and join them! And if he didn't show, well, it might mean he was more upset than he'd appeared. After confirming the reservation, the concierge asked, "Is there anything else I can do for you today?"

Ellie glanced down at the newsletter on the counter. *Cruise News You Can Use* listed every activity happening on board the ship, and that gave her an idea. "Actually, there is. I bumped into a guest earlier, and I promised to touch base with her, but I forgot to get her stateroom number. Can you direct me? Her name is Melanie and she's traveling in a party of two."

The woman's gaze flicked uneasily to Ellie's crew badge. What she was asking wasn't against the rules, *exactly*, but it was unusual. "And her last name?"

"I'm afraid I didn't get that either."

"Would you prefer to leave the information with me? I'd be happy to leave her a message."

Why did Suzie of Guest Services have to be so flipping considerate? And so cautious? This was Paul Gumbs' fault. Their chief of security was always lecturing the staff about security practices. Obviously, the staff shouldn't be giving out room locations to just anyone, but she was a trusted crewmate!

Granted, if Paul had his way, every guest would walk around wearing a GPS tracker strapped to their foreheads and there would be cameras posted in every hallway. But the owners had nixed the camera request, saying that no one liked to feel surveilled on vacation. On that topic, Roberta and the Picklewicks had been a united front.

"Oh, that's very nice of you to offer," Ellie said sweetly, "But I'm afraid this might involve a longer conversation. I figured I'd pop by her stateroom before the dinner hour."

Suzie's fingers flew across the keyboard. "Melanie Young. Party of two? She's staying in room 1289."

Room 1289 was in the ship's more luxurious section, *The Suites.* Ellie thanked her, snagged an extra copy of *Cruise News You Can Use* off the concierge desk, and made a few quick notations on the newsletter with the black plastic pen chained to the desk. Then she headed toward the front of the ship where the suites were located. She pressed her key card against the reader to enter the restricted hallway and ducked into a housekeeping closet to grab a stack of fluffy white towels.

The guest towels in *The Suites* had a large letter S monogrammed on them. The luxury rooms were full of small flourishes to make travelers feel extra-special. The soap in the shower was from a luxury brand, and the rooms were more spacious with fancier furniture. Ellie glanced around the hall in appreciation. Would it be nice to live here? Yes. Did she need to? No.

She paused outside room 1289 and knocked briskly on the door. It wasn't until her knuckles touched wood that she felt a tremor of uncertainty. Was she really going to do this?

Yes, I am.

She called out, "Housekeeping!" and her voice was loud and perky. Possibly too loud? She looked down at her casual shorts and pink tunic. Perhaps she should have given this plan more thought. But it would be fine! After all, who didn't appreciate some extra towels? All she wanted was to set her friend's worries at ease. Violet had built up this Melanie person so large in her mind that she was expecting some sort of confrontation. And if she knew more about her ex's situation, perhaps she'd feel less apprehensive about bumping into her.

Light steps approached the other side of the door, and a friendly-looking woman in her early fifties opened it. Melanie had a heart-shaped face, a curvaceous figure, and curly reddish-brown hair that rested atop her collar bones. Her black sleeveless dress was tightly fitted to her body and she wore a long, double string of pearls that went almost down to her belly button. When she spoke, her voice was melodious. She had a magnetic quality, but it was a subdued kind of magnetism. This was the kind of woman who could disappear into a crowd but when you saw her up close, her charisma became more apparent.

"Hello?" Melanie said, forming the statement into a question with a quizzical glance.

Ellie felt something click into place. *Yes, I can see those two together.*

Melanie was staring at her. Right! She was supposed to be a housekeeper. For a moment, she'd almost forgotten her task. "Hi! I thought you might like some extra towels. Are you settling in okay? Where can I put these for you?" Ellie took a small step forward, babbling her questions, and Melanie stepped aside to make room. Ellie walked inside and looked around. The suite had two bedrooms, one to the left of the living room and one to the right. There were black roller board suitcases resting on luggage stands in both rooms, visible through the open doors. Beyond the living room there was a small kitchenette and a sliding glass door leading to the balcony. Someone was standing outside, framed in light. The edge of the sheer curtains billowed into the room where the sliding glass door was partially open. The silhouette she saw was short and round. *That must be the Prime Minister of Peanut land,* she thought.

"You can sit those on my bed," Melanie was saying. She pointed to the room on the right. "Do you work with Rafael?"

Ellie spun around. "Who?"

"Our housekeeper." Melanie shot her a skeptical look. "He introduced himself about an hour ago. And he already brought towels."

Ellie smiled as brightly as she could. "Oh! *That* Rafael? Yes, sorry. I got my wires crossed. I heard they needed some help in *The Suites* so I came by to pitch in." She stepped into the bedroom and set the towels on the blue velvet coverlet. The room smelled like floral perfume and there was a large makeup case on the dresser. She quickly stepped back out into the living room and offered her hand. "I'm Ellie Tappet."

"Do you always introduce yourself with your first *and* last name?" Melanie raised an eyebrow.

"Maybe. I hadn't thought about it. Why?"

"Oh, you just reminded me of someone else for a second." Her gaze flicked in the direction of the balcony, then she seemed to catch herself. "I'm Melanie."

"It's nice to meet you. Is this your first time cruising with us? You and your husband, I mean?"

"Yes. And I'm traveling with my employer." Her lips compressed. "Although I'm well acquainted with cruise ships."

"Ah. Well, I have one more thing for you." She handed over the copy of *Cruise News You Can Use* that she'd prepared. "We have so many entertainment options on the ship that it can be difficult to choose! I circled the ones our guests seem to enjoy the most."

Melanie took the newsletter and glanced down at it. "Thank you." Her forehead furrowed. "Napkin folding demonstration. Acupuncture with Stevie. Morning Bible study?" She glanced up. "Seriously?"

"Oh, the napkin folding is quite extraordinary. They've added several exotic animals to the demonstration. Imagine this: you're having guests over for dinner, and they're expecting regular rolled up napkins, and – Pow! – They find a hippo on their plate. That's a real conversation starter." Ellie's words tumbled out too quickly, and she tried to stem the pace, but her heart was racing. "Oh! And don't forget the spa. They have a seaweed wrap that's quite popular."

Melanie nodded.

"I'm sorry to say I can't recommend the Karaoke show," Ellie blurted. "It's not very good."

Melanie's response was a flat stare.

Ellie felt heat pricking at her face. "Well, I'll leave you to your evening. Have a wonderful vacation and dial the concierge desk if you need anything at all. We're at your disposal, twenty-four seven." She smiled brightly and backed swiftly out of the room, shutting the door behind her. She pressed her back against the door and closed her eyes. That hadn't gone *too* badly, although she might have tipped her hand with the karaoke comment. And she'd gathered a valuable bit of intel. Melanie was traveling with her employer, not a lover. Perhaps that would make Violet feel a tiny bit better?

Inside the stateroom, she heard a screechy voice call out, "Who was that?" She took the hint and pushed herself off the door and strode up the hall and out toward the atrium. It had been a busy day, full of surprises, and it was time for a nice cup of Earl Grey before dinner. Perhaps she'd have a message from Ben when she got back.

Holding that hope like a prayer, she hurried back to her room to find out.

Chapter Six

DINNER WAS A FAMILY AFFAIR. The steakhouse was lit by amber-swirled sconces; electric candles flickered convincingly atop the white-sheeted tables. The scents of sizzling steak, baked potatoes, and fresh bread floated through the air. "This is really nice, Ma." Junior said, looking around the restaurant with an appreciative gleam in his eye. He patted his flat stomach with one hand. "Although if I ate this way every night I'd be as big as a house!" He loaded up his fork with his last bite of mashed potatoes and ate them with a moan that bordered on scandalous.

Marcie shot her husband a fond look and turned to Ellie. "I have to say, it's a treat to go a whole week without cooking. Although I expect most of the food is high in salt and fat." She shot Ellie a concerned look. "How is your health, by the way? I noticed that you're not using your cane anymore. The cane your doctor gave you to use? And you look great, but—"

Ellie held up both hands. "I'm in excellent health. No need to worry. Doctor Strunk has me on a nice anti-inflammatory for my arthritis and I haven't needed the cane. In fact, I gave it to a charming young man who sprained his ankle last month. We went ziplining, and he tripped and fell down in the parking lot on his way back to the bus!" She chuckled. "It's strange, but a lot of vacation injuries go that way. People are cautious when they snorkel and hike, but then they face-plant walking down the ramp to the dock."

"You went ziplining?" Marcie's baby-blue eyes widened as if this were the most shocking revelation she'd heard all year.

Here we go, Ellie thought. *Worry-wart Marcie, arriving right on schedule.*

"I had these two guests," She explained, "William and Sofia, and you could tell they were attracted to one another, but they were both so very shy. They both wanted to go zip lining, and they practically dragged me along with them. I think they felt like it wasn't a date if I was there?" She felt a flush of pride at the memory of William offering to hold Sophia's hand 'for safety' while she got buckled into her harness. "I can't say that I love heights, but it wasn't too bad. And they did exchange numbers before the cruise ended, so who knows?" Marcie was still staring at her, so she added, "Why? Is it so inconceivable that I could go ziplining?"

Marcie looked abashed. "No! Not at all. I'm just glad to see you getting back to your old self."

She seemed sincere, so Ellie nodded, her irritation melting away. "Well, thank you. It has been nice. But you're right about the food. I've taken to walking around the promenade deck every afternoon and evening. Plus, I use the weight room twice a week with Kameron. She's our junior security officer, and she's teaching me how to dead-lift. It's good for the joints. The idea is, you surround weak joints with muscle, and your bones don't need to do all the work. She's a lovely woman. Very encouraging, but tough too."

Junior's eyebrows lifted. "You're weight training, Ma? That's great."

Marcie cut a few small pieces of chicken from her plate and shifted them to Clara's. The little girl carefully stabbed one with her fork, concentrating as if the task were the most important thing on Earth.

"Does it ever get old?" Marcie asked. "Working here, I mean. When we looked at the website it said you guys were doing the same itinerary over and over again."

"Not really. It gets familiar, but that's not the worst thing. We're heading to Mexico soon. That will be something new!" She glanced at the empty chair at the table. Ben hadn't yet made an appearance, and it was almost time for dessert. She kept her smile on, not wanting to worry the kids, but the truth was, she was getting more anxious by the minute. It wasn't like him to ignore one of her notes.

Marcie followed her gaze. "You said a friend was joining us?"

"Bossy Bee is my friend," Clara declared, pounding one fist on the table. "Mine."

Grateful for the distraction, Ellie turned to her. "And who is Bossy Bee, my love?"

"My friend," Clara said, before picking up a piece of carrot and putting it in her mouth. She chewed with a thoughtful expression, then swallowed with a small nod of approval. It was too cute.

"We all need friends," Ellie said.

"The Bossy Bee is Clara's favorite TV show." Junior said. "You might even say the Bossy Bee is her inspiration." He pinched his fingers in the air and shook them. "Her muse."

Marcie's ears turned a faint shade of pink. She'd put on a cute cotton dress for dinner and her ears matched it perfectly now. "Clara's just testing boundaries. According to the doctor, it's normal behavior."

Junior sighed wearily. "I wasn't complaining, Marce. Just joking around." He reached for the bread basket at the center of the table. "So, Ma. We've been wondering. When are you coming home? After Mexico, maybe?"

"What do you mean?'"

"Well, when you said you accepted a short-term contract to work aboard the ship, it sounded like a fun adventure. And I can tell you're doing well here. But you obviously won't be working here *forever*. So now that you've had a nice long break, I'm just wondering, what are your plans? You're not as young as you once were, and I'm sure you're thinking about your future."

Oh. She wasn't as young as she once was? Well, no one was. That's how the flow of time functioned. She was about to say as much, when Marcie blurted out, "We'll support you no matter what you do. And all Ron meant was—"

"Hon. I think I'm capable of speaking for myself." Junior's voice was polite, but Marcie recoiled like he'd slapped her.

"No. No-no-no-no-no!" Clara's sudden outburst gave Ellie an excuse to look away from the awkward exchange.

"No what, sweetie?" She leaned over to take one of Clara's hands.

"No carrots," Clara said. She brushed her blonde curls back. It was such a grown-up gesture, and so reminiscent of her mother, that Ellie smiled. She picked up a spoon and began pushing foods around on the little girl's plate. "Well, let's see what our options are, shall we?" As she helped Clara with her dinner she tried not to eavesdrop on the kids. They were speaking in low voices, not fighting exactly, but the tension was palpable. She wasn't sure what was more surprising, hearing Marcie come to her defense, or listening to Junior admonish her about *her future* like she was an irresponsible teenager.

Movement caught her eye. Near the entrance to the kitchen a server was waving her hands, trying to get her attention. As soon as Ellie looked over, the dark-haired woman pointed toward the hostess stand at the front of the restaurant. Ellie sat up taller and looked. Ben was standing just inside the entrance! He beckoned her over and held a finger to his lips.

"Will you three excuse me for a moment?" Ellie got up, set her napkin in her chair, and bent over to kiss Clara on top of her head. "I'll be back in a jiffy."

Ben ducked outside when he saw her coming. She exited the restaurant and turned the same direction, and she almost ran right into him. And thank the Lord! He was smiling at her. "Hey! I'm sorry I missed dinner. I just found your note and I wanted to come by and see if the coast was clear."

The words she'd been holding all day came bursting out like water from a broken pipe. "I'm so sorry about this morning! It's all my fault. I was going to talk to the kids when I got home. And the surprise was lovely. It really was! I was just caught off guard. They'll love you. I know they will. And I wanted to introduce you tonight. Now. Right away. Because I care about you, and—"

Ben grabbed her hands. "El, calm down, will you? I'm not mad."

"You're not?"

"Well, I was surprised! But it was obvious that you hadn't told them yet, otherwise you wouldn't have sprung straight up in the air like a horror movie victim when I came over." He glanced down at her hands. "I just... I hope you're not embarrassed by me."

"Never," she said fiercely. "I was just mortified that I hadn't told my kids yet. And when you ran off like that—"

"Ran off? No way! I was trying to keep up your ruse. I figured if I stayed, I'd end up making googly eyes at you and the jig would be up!" He smiled, but then his expression grew more serious. "But you *are* going to tell them. Right?"

She pulled him closer and stood on her tiptoes to kiss him. "Yes, I'm telling them. I was going to tell them on the way to dinner but then you didn't show, and I chickened out, and they seem a bit cranky tonight, and—"

"Gamma!" A high-pitched voice shouted right behind them and Ellie spun around. Clara was standing there in her little blue dress.

"We seem to have an escapee," Ben said, crouching down to put himself at her eye level. "You must be Clara. I'm Ben."

"Hi Ben."

"How old are you, Clara?"

She held up two fingers. "I'm two *and* a half." Then she held up two fingers in her other hand and giggled. "No! I'm twenty-two!"

Ellie stifled a laugh, but Ben pretended to consider this bit of information with all seriousness. "Well, young lady, I'll still need to see some ID if you want a beer."

Clara giggled, and Marcie came through the doorway, breathing hard. "Oh, Thank God! She wanted down from the chair and I turned around for *one second* and she was off like an Olympic sprinter." She picked the little girl up. "You can't run off like that, sweetie. It's not safe."

Clara nodded. “Okay.” Then she leaned into Marcie’s hair and whispered something.

Marcie nodded. “That’s fine. Come on. Let’s see about ordering you some dessert.” She looked over at Ellie and Ben. “Captain Spark, right? It’s good to see you.”

“Call me Ben. Your mother invited me to join you for dinner, and I just came by to say that I can’t make it. But perhaps tomorrow? I’d love to get to know the rest of the Tappet clan.” He waved at Clara with his fingers. “See you later, kiddo. And bring your driver’s license.”

Ellie said goodbye, feeling her heart soar when Ben winked at her. She followed Marcie back into the restaurant.

“What was that about?” Marcie asked.

“Clara told him she’s twenty-two.”

“Ah,” Marcie said. She looked back in the direction he’d gone. “He seems nice.”

“He is,” Ellie said. “He’s great. Say, I was thinking of introducing you to some of my friends tomorrow. We can go to the beach, and then we can see my friend Violet’s karaoke show tomorrow night after dinner. Maybe Ben will come. How does that sound?”

Marcie glanced at Clara. “That sounds great. But maybe you should take Ron. I’ll need to have her in bed a bit earlier than that, I think.”

"Oh, don't worry, I can line us up a babysitter. In fact, I've got the perfect person in mind." She looped her arm over Marcie's shoulder and felt Clara squeeze her hand. "Come on, girls. Let's get some dessert."

AFTER DESSERT AND A SLOW walk around the promenade deck, Ellie walked her kids back to their room. "Did you have a good time tonight?" she asked.

They both nodded. Clara was already dozing on her father's shoulder, her curls bouncing with his every step. Marcie yawned and Junior smiled at her. Whatever tension they'd been feeling earlier seemed to have blown away with the cool ocean breeze. The water surrounding the ship was smooth and dark, and the nearly full moon spilled light in a long glimmering path that led from the ship to the horizon. Now that they both looked so relaxed, this might be a good moment to share her news. Ellie took a breath. "So, there's something I want to talk to you about."

Marcie nodded. "Sure."

But before she could say more, she was interrupted by the squawk of the radio she'd shoved into her purse. "ET. Phone home." Kameron's voice was crisp and professional.

"ET?" Junior looked down at her handbag.

Ellie nodded. "That's my code name." She fished around in her bag for the radio and pressed the button on the side. "ET here. Go ahead."

"I need you to meet me at the atrium. Code orange. Songbird."

Songbird was Violet's code name! But what was the situation? It had to be something important, or else Kameron wouldn't have called. She racked her brain, but she couldn't remember what code orange meant. Code red was fire. Code black was a death. Code blue was a medical emergency, and code white was a man overboard. But orange? If she'd heard that one before, it had slipped her mind. She keyed the radio again. "Orange?"

There was a pause, then Kameron spoke again. "Altercation."

Ellie stared at the radio and put the pieces together. Violet. Having an altercation. In the atrium. This was like the world's worst game of Clue, a version in which you had all the answers, but the solution only raised more questions. She keyed the radio. "I'm on my way."

Junior was staring at her like she'd just sprouted a second head. "Ma. Who is Songbird? Is everything okay?"

"Songbird is my friend Violet," she explained. "I need to run. But I'll pick you up for breakfast, okay? Eight sharp! Wear sunblock." She shot Junior a *don't-worry-about-me* smile and turned tail, jogging toward the center of the ship. She held up the radio again. "ETA, two minutes."

Chapter Seven

ELLIE RAN UP TO THE wooden railing, put her hands on the smooth varnished wood, and looked down into the big, light-filled space below. While she caught her breath, she checked the dance floor. The piano player was down there. There were no dancers. But to her left and right, and on the levels above and below, guests were lined up at the wooden railings, staring down at the empty dance floor. A woman's voice floated up through the air, angry and echoing. Violet's voice!

"Excuse me," she said, heading for the grand staircase, turning sideways to move through a cluster of gawkers in formal wear. She raced down the stairs as quickly as she dared, keeping one hand on the railing for stability. At the lower level, she stepped on the tiled floor. From his bench seat, the piano player looked at her with desperation in his eyes. His fingers continued to dance across the keys with cheerful agility, but as soon as he noted her crew badge and the expression on her face, he jerked his chin toward the other side of the room. *There*, his gesture said. He raised his eyebrows, and she knew he meant, *hurry*.

That's when she saw them. Standing between two decorative columns, just off the dance floor, a pair of well-dressed women were arguing in raised voices. The silk ivy leaves and plastic grapes hanging off the columns reminded Ellie of set dressing, as if the argument might be nothing more than a stage play. But she knew better.

Violet and Melanie had found one another.

"What do I want? I want an explanation! You owe me that much." Violet's green eyes flashed with frustration and she flung her arms outward as she spoke.

Melanie was in the same little black dress she'd worn earlier, and she had a cocktail in her hand. She flicked a contemptuous glance at Violet, and her cheek was bright pink. At first, it looked like Violet had slapped her! But as she turned her head it became obvious that her entire face was lit up with some intense emotion. Embarrassment? Or was it anger?

"Oh?" Melanie said coldly. "And why is that?"

The piano player switched to a dramatic song, reminiscent of a daytime soap opera. Did he think this was *funny*? Ellie turned to glare at him, and he jerked as if he'd been stung by a bee. Quickly, he transitioned to a Disney song: *Under the Sea.* Ellie nodded, once, and as she turned back, she caught a glimpse of some of the assembled guests watching the 'show.' Most of them seemed entertained, and perhaps that's why the piano player had chosen that song. Couldn't they see these women were upset? Mocking them didn't help.

"We were together for seven years," Violet said, projecting her voice to carry. "We had a home. A life. A history. We had *plans.*" Violet's face screwed up like she might cry, but she took a shaky breath and continued. "When I landed at the airport, you weren't there. That was fine. I knew you had auditions. But when I got home, and I saw..." Her chin trembled but she clamped her jaw down. "The house was torn apart! Your stuff was gone. There was spoiled milk on the counter, and the desk drawers were all pulled out. I thought you'd been..." Violet wiped her eyes. "I thought you'd been abducted!"

"I left you a note," Melanie said, brushing her reddish-brown hair back over one shoulder. Her pose was casual, but she glanced away, at the carpet, uncomfortable now. "You *knew* why I left."

Violet laughed bitterly. "Oh, the note! Let's not forget the note! That was my favorite part. The police were at our place, in the kitchen, interviewing me about *your disappearance* when they found the note you left." Violet flung her hands up in the air and made quotation marks with her fingers. "I'm breaking up with you. Don't look for me." She dropped her arms to her sides. "Two sentences? Nine words? That's what I get after seven years? Nine whole words! I loved you. I wanted to *marry* you." She was shouting now. "But you never cared about me, did you? You just disappeared. Fine. You're awful. You're heartless. I should have known better. But now you're here. And why? To show off your *boyfriend*? Did you wait just long enough for me to get over you before you came back, ready to stick the knife back in?"

A distinguished looking man in a dark gray suit was walking out of a nearby cafe. He watched the women for a moment, shot them a look of pure disgust, and walked away. Ellie's heart sank. She knew that look! He was going to file a complaint at the service desk! That meant Roberta would hear all about it. And what would Roberta do, once she'd heard that Violet had been shouting at a guest in the atrium?

Ellie walked toward the women, one arm out. She kept her voice low. "Why don't we—"

Melanie strode over to the piano and dropped some cash in the tip jar. "Hey," she said, matching Violet's volume. "Piano man, how about a sad song for my old friend? Something to make us feel sorry for her. Go ahead!" She lifted her glass in the air. "You've got the big dramatic scene you've been craving. May as well make it a musical number. Isn't that your thing?" She gestured theatrically in Violet's direction. "Violet Wolfe, everyone, your cruise director! She's never satisfied with life unless she's on a stage, somewhere, receiving the adoration of random strangers."

Violet's big green eyes were narrowed in a squint. She took a step forward. And another.

Melanie set her drink on the piano, her spine straight, her shoulders back.

For a moment, they stood there, three feet apart on the dance floor, eye to eye, glaring, looking like they might fight or scream or even kiss. Ellie saw Kameron loping down the steps like a hunter in search of prey, her expression grim. Maybe she'd been waiting and watching, but she was done with that. Unless this confrontation ended, and fast, Violet was about to get dragged out of the atrium in front of everyone. Ellie's gut twisted. Who knew what Roberta might do when she learned her cruise director was fighting with a guest? And in front of everyone? Working aboard the ship was Violet's passion. Singing was her life! She was out of line, and she needed someone to rein her in. And quickly, before one of them did something they couldn't take back.

Ellie ran forward, putting her body between Melanie and Violet, her arms and legs spread out, creating a physical barrier. "Hey, ladies! Wow. It's always exciting when we run into old friends on board, isn't it? Man. Is it getting stuffy in here, or is it just me?" She laughed awkwardly, and her laughter echoed up toward the ceiling. The assembled guests were staring at her now, not at the women. *Good.* Ellie grasped for something to say. Anything, to keep those two apart. "Yes, it's very warm in here. And on a hot day, there's nothing better to cool a person down like our daily drink special!"

Melanie was looking at her like she was an escapee from a lunatic asylum, and Kameron had stopped moving at the bottom of the stairs. Ellie's shoulder muscles ached in protest. She was splayed out like a starfish, and the piano player was still playing that Disney tune. She looked ridiculous, and she could feel everyone staring at her from above. Good! So long as they were staring at her, no one was looking at Violet, who still looked ready to spit nails. She dropped her arms, slowly, and the ache in her shoulders faded. She stepped toward Violet, getting too close, forcing her friend to take a small step backward. "Violet, have you heard about today's drink special?"

"What?" Violet's eyes focused on her.

"I *said*, have you heard about the new drink special?" She glanced upward, hoping Violet would take the hint and notice the audience surrounding them. "It's *amazing*. It's called the... The coconut crocodile, and it's made with coconut, and lime, and a special kind of rum, and..."

Was Violet backing off? She seemed to be. But Melanie was still right behind them. "And it's got — um — gummy crocodiles in it! Real gummy crocodiles! And fish sauce. And hey," She loosened her stance, and turned around to speak to the assembled crowd, looking up, "if you want to experience the coconut crocodile with less bite, skip the rum! Here on the *Adventurous Spirit*, it's never been easier to get your croc on."

"Fish sauce?" That came from a twenty-something guy near the bottom of the stairs. He wore a baseball cap, shorts, and a tropical shirt with palm leaves. "That sounds disgusting."

Ellie turned and nodded enthusiastically, keeping her body between the two women. "Yes! Yes, sir, it does sound disgusting, doesn't it? But it tastes amazing. We... err... we can't include real crocodile, obviously. So we had to improvise." One level up, at the railing, a woman with long white hair was whispering in her companion's ear, her expression full of cruel amusement. Was she talking about Violet? Ellie pointed up at her. "Ma'am! You look like you could use a refreshing beverage. How about it? Head right upstairs and talk to my friend Manny at the Seabreeze Bar. Tell him Ellie sent you!" The woman, perhaps embarrassed to have been caught gossiping, nodded and stepped back from the railing.

Violet shot Ellie an irritated look. A *I-know-what-you're-doing* look. But there was a faint flicker of amusement in her eyes. And that was a cause for hope. "Ellie," she said loudly. "You can't put fish sauce in a cocktail. That's vile."

Ellie pretended to think. "You know what? You're right. In fact, I'm going to go upstairs, *right now* and have them take out the fish sauce." She glanced up and saw that some of the crowd was starting to disperse. Not all of them, but most. She looped her arm through Violet's and tugged her toward the back of the ship, away from the atrium. "Come on," she said. "You can give me a hand with that."

Once they'd passed the opposite side of the dance floor, she leaned close to Violet. "What were you thinking? Kameron called me." She jerked her chin toward the far side of the room, where Kameron stood, her arms crossed like a bouncer. "Did you even stop to think about how devastated I'd be if you got *fired*? You can't go screaming at our guests like that. It's not—"

"Ellie," Violet sounded apologetic, but before she could say more a pompous male voice rang out behind them, echoing in the atrium like the call of a circus announcer.

"Darling, where have you been? I've been looking *everywhere*."

Violet's body stiffened and she stopped moving. *Great. Just... Great*, Ellie thought, turning around but keeping a hold of Violet's arm in case she tried to move. A dumpy-looking little man was approaching Melanie, swinging a black cane back and forth as he went. He was five foot four and shaped like a turnip, wide in the hips and skinny in the neck and shoulders. He had a thick thatch of dull-looking black hair and a matching goatee that tapered into a point below his chin. Thick, dark, eyebrows crawled across his forehead like furry caterpillars. He wore a pitch-black suit with a shiny red vest, and as if all that weren't enough, there was an enormous green and blue parrot on his shoulder! The bird's spectacular blood-red tail feathers matched the man's vest perfectly. The parrot opened its wicked-looking beak and bobbed its head enthusiastically at the piano player, who had switched back to a waltz.

The man with the cane spoke to Melanie like a king addressing his favorite servant. "You said you'd be right back, my girl, but it's been ages. Did you find the porter?"

"I'm sorry, Murray," Melanie said. Her formerly confident pose melted away like it had never existed. "I just ran into..." She shot a disgusted look at Violet. "It doesn't matter. What do you need?" She quickly walked over to him, her expression simpering. "I'm right here."

"See what I mean?" Violet muttered.

Ellie squeezed Violet's arm and let go. "Stay right here. Let me take care of this." She strode over to the couple, her hand stretched out. "Hello! You mentioned you needed some assistance?" She pointed at her name badge and gave the man a sunny smile, then reached out again, pumping the guy's hand enthusiastically. He had a firm grip. "Ellie Tappet. Guest relations. What can I help you with?" Out of the corner of her eye, she saw a couple with a young boy standing near the elevators. The boy pointed at the parrot and smiled. She didn't blame him. It was a beautiful animal.

Melanie's companion stepped back with one foot and gave a courtly bow. As he did so, the parrot squawked and danced back on his shoulder to avoid losing his footing. "Murray the Magnificent, at your service. As Los Angeles's *premier* party magician, I've been dazzling audiences all over the world for thirty magical years." He shot her a perplexed look. "Wait. I've seen you before, haven't I?"

Had he noticed her when she'd visited his stateroom? If so, she wasn't sure how. But she was almost certain this was the figure she'd seen out on the balcony. He had a rather distinctive shape. Her brain served up a sudden image of Violet mouthing the phrase *Prime Minister of Peanut land*, and it took all her willpower not to react.

Murray reached forward as if to touch her shoulder but at the last moment his hand darted to one side and upward. He produced a business card from behind her ear. Then he laughed merrily as he handed it over. "Here you go, young lady."

Melanie looked amused. Probably she'd seen this trick a thousand times before, but she was looking at Murray with a fond expression. Ellie glanced at the card, which bore the magician's photograph and contact information.

"Wait," Melanie said, frowning slightly. "I remember you! You said you were a housekeeper."

Ellie felt her cheeks heating up. "Ah, well, I help out wherever I'm needed." She wanted to turn around and make sure Violet was keeping her distance, but it was best to stay focused.

"Perfect!" Murray clapped his hands together. "Then perhaps you can help me. One of your porters — fine young men, to be sure — left a suitcase outside my room, but it's not mine. And I've gotten tired of walking around it. Can you have one of your," He made a fluttering motion with his fingers, "Magical elves spirit it away for me?"

"Sure. We can—" Before Ellie could say more, Violet was at her side again.

"So, you're a magician, huh? What kind of magic do you do?" Violet's voice was as sweet as pie, but still, Ellie winced.

"I specialize in corporate events, my dear. Company picnics. Board meetings. Product expos. Murray the Magnificent is at your service." He bowed again and the bird squawked in protest as he was dipped forward a second time.

"Murray the Moron! Murray the Moron!" The bird called.

His face turned dark red. "Ah, pay no mind to Sal. He's in a bad mood this evening."

Ellie caught a familiar face in her peripheral vision. Kameron was still standing a respectable distance away, but now she was glaring at the parrot like it was a criminal in need of capture.

"I'm happy to help you with that," Ellie said. "Where are you staying?"

"You know where we're staying," Melanie said, raising one eyebrow. "You were just there." She glanced from Ellie to Violet as if putting two and two together.

"Ah, yes. I forgot. Well, if you'll follow me—"

But before she could finish the thought, Kameron was suddenly *there*. Now, with Violet on her left and Kameron on her right, she felt like a potted plant flanked by two angry statues. Why wouldn't they let her handle this situation? The last thing they needed was another episode of *Drama in the Atrium.*

"Sir, you can't have that bird on board. It's against regulations." Kameron's tone was matter of fact.

The magician's face turned an ugly shade of red. "Well, I'm afraid that's simply unacceptable, Miss. Sal is not only my business partner, he's a registered emotional support animal. And I already explained this to the port staff. My paperwork is in order! I have a note from a doctor. The law is clear in this matter; you cannot deny him passage. Or me."

"You have an emotional support parrot?" Kameron sounded skeptical.

"Murray the Moron! Murray the Moron!" the bird crooned in a softer voice.

"Let the bird stay," Violet quipped. "I like him."

"Sal isn't an ordinary parrot," Murray said. "He's a rare African rainbow parrot, one of the most intelligent birds in the world. And, like I said, I do have a permit. It's in my room with his cage. I travel with Sal at *all times* you see. We've never been separated." A thin sheen of sweat made Murray's forehead shine.

That poor man! Murray looked pale and sweaty now. He couldn't bear the thought of being separated from his parrot. Still, Kameron was right, the only animals allowed aboard the *Spirit* were registered service animals, like trained service dogs. She glanced at Kameron to see what she'd do.

Kameron's stern expression flickered for a moment. She glanced at Ellie, then at Violet. "Is everything okay here?"

Ellie nodded.

Kameron waited, staring daggers at Violet.

"Yes," Violet said, keeping her voice even.

"Good. Then I will speak to our security chief and see what can be done to accommodate our feathered guest," Kameron said, taking a closer look at the parrot. Her stern expression softened when he tilted his head at her. "He's quite extraordinary."

"He is, isn't he?" Melanie made a soft chirping sound, and the parrot swiveled his head to her.

"Pretty lady. Pretty pretty."

Melanie glanced at Violet before turning away. "Murray, let's go for a walk. Let the staff take care of the luggage." She turned to go.

He nodded. "A fine idea. I could stretch my legs. But let's take Sal back to his cage. We wouldn't want him going outside and getting any ideas!" He grinned at Ellie and winked as if this were a hilarious joke. "If you will lead the way, Madame?"

Violet made a huffing noise.

"Violet," Ellie said. "Why don't you head out? I can find the porter for Mister..." She realized that she didn't know his real last name. "Mr. Magnificent."

But Violet was already striding up the hall in the direction of *The Suites*, her shiny black hair bouncing with every step, her arms pumping back and forth like a power walker.

Chapter Eight

"VIOLET, WAIT UP!" ELLIE HURRIED, trying to close the gap. She glanced back. Murray and Melanie were following. The magician's head went up to Melanie's shoulder, and they chattered companionably as they walked arm in arm. Melanie's diamond and ruby necklace looked far too gaudy to be real, but the red stones matched the red silk of Murray's vest perfectly. The magician and his assistant. They might not be a couple, but they certainly seemed to get along.

Violet must have heard Ellie huffing and puffing, because she slowed down a little. And as soon as they were walking shoulder to shoulder Ellie leaned closer and spoke low. "It's not what you think — the two of them, I mean."

"Why would I care? She's dead to me." Violet didn't bother to lower her voice. She tapped her badge against the black plastic pad outside *The Suites* and pushed her way through, hands out, flinging both doors open simultaneously, letting them bang against the walls. She pointed ahead. "There. I see the suitcase. Let's get this down to lost luggage. Wouldn't want to keep *our guests* waiting."

Despite her sarcasm, Violet's fury seemed to be winding down. Her voice was tired, and she was moving more slowly. She'd worn herself out, just like Clara did after a full-throated tantrum. Adults were basically toddlers running a more sophisticated kind of software, and it was hard to sustain anger for too long. Poor Violet! That breakup sounded terrible! Far worse than she'd let on. And as for Melanie, well, she seemed rather cold.

No wonder Murray had wanted the suitcase moved. It was huge! At nearly four feet tall and three feet wide it was one of the largest pieces of luggage Ellie had ever seen. Cruisers weren't light packers as a rule — why leave the comforts of home behind when your accommodations traveled with you? — but still, this suitcase was ridiculous.

Violet went around to the back of it and raised the telescoping handle. It went up smoothly and stopped at the highest position. She pulled the bag back, trying to tip it onto the wheels, but it didn't budge. The handle bent like it was about to snap. "What in the heck?"

Ellie looked at the base where it bit into the thick blue carpet. She pointed. "One of the wheels snapped off. That's why it won't roll. Why don't you grab the other handle up top? I'll get the bottom. We can get it out of the way at least, until we get a cart." Violet gripped the top handle and Ellie squatted to grab the bottom, reminding herself to lift with her legs and not her back. Kameron would be proud of her form! She groaned with the effort of the lift and felt her shoulder muscles pulling like her arm was about to leave the socket.

"Ellie—" Violet gasped.

"Put it down! Before I drop it!" Ellie let the bag slip back down and it hit the ground with a thump. Now it was lying flat, blocking most of the hall, with the solitary scuffed wheel facing her. "What's in there? Bricks? Maybe a baby elephant?" She rubbed her lower back. With all the running and lifting tonight, she wouldn't feel bad about skipping her workout with Kameron tomorrow.

"Ah, yes. It's very heavy," Murray said. He and Melanie had reached them at last. He paused for a second, as if wondering if he should help, then he dipped his hand into the inner pocket of his jacket. "Good luck with that." Sal the parrot chortled something too low to hear.

"Maybe if we take some stuff out of it, we can move it out of the way at least?" Violet crouched down. She unzipped the front panel and flipped it open.

She yelped like a dog with a stepped-on-tail! Then she scrambled back, almost tripping in her eagerness to get away from the suitcase.

Ellie stepped forward, her heart in her throat. The luggage flap had fallen back down, but not before she'd caught a glimpse of a woman's wrist and hand, pale and still, surrounded by silvery blue fabric. She lifted the flap of the suitcase gingerly and flung it over, not wanting to touch it any more than she had to.

"Ellie, don't—" Violet choked out.

Behind her, Melanie gasped softly.

The young woman was curled up in the fetal position. Her arms were bare and bluish white, and her dark hair streamed down over her bloated-looking face. An angry purplish line ran around her throat. She wore a pale yellow t-shirt and jean shorts, and her well-defined muscles gave her arms a shapely beauty even in death. Had she been an athlete? Whatever she'd been in life, her spirit had long since fled. "Oh, you poor thing," Ellie murmured. She glanced up. Violet looked pale. Turning around, she saw that Melanie had one hand flat on the wall, as if to hold herself steady. Her face was blank.

Murray the Magnificent looked like he'd just seen a ghost. He had one hand over his mouth, and he was frozen in place, his eyes sweeping over the suitcase like he couldn't quite believe what he saw. His eyes rolled upward, and his shoulder dipped. Sal squawked in alarm and began flapping his wings.

"Catch him!" Ellie called, rushing forward.

Murray's knees buckled and he dropped to the ground like a sack of potatoes. Melanie managed to soften his fall by throwing her arm behind his shoulders, and Sal had lifted off, flapping his wings furiously. A long green feather drifted down and landed on the carpet. Up on the wall, Sal was struggling to grip the curved edges of a frosted-glass sconce, his wings beating hard. Melanie was kneeling, running her hand alongside Murray's face. "Murray! Wake up!"

"Is he breathing?" Ellie asked, preparing to drop down and administer CPR.

Melanie looked up, her eyes frightened. "Yes, I think so." Murray stirred slightly, and he reached up and touched his head with one hand, groaning.

Ellie tried to recall her first aid training. *Assess the scene. Render aid. Call for help.* She turned to Violet. "Violet, help Sal before he hurts himself." She rummaged in her purse for the radio and lifted it. She pressed the button on the side. "ET here. I have a..." She looked at the scene in front of her. Violet had made her way over to the terrified bird, stepping over Murray in the process. Her arm held steady beneath his feet, and she winced as his wings beat the air just inches from her face. Ellie looked again at the open suitcase on the ground, and the dead body inside. Down on the carpet, Melanie looked anxious, but Murray's eyes were fluttering open and his chest was rising and falling as he breathed. "I'm in the Suites. Code black. Code blue. Code..." She winced, wondering how many people were listening to the transmission. "Just get me Gumbs and a medic. ET Out."

Ellie lowered her radio. Sal, after a few moments of terror, stepped down onto Violet's hand and hopped along her arm until he was resting on her shoulder. She stood stiffly, her eyes squeezed shut, as if she feared the bird might peck her eyeballs out.

Melanie was helping Murray sit up. He seemed okay. Ellie couldn't help but look at the body in the suitcase one more time. How did she get in there? Had she intended to stow away? Except that couldn't be it. The ligature marks on her neck meant she'd been strangled. There was clothing wrapped around her body, and most of it was evening wear. It looked like someone had shoved the dresses all around her body to keep her in place. Whoever had killed her had put her in the bag, most likely to hide their crime. Lost luggage was eventually returned to the port of departure, and they might never have known she was inside.

As she inspected the suitcase. It was dark blue, with big, zippered pockets in the front. There was something small and white shoved into the dead woman's hand. Ellie gently worked it loose, taking care not to touch anything else. It was an *Adventurous Cruises* luggage tag, folded in half! She opened it and saw that someone had filled it out in rounded cursive handwriting. It read: "Melanie Young. The *Adventurous Spirit*, room 1289."

Chapter Nine

A SHORT TIME LATER, ELLIE sat on Violet's bed and kicked her tennis shoes off, pulling her sock-clad feet up onto the clean white comforter. "Will you sit down?" she asked. "You're making me dizzy."

Violet was pacing back and forth like a tiger in a cage. Her long strides were at odds with the short stretch of carpet that ran from her dressing table to her bathroom door, and she only managed five or six steps before spinning around and heading in the opposite direction. Ellie adjusted her position and pulled a pillow into her lap. Violet had a whole row of plump pillows along the wall, turning the bed into a daybed of sorts. But most of the bed was covered in clean laundry. She'd started to fold it up, but Violet had insisted she leave it alone. So she sat with the pillow in her lap, watching Violet grow more agitated by the minute.

"I don't see why Paul wouldn't let us stay," Violet said irritably. She stopped pacing, but instead of sitting she put her back against her bathroom door. Her black silk bathrobe was hanging on a hook, and it brushed against her face as she backed into it. She batted it away and it fell to the ground.

Ellie got up. "Come. Sit on the bed. Now."

Violet obeyed. Ellie walked over and picked up the bathrobe, giving it a little shake before hanging it up. "You know why Paul sent us away. He needed to secure the evidence, and he wanted to talk to the witnesses without any extra drama. And you haven't exactly been..." she searched for the kindest words, "You haven't been your usual professional self."

"I don't know what you're talking about." Violet's nostrils flared.

"Is that a fact? Not only did you point at poor Murray and accuse him of killing that girl, *without evidence*, you were having a shouting match in the middle of the atrium when I arrived. And did you even think to ask why I was there? Kameron got calls from *three different crew members* saying that you were harassing a guest. What would have happened if I hadn't shown up when I did? Would you have started hair-pulling? Swearing? Tossing drinks in each other's faces? Honestly, Violet, I've never seen you behave that way." She picked up a mound of clean socks and set them on Violet's dresser to make room. When she sat back down, she ignored the little throb of pain in her hip.

Violet exhaled and leaned back against the row of pillows. Ellie sat next to her and did the same. She pulled a small midnight blue pillow into her lap and hugged it, enjoying the softness. "Why don't you tell me what's on your mind?"

"I'm sorry about how I acted. Actually, no. I take that back. I'm *not* sorry. I've been rehearsing that speech in my head for well over a year, and if I didn't let it out, it was going to kill me. Literally. I was going to burst and leave guts all over the ship. And I never touched her, Ellie. You know I'd never do that. No matter how mad I got."

"I know. But you had me worried."

Violet shrugged. "It's fine. It's done. I said what I needed to say. And now she can go live happily ever after with her weird little boyfriend. I couldn't care less."

That was a lie, but Violet said it with such ferocity that Ellie almost smiled. "Well, if you'd waited for me, I could have told you what I discovered earlier when I went to their room to drop off some towels."

Violet glanced over. "You did what?"

"Who doesn't like extra towels? Anyway, I went into their room for just a minute. I gave her some towels and some recommendations for events to attend. You know, all the events where *you* won't be present? They're sleeping in separate rooms. Also, she referred to Mr. Magnificent as her *employer*."

"Oh." Violet had the grace to look embarrassed. "That's good, I guess. But can we not call him that? It squicks me out."

"Sure." Ellie chuckled. "Granted, this doesn't make what she did to you any better, but maybe–"

"I know. I'm being petty. It was just salt in the wound, you know. Leaving *me* for someone like that." She gestured up and down her body. Her purple *Adventurous Cruises* polo shirt had come untucked at some point, but she still looked remarkably put together. "I mean — Have you *seen* me? I'm–"

"Magnificent?" Ellie teased. "Well, if your ego is back, perhaps your heart is on the mend after all. Now, about that poor girl in the suitcase, what do you think we're dealing with?"

Violet looked down at her hands. "I wish I knew. It was horrible. It looked like she'd been strangled, didn't it?"

"Yes. And I wonder what was up with her clothing."

"What do you mean?"

"Well, her suitcase was full of fancy clothes. I saw sequins, and some shiny fabric. Most people bring a nice outfit or two for the cruise, but a whole suitcase full? And that luggage tag in her hand must be a clue. I wonder if she had it in her hand when she died, or if the killer put it there. Either way, it's suggestive, don't you think?"

"Melanie didn't kill anyone," Violet's green eyes met Ellie's with full sincerity. "Don't get me wrong. I *hate* her guts and she can get eaten and pooped out by a shark for all I care, but she's not a killer. She..." Violet closed her eyes for a moment, then opened them back up, her expression tender. "Look. When we were together,

Melanie fed every stray cat in the neighborhood. There would be someone asking for money outside the grocery store and she'd empty her wallet for them and come home empty handed. She loved little kids, and dogs, and she volunteered at the juvie center. She doesn't have a murderous bone in her body."

Ellie nodded.

"But I do wish a shark would eat her," Violet added. "Just to be clear."

Ellie chuckled. "Understood. But what about that luggage tag? The one with her name on it?"

Violet scoffed. "So there was a luggage tag in the suitcase. It doesn't mean anything."

"Well, it probably means *something*," Ellie said. Violet looked ready to argue, so she quickly added, "I'm not saying Melanie killed her. If you say she's not the type, I believe you."

"That's it? You believe me?" Violet sounded skeptical.

"Sure. But it's not me you'll need to convince."

And as if to prove that statement true, a knock on the door made them both jump. Paul's deep voice called out. "It's me. Can I come in?"

PAUL GUMBS DUCKED HIS HEAD as he passed beneath the threshold. Once he was inside and the door was shut behind him, he got right down to business in his soft Jamaican-accented English. "I'm sorry to keep you two waitin'." He looked around for a place to sit and chose the only remaining seat: the small stool at Violet's dressing table. The surface was littered with magazines and bottles of nail polish in a dozen different shades of red. A bra hung off the mirror by one thin strap. If Paul noticed, he didn't show it. "Let's start from the beginning. Why don't you tell me what happened, and I'll share what I can."

Ellie told him about finding the luggage, their futile attempt to move it, and the discovery of the body. "Murray fainted, and then I called for help. Is he going to be okay?"

Paul nodded. "He's fine. Doctor Strunk said it was stress-induced syncope."

"What's that?" Ellie asked.

"He panicked and passed out." Paul said.

"What a hero," Violet muttered.

"Why were you two moving luggage in the first place? Isn't that a job for the porters?"

"Ah," Ellie said, choosing her words carefully. "Well, I happened to be in the atrium when Mr. Magnif—" Violet was glaring, so she stammered, "I mean, when Murray asked for help moving the suitcase out of the hallway. And I figured, why not just go take care of it?" She glanced at Violet, who was studying her fingernails. "And Violet was there too, so she went with me."

"Violet was there too," Paul said flatly. "That's your story?"

Violet shot Ellie a pained look. "I had a discussion with Melanie, and—"

"A discussion," Paul repeated.

"Fine. I had a *heated* conversation with Melanie, and then the conversation was over, and that's when that jerk with the bird came over. He was complaining about the luggage, and I felt kind of bad about my, um—"

"She wanted to offer an olive branch," Ellie said. "A guest wanted the luggage moved, so we went to move the luggage."

"You offered," Paul said, his voice neither believing nor disbelieving. "Because you felt bad. About your heated discussion."

Ellie's hands were two tight knots in her lap. With effort, she loosened them. "Paul, no doubt you heard about the disagreement Violet had with her ex. But that's all it was. And then Melanie's boss showed up, and we went to take care of his luggage problem. That's what happened."

"I see." He pulled a small notepad out of his shirt pocket and made a notation. "You say that the magician is her boss?"

Ellie nodded. "That's what she said when I talked to her this afternoon."

Paul's glance betrayed his surprise. "You spoke to her this afternoon? When? And why?"

"Um. I *may* have dropped some towels off, as a courtesy," Ellie said. Paul was staring at her and she felt moisture run down the back of her neck. "Fine. *Fine!* I admit it.

I dropped off the towels because I wanted to meet her. Violet was upset that her ex was on board, and I wanted to do some... um. I wanted to—"

"You were snooping," Paul said. He managed to keep his expression neutral, but one corner of his mouth lifted before he smoothed it back down. "And what did you discover, exactly?"

She shot him a guilty smile. "Not much. I saw that they had separate rooms. And Melanie said she was traveling with her employer. I was going to tell Violet all about it because she's freaking out—"

Violet's elbow nudged her. "I was *not* freaking out."

Paul cleared his throat. "May I make a suggestion, ladies? Off this ship, never speak to any member of law enforcement without a lawyer present. Because you'd both fall apart during cross-examination and end up serving consecutive life sentences for a crime you didn't commit."

"Hey!" they said simultaneously.

Paul barked a laugh, and Ellie felt the tightness in her shoulders loosen. Why was she worried about what she'd done? Paul was just doing his job. And what were they going to do, fire her? As soon as that thought came to mind, she felt a flash of guilt. Just because she was a part-owner of the cruise line now, it didn't mean she should be flouting the rules. Hadn't she taken Roberta to task for doing the same thing? She winced. "Sorry, Paul. We'll tell you everything." She aimed an insistent look at Violet, who pretended not to see it, then turned back to Paul. "What else do you want to know?"

"Ellie, you found this in the deceased woman's hand, is that correct?" He reached into his other shirt pocket and took out a plastic bag. Inside was the paper luggage tag. It was the kind emailed to guests prior to their voyage. After folding it into quarters and filling in the information, it could be stapled over a suitcase handle. The tag was torn along one side, as if it had been yanked off another suitcase by force.

"Yes," Ellie said.

His eyes flicked to Violet. "And I understand you had a prior relationship with this Melanie Young?"

Violet's mouth compressed slightly. "Yes."

"And when was the last time you were in contact with her?"

"Prior to today? It's been over a year."

He held out the luggage tag. "Is this Ms. Young's handwriting?"

Violet's mouth twitched. "No."

She's lying, Ellie thought, her heart heavy. *I'd bet my monthly shopping budget on it.*

If Paul noticed, he didn't say anything. He asked, "And what was your argument about?"

Violet scoffed. "Paul, don't talk to me like I'm one of your suspects."

Paul shot Ellie a *talk some sense into her* look. Ellie glanced over. "Violet, you know he needs to ask these questions of everybody. It's not personal."

Violet told him everything. She told him about the breakup, the shock of seeing Melanie on board, and the way they'd argued in the atrium. In the end, she sighed and sat up straighter. "You can go talk to the crew at *Cuppa*, or the piano player. I imagine they overheard everything."

Paul nodded. "I'll do that. And what did Ms. Young do for a living when you knew her?"

"She was an actress. Theater, mostly, although she had a few small parts on television. She played a dead body on CSI once. And she gave walking tours in Hollywood to supplement her income. Come see where your favorite movie stars live, that kind of thing. It wasn't much fun, but it paid the bills. We kept a place in L.A., and I flew home between contracts."

"And neither of you recognized the woman in the suitcase?"

They shook their heads.

"And what can you tell me about Murray the Magnificent?"

"Very little," Ellie said. "I only just met him myself."

Violet glowered at him. "Same here. He seems like a jerk. He bosses her around and she flutters her eyelashes at him like he's being charming."

"Well, it sounds like she's his assistant," Ellie said. "That might be her job."

Paul frowned and closed his notebook before tucking it back into his shirt pocket. "That's all I need for now. But I may have more questions later."

Ellie nodded. "Paul, what can you tell us? Do you know who that poor murdered woman is, or where the suitcase came from?"

"We don't know much yet. The body is with Doctor Strunk, and he'll do a more thorough examination this evening. There was no identification on the body or in the suitcase. Kameron is combing through our guest list to see if anyone failed to show up after checking in at Port-Miami. Ms. Young and," he checked his notepad, "Murray Nickles, stage name: Murray the Magnificent, claim they don't know who she is either."

"Do you believe them?" Ellie asked.

Paul nodded. "At first glance, yes; their denials seem credible. At the moment, our only clue is the luggage tag."

Violet crossed her arms. "Well, if this Murray guy managed to sneak an entire parrot on board, maybe he got that luggage on board too," Violet said. "In fact, maybe he's trying to pin the murder on Melanie."

"And why would he do that?" Paul asked.

"I don't know," Violet snapped, tossing her head to one side.

"So why would you suggest it?"

"Well, obviously *Melanie* didn't do it. Who else is there?"

"Ah. Well. There is that," he said dryly. "And as for the parrot, Mr. Nickles presented his medical paperwork to the crew at port, and they made an exception for him." Paul shrugged. "I told him that so long as he leaves Sal in his room there won't be any trouble."

"You're already on a first name basis with the parrot?" Ellie teased.

Paul preened a little. "Well he *did* call me a handsome fellow."

Ellie chuckled. "Flatter the man and he rolls right over. So, what's our next move?"

"*Our* next move?" Paul looked amused. "Ellie, you have company, *and* you're covering for Roberta. That's plenty. I've got the investigation handled. Of course, if you notice anything out of the ordinary, come to me immediately. Thankfully, Mr. Nickles and Ms. Young have agreed to keep the matter to themselves. I'll be looking into their backgrounds more closely, and I may have more questions for Violet, as she has some prior knowledge of Ms. Young." He shot Violet a questioning look. "Assuming that's okay with you."

"Why wouldn't it be?" Violet shot back.

"Very well," Ellie said, hopping off the bed and stretching her legs, picking up one foot at a time, feeling the tension in her quadriceps muscles tighten then release. "Paul, in the absence of Roberta, please keep me informed of your investigation. And I'll notify our attorneys in the morning." She sighed. There were some aspects of being an owner that weren't any fun at all, and lawyers and paperwork were right at the top of that list. Roberta couldn't get back too soon! It would feel great to hand that radio back over to her, and all the responsibilities that came along with it.

Paul raised an eyebrow. "Yes, I'll keep you informed *during Roberta's absence.* As if you'd stop pestering me anyway."

Ellie winked at him. "Well, now my meddling is on the up and up. As an owner, I'm officially allowed to poke my nose into shipboard affairs." She turned toward the bed. "Violet, are you going to be okay?"

"Yeah. I'll be fine." But as she said the words, she sounded defeated, and her head slumped down. Ellie and Paul exchanged a worried look. Should she tell Paul that Violet had lied about the handwriting? No, that wouldn't be fair. For one thing, she wasn't a hundred-percent sure. And for another, it might not matter. If it did, she'd bring it up. She reached out and grabbed Violet's hand. "Come on. I'll buy you a drink." She pulled Violet into a standing position. "Paul, I'd ask you to join us but..."

He smiled at them. "That's okay. I have work to do." He opened the door and paused in the opening, looking back at Violet. "I recommend that you stay away from your ex, for everyone's sakes."

Violet's smile was as brittle as old glass. "You don't need to tell me twice."

Chapter Ten

AFTER BREAKFAST THE NEXT MORNING, Ellie took her family to Beachcomber Key, the small private island owned by the cruise line. After a stop at the shops to buy a mermaid costume for Clara, and a bite of lunch at the Crab Shack, they located some lounge chairs in a shady spot beneath a cluster of palm trees. Ellie offered to get some cold drinks from the stand nearby, and by the time she returned, balancing a cardboard tray in her arms, Junior had dozed off in his chair. He was on his back, sunglasses on, his mouth slightly open, snoring softly. Clara was face-down on his belly, fast asleep, her body rising and falling with the movement of her breath. Marcie looked up from the paperback book she'd brought and lifted a finger to her lips. "Sorry," she whispered. "Clara had a rough night, and he was up with her. I don't think they got much sleep."

Ellie set her bounty down on her beach towel and handed Marcie a Piña Colada. Then she took one for herself and pointed toward the water. "Let's take a little walk," she whispered.

The water was a deep aquamarine blue in the distance, and the sunlight threw up glittery lights where it reflected off the waves. The waves lapped the shore, transparent and thin, and palm trees hung lazily over the blue beach chairs in the distance. A couple, holding hands, walked further ahead, leaving footprints that melted away as the waves came in. The low roar of the water was punctuated by the laughter of snorkelers out further in the surf, happy screams of children chasing one another along the beach, and the occasional call of a seabird. "This is beautiful," Marcie said, once they'd been strolling along the damp edge of the sand for a while.

"So," Ellie said, choosing her words carefully. "Do you want to tell me what's been going on with you and Junior?" She half expected her daughter-in-law to deny there was a problem, but Marcie only sighed.

"You noticed that, huh?"

"Well, I don't know what I saw, exactly. But you seem tense. Have you been fighting?"

Marcie frowned. "Not exactly. It's more like he's always on edge. I'd blame his work, but that hardly seems fair. I'm married to a cop. He's going to bring some stress home with him from time to time. I'm not upset about that; it's part of the package. But..." Marcie paused to take off her flip flops. She let them dangle in her fingers and she squished her pink-painted toes into the sand.

"Yes?" Ellie took her sandals off too. It felt good to have the warm sand beneath her feet. They resumed their slow walk along the edge of the water.

"Well, he bottles up what he's feeling. And then he gets short-tempered. And even though I should know better, I try to drag it out of him, and that makes him even crankier. He thinks I'm nagging him to death. And — who knows — maybe he's right? You know me, Mom. I get worried, and then I try to keep it to myself, but then everything I'm worried about comes leaking out of my mouth, and the next thing I know I'm treating him like he's a stubborn little boy. I swear, it's like I have two kids sometimes, him *and* Clara. And at least Clara doesn't hold out on me." Marcie laughed weakly.

Ellie remembered something. "When Junior was six, he broke his big toe, but he refused to let me look at it for days. He seemed to believe he could wish it away if he tried hard enough." She sipped her drink. It was too sweet, so she swirled the plastic cup around to help the ice melt faster.

Marcie's smile was half-hearted. "I *know* Ron. But something has changed. Lately, I never know what's going to set him off."

"Hon, if he's being mean, that's *not* okay. You're his wife, and he needs to—"

She held up her hands. "Oh. No! It's nothing like that. He's never mean *to* me. It's more like he's always frustrated. And lately, he's been acting strangely. Like, he'll be in a fantastic mood all of a sudden, which is great, but he won't say why. And if I dare say that I'm glad to see him in a good mood, it's like I burst his bubble. He sulks! And a few times..." Marcie took a deep breath. "I think he sent my call straight to voicemail. He's never done that before. When he's at work, he leaves his ringer off. But now it does that thing where it rings twice and it goes to his voicemail. It's like he's rejecting me."

Poor Marcie! She certainly did look miserable. It was too bad that marital issues couldn't be fixed by having your mother tell you to straighten up. Otherwise she'd go to Junior right now and demand he apologize to his wife! But that could only make things worse. So she said, "I'm sorry, hon. That sounds really hard. For both of you. Is there anything I can do to help?"

Marcie shrugged. "I can't think of anything. But don't worry. We'll figure it out." She stepped toward the water, letting the crystal-clear waves rush over her feet. She looked back, the blue sky surrounding her body like a living postcard. "I'm sorry. I'm ruining our lovely day. You shouldn't have to worry about this stuff."

Ellie stepped into the surf too. The water was as warm and soothing as a bath! So different than the beaches at home. "Nonsense, kiddo. I love you both and worrying about you is my job." Her heart sank, "I just... I wish I had been around more. You probably feel like I abandoned you, and that's not too far from the truth."

Marcie tried to untangle a knot from her long mouse-brown hair, and she shot Ellie a disapproving look through the strands. "Now you're the one being silly. Think it over, Mom. First, you watch your granddaughter, for free, for more than a year. Then you loan us your enormous house so we can save up money for our own down payment. We're not angry, Mom, at all. We're grateful."

Ellie's eyes stung a little. The sun was very bright! She gave Marcie a grateful smile. "I can't tell you what a relief that is to hear."

"Good," Marcie said, nodding once. "Now, I want you to tell me all about that nice man you're dating."

Surprise jolted her like a jellyfish sting. "How did you know?"

"You're not as sneaky as you think you are. I saw the way you two looked at each other. Besides, Clara informed me that 'Gamma kissed Gampa' and it doesn't take a cop to figure out what *that* meant." Marcie laughed. "So, when do we get to meet him? For real, that is."

"Tonight. Assuming I get up the courage to tell Junior. I was going to tell you last night, and then I was going to tell you this morning, but—"

"But Ron has been a grumpy-butt and you bailed. Don't worry about it." Marcie sipped her drink and used her hand holding the flip-flops to itch her forehead, leaving a streak of wet sand behind. "But tell me about him. What's he like?"

"Ben? Oh, he's wonderful." Ellie felt her heart lifting skyward like a kite. "He's funny, and smart, and kind. He loves to read, and he's got this amazing gift for navigation. Did you know you can sail a ship using nothing but the stars as a guide? His father taught him how, and he's spent most of his life on the water." She felt herself smiling. "And he's one of those men who keeps it all buttoned up, you know? He's got a lot to say, but he keeps it inside until he knows you better. He's never been married, and he spent eight years in the Navy, and have I mentioned how *fun* he is? He's just—" She was babbling, and so she forced herself to stop.

Marcie looked thoughtful. "How serious is it?"

Ellie glanced down at her wet toes. "I think I love him."

"Wow."

"Yeah. Who knew? I never thought it would be possible to..." She took a shaky breath. "I thought you only got one true love, you know? And it wasn't something that I was looking for, but it crept up on me. For a while, I tried not to believe it. But..." She glanced nervously at her daughter in law. "I don't want you to think I love Junior's dad any less. Because I don't."

"I know, Mom. And I think it's good. I really do!" Marcie's smile faded as quickly as it came. "You were so broken after Dad passed. It's like your flame went out, and we were afraid we'd lose you too."

Had it been that bad? Maybe it had been, but it was hard to tell what a storm looks like when you're standing in the center of it. "Well, there was no chance of that. Not with you keeping such a good eye on me. Making sure I don't fall and break a hip. Bringing me a daily calcium chew with my morning tea. Nagging me about my doctor appointments with religious fervor." She raised an eyebrow and Marcie laughed.

"Yes, I went a bit overboard, I'll admit. But I got that from you, didn't I? You're a tough act to follow. You Tappets have such a bossy form of love. And it's hard to match that energy."

Ellie reached her arms out. "I'm so glad you're here, love. Not just here visiting, but here in my life."

Marcie hugged her, hard. "Me too. Now, what do you say we go wake up the sleepyheads and build a sandcastle. And then I'll turn to Junior and say 'Hey, did you hear Ma has some *really good news*' and you'll say..." She pointed at Ellie.

"I'll tell him about Ben."

"Good." Marcie said. "Let's rip the band-aid off. You'll feel better in no time."

Chapter Eleven

VIOLET AND KAMERON WERE WAITING at the restaurant when the family arrived that night. "Hey," Violet said, reaching out to give Ellie a hug. "The captain is running a few minutes late, but I told him I'd fill in during the appetizer course." Violet turned toward the younger Tappets. "You must be Ron and Marcie. And this little queen must be Clara!" She beamed at them all. "I can't tell you how pleased I am to meet you. Your mom talks about you constantly, and I feel like I know you already. I hope you don't mind me crashing your meal to say hello."

Junior smiled at her, "And you must be Violet, the singer."

She tilted her head, "How did you know?"

"Ma said you have a lot of charisma," Junior said, reaching out to shake her hand. "Pleased to meet you. It's nice to finally meet all of mom's friends in person." His voice held a hint of reproach, and Ellie grit her teeth but didn't say anything. He'd taken the news about Ben rather well, but ever since she'd spilled the beans Junior had been less talkative than usual. She looked over at Marcie, who seemed completely at ease. Well, if she hadn't noticed anything, perhaps Junior's tone was just her imagination.

"We're coming to your show tonight," Marcie said. "Karaoke Crush? Mom said it's the best show on the ship."

Violet grinned at the compliment. "Well, I'd pretend to be modest, but why pretend?" She gestured at the young black woman next to her. Kameron had traded in her security uniform for dark jeans and a sleeveless gold top that warmed up her deep brown skin. Her long hair was plaited in a detailed-looking braid nearly as thick as her wrist. "And may I introduce Kameron Achebe, your babysitter for the evening."

Marcie smiled at Kameron and bounced Clara lightly on her hip. "Are you sure you don't mind? I don't want you to feel obligated."

Kameron's smile was pure happiness. "No, ma'am. It's no obligation at all. Before I took this job, I was an au pair in my home country, and I miss spending time with little ones." She leaned forward and shot Clara a playful look. Clara turned her head away, suddenly shy, and Kameron tweaked her foot. Clara spun around but Kameron had stepped back, and she was looking up like nothing had happened. Clara laughed.

Marcie grinned. “Oh, I think you two will get along just fine. Thank you so much. I can’t remember the last time we had a grown-up evening out.” Marcie handed Clara over, and the little girl immediately wiggled like a fish out of water.

Kameron didn’t seem to mind. She said, “Oh, you want to wiggle? Very well. But don’t stray.” Kameron set Clara on the ground, and she immediately took off running toward the restaurant door. “I’ll get you!” Kameron called, chasing her with an easy jog, staying two steps behind on purpose. She turned back and gave Marcie and Junior a wave before they disappeared around the corner.

Marcie put her arm around Junior’s waist and sighed. “A whole night off! This is heaven.” He smiled down at her and brushed a lock of her hair off her shoulder.

Ellie felt a tiny wave of relief. The kids were fine! They might be having some stresses – what married couple didn’t? – but there was plenty of love in their hearts. She could see it there, in the way they interacted.

The host brought them to a table near a big picture window and lit the candle in the center of the table before wishing them a good evening. Violet sat across from Junior and put her elbows on the table. “So. What do you two think about your mother running off to join the circus?”

Junior stammered a reply, insisting that it was all just fine, whatever his mom wanted to do was her business.

"Don't mind Violet. She's direct like that," Ellie said. "It's one of the things we love *and* hate about her." Violet winked at her, and Ellie's heart lifted. It was good to see Violet back to her old self! Just as she'd suspected, a good night's sleep had done her a world of good.

"Well, I'll admit it was a shock," Junior admitted. "What was that old TV show where a bunch of people went off for a three-hour tour and they didn't come home for years?"

"Gilligan's Island," Marcie said. "I used to watch it on *Nick at Nite* with my dad when my mom worked swing shift at the hospital. Gilligan's Island was his favorite."

Junior laughed. "Right! When Ma left, it was kind of like Gilligan's Island. She went off for a one-week vacation and she basically never came back." He frowned slightly, but he noticed Marcie giving him a stern look and he quickly added, "But it's good to see her so happy. That's what's important."

"Being away from home is the worst part of working on a cruise ship," Violet said, perusing the wine menu. "Sometimes it can feel like being torn in two." She looked sad for a moment, but then she rallied. "Your Mom wanted to come home earlier, but Roberta asked her to help host her friends' funeral, and she agreed, as a favor to Roberta. When you meet Roberta, you'll understand. She's a hard woman to say no to."

Marcie shot Ellie an amused look. "I know a few women like that."

"Hush," Ellie said, smiling.

The server came by and took everyone's drink orders. After he left, Junior turned to Violet. "So, what can you tell us about the captain? Does he have a history of dating his employees?"

Ellie choked on her ice water.

"Ron!" Marcie said.

Violet laughed. "Hey! I think it's a fair question. And no, Captain Spark has never dated anyone in the years I've worked for him. Besides, he technically works for your mom now, so if anyone will be on the wrong end of a sexual harassment lawsuit, it's her." She shot Ellie a look of disapproval. "And to think, *I* recommended you for this job." She turned back to Junior, her expression bland and her eyes dancing with amusement. "Truly, she's disappointed us all."

Junior laughed, and Ellie shot Violet a grateful look. She was certainly taking the pressure off tonight!

"No one is suing anyone," Ellie said.

"Well, now that you're dating someone on the ship," Junior said, "what does that mean? Are you staying here forever?"

Ellie blinked. "Well, I haven't given it much thought. I'm just taking the days as they come."

"I see," Junior said, frowning a little. She waited for him to say more, but he didn't. He just sipped his water and browsed the dinner menu in silence.

"I understand you're a police officer, like your father was?" Violet asked, leaning forward on her elbows. "What's that like?"

He shrugged. "It's okay."

"Your father must have been very proud of you," Violet said.

Junior's jaw seemed to harden. Violet shot Ellie a *what-did-I-do look*. Ellie shrugged, and Violet turned to Marcie. "And you work for the school district?"

Marcie nodded. "I do. I'm a part-time math instructor. In fact, that's how Ron and I met. His brother Cole is a coworker of mine. He introduced me to Ron at a middle school band recital, of all places." She smiled at the memory. "Cole was trying hard to fill up the audience so his students wouldn't feel bad, and he roped his brother into attending. The theme was 'Spring Fling'."

"Music has a way of working miracles," Violet said. "Did your mom ever tell you about the time she brought someone back from the dead with a sing-along?"

"What?" Marcie and Junior spoke as one, and their heads turned in her direction.

"She exaggerates," Ellie said. "We had a young woman who'd been poisoned, and she was in the hospital, and all I did was—"

"Someone was *poisoned*?" Marcie flattened her palm against her chest and squeaked the words aloud. Her voice was loud, and a foursome at a nearby window table turned to stare.

Ellie laughed as if the matter were a funny joke, "Oh, you're a kick in the pants!" She turned to the guests watching them and added, "I recommend the raspberry chocolate lava cake if you're having a hard time deciding.

It's *so* delicious." She waited until they'd turned away before she turned to Violet and glared. Was this topic really the best dinner conversation?

Violet looked abashed. "Oh, we have an occasional mystery on board, that's all. Whenever you have a lot of people together, you have human nature at work. Your mom is the helpful type. Sometimes she helps Paul with his investigations. Paul Gumbs, that is, our security officer. He's Kameron's boss."

"Investigations," Junior said, lifting his eyebrows. "Plural?"

"Good evening." Ben was at Ellie's shoulder, as if he'd been there all along. She glanced up at him, surprised, and he said, "Oh, am I interrupting a story? Please, don't let me." He beamed down at Ellie. "Are you telling them about the time you found Morgan Picklewick's killer by—"

Ellie shook her head rapidly and crisscrossed her hands over her body, low where she hoped Marcie and Junior wouldn't see them. Ben's mouth snapped shut. "Oh? Never mind. I must have been thinking of someone else." He pulled out the chair next to Ellie and sat down, pulling the napkin into his lap with a flourish. "Have you ordered dinner already? I'm famished, and Devon tells me the latest batch of king crab is to die for."

Ellie lifted her menu and studied it. Junior was staring at her like she'd grown a second head, and she lifted the menu even higher, to eyebrow level. "Yes. I think I'll have the crab," she said.

"Ma. How many crimes *have* you gotten mixed up in?" Junior asked.

"Oh, just a few!" Ellie said brightly. She set her menu down on the table. "Oh, and before I manage to mess this up again, Marcie, Junior, I'd like to introduce you to my boyfriend, Ben."

"It's a pleasure," Marcie said, smiling at him. "Mom's told us all about you."

Junior stood up to shake his hand. "Ron Tappet," he said.

"Well, we ruined your Mom's plans to break the news gently," Ben said, smiling at Ellie. "But I'm glad the cat is out of the bag." He looked around the table. "Where's Clara?"

Marcie smiled. "She's with Kameron. Mom thought we might like a grown-up evening, and Kameron was nice enough to volunteer."

Violet checked her watch with an exaggerated gesture. Actually, she checked the spot where her watch should be. Her wrist was bare. "Well, I've warmed them up, Captain, but now you're on your own. Paul asked me to stop by and see him before the show. But don't worry. I told them that while you collect shrunken heads in your spare time, the doctors say we need not be concerned."

Ben threw back his head and laughed. "One head! Just one! And it was a carving made by an incredibly talented artist in Bali. No actual craniums were harmed. I swear."

She saluted him, winked, and said her goodbyes. The server came back with drinks and everyone ordered dinner. Ben looked around the table and asked, "So, what did I miss?"

The food was good, the candles in the restaurant flickered and spread warm light across the white-sheeted tables, and Ellie watched as Ben gave the kids his full attention, asking questions and telling little stories about his life at sea. As he talked, she saw that Marcie liked him, and that Junior's polite reserve was starting to melt away. When the waiter came to take their dessert orders, Ben reached over and squeezed her hand beneath the table. She smiled at him, not bothering to hide the joy surging beneath her breastbone. Why had she been keeping these two halves of her life apart for so long? In retrospect, her old worries made no sense at all.

Chapter Twelve

STEPPING INSIDE THE MOONLIGHT LOUNGE was like being swept into a dark and velvety hug. The familiar semi-circular booths faced the front of the room and the dark leather seats gleamed softly beneath the sparse overhead lights. The low stage was lit with two spotlights, and each spotlight illuminated a microphone in a skinny metal stand. Purple velvet curtains hung to either side of the stage, and soft jazz music played over the speakers at a low volume. Servers circulated through the room, smiling, welcoming, and taking drink orders. Violet was nowhere to be seen, but a woman in a dark uniform sat inside the small DJ booth to the right of the stage. The DJ looked down at the glowing screen, preparing for the evening's festivities.

They settled into a booth and put in their drink orders. Marcie leaned back against the plush backing of the booth with a happy sigh. "This is really nice," she said.

Ben nodded. "Normally I don't get to attend guest events, so this is a special occasion. And Violet's show is always packed. She has a knack for getting shy singers up on stage. Just ask your Mom."

Junior looked at her. "Are *you* going to sing?"

She chuckled. "No way. That was a *one time* deal. Besides, I wouldn't want to take up a slot that could go to one of our honored guests. Like you and Marcie." She half-rose from her seat. "Should I put your name in the bowl?"

Marcie grabbed her wrist and tugged her back down. "No thank you! The only music I'm interested in is—"

Marcie's words were interrupted by an excited squeal. It sounded so much like a young child that they all swung around to see. Behind them, at the closest table, Murray and Melanie were just arriving. And Sal the parrot was making a racket on Murray's shoulder. So much for leaving the bird in his room!

"This is bad, isn't it?" Ben asked quietly. Ellie nodded. She'd made a point of suggesting Melanie go elsewhere. And after that fight, why would she even want to be in here? Violet's name was right on the newsletter! Melanie had to know that her ex would be present.

Junior accepted his beer from the server with a word of thanks, then looked over, speaking low. "What do you mean?"

Ellie leaned in close. "Remember how my friend Violet had an argument with her ex? Well, that's her ex."

Marcie sipped her drink and turned her head, taking a sneaky look back at the couple. She faced forward and put her drink down. "Him? Seriously?"

"No. Not the gentleman. The lady with him. That's Violet's former partner." She whispered in Marcie's ear. "Melanie. The magician's assistant."

Marcie looked perplexed, then her eyes widened. "Oh. *Oh*! I just didn't realize that, well, you know..."

"It's fine." Ellie smiled at Marcie because she knew exactly what she was feeling. It was natural to feel uncertain how to react when meeting someone from a different background than your own. But the more time Ellie had spent aboard the *Spirit*, with guests and crew from all nations, all faiths, and varying cultures and experiences, the more it affirmed what she'd always been taught: that every human being was a child of God. Still, it could take a person a moment to wrap their head around those differences!

"Who let that parrot on board?" Ben asked.

"Sal is an emotional support parrot," Ellie said. She glanced back, hoping that their gossip wasn't being overheard. Thankfully, the twosome seemed embroiled in a conversation of their own. Neither one looked entirely happy, and Melanie was studiously avoiding looking up at the stage. Perhaps Murray had insisted she come? She looked back at Ben. "I've heard of emotional support animals, but I didn't know parrots qualified."

Junior looked puzzled. "I'm surprised he lets the bird sit on his shoulder. Can birds be potty trained? I'm not sure how emotionally supportive it would be to have a parrot take a massive—"

Ben laughed out loud. He tried to turn his laugh into a cough, but out of the corner of her eye Ellie caught the magician watching him with an irritated expression. Ben whispered to Junior, "Just in case, we should have a plan. If he flies overhead, let's duck under the table."

Junior nodded. "Or we could use the drink menus as shields."

Marcie and Ellie exchanged an amused look. It was nice to see the menfolk getting along.

The lights dimmed, and Violet stepped on stage. Her raven-black hair shone beneath the spotlight but instead of her officer's uniform she was wearing a fantastic cocktail dress. It was covered in silver sequins that dangled down, and each sequin was shaped like a curved dagger, giving the fabric a shaggy appearance. Wherever the light hit the dress, it reflected, sending spots of light onto the floor and walls like she was a human disco ball. Her voice was low and velvety, and her dark red lipstick and short black hair gave her a look almost out of the nineteen twenties. "Welcome, everyone! I'm Violet Wolfe, your cruise director extraordinaire. And here, tonight, on this stage, legends will come to life." She paused, holding one hand up high in the air. Then she swept her arm from left to right, pointing at the audience. "Who's ready for Karaoke Crush?"

The crowd cheered appreciatively, and Ellie felt a tiny thrill of anticipation. This was Violet in her element! No matter how many times she'd heard that same introduction, Ellie always arrived at the show expecting a good time, and some surprises along the way. That was one of the best things about karaoke. Every show was different than the last. Ellie leaned over to Ben. "She put on a new outfit. We must be in for something special."

Violet walked back and forth across the stage, her spike heels tapping with each step. "Tonight, we'll be enjoying karaoke. But not just any karaoke! For each song, we'll have two brave singers come up and share the song. When I point left," She demonstrated by pointing at the left microphone, "the first person will sing. And when I point right," she pointed at the other microphone, "the second person will sing." She beamed at the audience. "But this isn't a sing off! We're not here to *compete*. Tonight we'll affirm that all our voices can be beautiful. Let's call our first singers to the stage." Violet was shading her hands with her eyes, looking out into the audience, and she opened her mouth but snapped it shut before saying another word. She stood stock-still, her microphone just below her lips.

Her eyes narrowed.

"Oh no," Ellie whispered to Ben. "I know that look."

Violet pointed at the crowd. "You!" At first, it seemed like she was pointing right at Ellie! But Violet's gaze went past their table and landed on the magician. She smiled wickedly. "Everyone! We're honored to have a very special guest aboard the *Adventurous Spirit*. He's a man so talented, so famous, so *admired*, that surely he requires no introduction. I'm talking about our visiting magician, Murray the Magnificent!" She flung her hand out, open to the sky. And then she jerked her head in the direction of Murray's table. A moment later, the spotlight had moved, and it blasted the table with light. Sal bobbed his head excitedly and said "Murray the Magician! Murray! Murray!" The magician blinked beneath the lights as if momentarily blinded. Next to him, Melanie was shooting Violet a look of pure fury.

Murray stood up and looked around the room, waving and smiling. "Good evening! I'm glad to be here!"

"Now, Murray, I know that magic is your talent, but what would you say to joining me on stage for a song? Will you come up and sing with me? Together, let's show everyone that it's nothing to be afraid of."

Murray's face looked pale behind his smile, and he looked like he was about to decline, but Violet was already pumping her fist in the air and chanting his name. "Murray! Murray! Murray!"

The parrot screeched and began swaying rhythmically on Murray's shoulder, his colorful head bobbing in time with the chants

The crowd chanted along with Violet. Ellie, seeing the stricken look on the man's face, waved at Violet, keeping her hand low in front of her body where the audience wouldn't notice it. Violet flicked her eyes in Ellie's direction but bounced her gaze away when she saw Ellie mouthing the word 'no'.

Murray stood and made his way to the stage. A bead of sweat ran down his temple, and he brushed it away with the sleeve of his jacket. Behind him, Melanie called out, "Murray, you don't need to sing if you don't want to." But he only shook his head at her and doggedly walked up to the stage, smiling at the guests as he went. When he reached the front, he stood by the microphone stand on the left and picked up the microphone. He blew into it and it made a high-pitched squeal. "Ah, hello, everyone. Murray the Magnificent here. I'm Los Angeles's *premier* party magician." He wiped his forehead. "I can't claim to have a good singing voice, but I'm always game for a challenge." He shot Violet an arrogant smile. "Shall we?"

"Excellent," Violet said. She stepped into the DJ booth and whispered something in the woman's ear. The woman seemed to argue, but Violet spoke again, and the DJ nodded. Violet stepped out on stage, and said, "Who enjoys The Eagles?" The crowd clapped and she nodded. "Good!" A rhythmic bass guitar began sounding out a beat. A familiar beat. Drums added to the complexity of the music.

"Oh no. I know this song," Ben said.

Ellie recognized the song too, and her heart sank. She looked around the lounge and saw the crowd was already swaying to the music. Melanie looked angry enough to bite through wood, but everyone else appeared immune to what Violet was doing. Well, perhaps everyone except for Murray, who was gripping the microphone like it might run away from him. He was being a good sport, all things considered. And this wasn't like Violet, at all. Since when did she put her personal feelings ahead of the comfort of their guests?

Never, until Melanie Young had come aboard.

Violet tipped her head back, held up the microphone, and began to sing *Witchy Woman* by the Eagles. After three full verses, she pointed to Murray. He stepped forward and sang. While his voice was high and squeaky, he gave the song his best effort and he stayed mostly in tune. The crowd cheered him on, even more loudly than they'd cheered for Violet. Every time Violet said the words *witchy woman* she stared directly at Melanie, her voice beseeching, her eyes full of contempt. Finally, the song ended, and the crowd applauded. Ellie cheered as loudly as she dared for Murray. That poor man! He hadn't noticed Violet was using him to make a cruel point.

"I can't believe she did that," Marcie said to Ellie. "At dinner, she seemed so nice."

Behind them, Melanie was getting up from the booth. She picked up her silver clutch purse, drained the last of her martini, straightened up, and made a beeline for the exit.

"She usually is," Ellie said.

Violet led the rest of the Karaoke show as usual, encouraging participants as they sang, and making sure they were well-supported by the audience. As the show went on, Murray sat alone with his parrot, drinking and bobbing his head to the music. If he was concerned that Melanie had left him there alone, he didn't show it. And after the show ended, he stuck around, shaking hands and answering questions about Sal. Everyone who approached him got a different object pulled out from behind their ear: a coin, a poker chip, another business card, a piece of hard candy. Compared to how uncomfortable he'd seemed on stage, Murray looked at ease now, performing within his element.

A couple in evening wear walked up to him. The woman wore a long blue silk dress and the man had expertly coiffed gray hair that reminded Ellie of cupcake frosting. He pointed at Murray and called out. "Hey! I remember you. We met at your office, about a year ago." Murray hurried forward with a big smile. "Of course! It's always nice to meet a returning customer. It's something with a J, right? Mr. Jones? No, Mr. Jackson. I never forget a face. Is this your lovely wife? Let me introduce you to Sal, my business partner. Say hello to the pretty lady, Sal."

"Pretty lady!" Sal responded, his long, beautiful tail feathers spreading outward.

Well, at least those two are happy, she thought.

Ellie excused herself for a moment and went up to the stage to look for Violet. She pulled the glittery curtain back, but the stage was empty. Violet had already left.

Chapter Thirteen

AFTER THE SHOW, ELLIE SAID goodnight to her kids and walked Ben back to his stateroom. She swung by the security office and knocked on the door; Paul answered.

She stepped into the room, turning sideways to make it through the cramped gauntlet of desk chairs. It seemed that every available surface was crammed with gear. The desks had multiple monitors on them, and a tall rack of portable radios rested along the wall near the door. One wall was covered in clipboards, and each clipboard had a cover sheet describing the procedure it contained. The room might be packed, but it was well-organized. The clipboards were hung on the wall in geometric precision, a testament to Paul's well-organized mind. The clipboard wall reminded her of the game show Jeopardy. And if Alex Trebek showed up asking questions, challenging the security team to "Missing Persons Procedure for four hundred dollars," surely Paul and his crew would win.

When they'd first met, she'd thought Paul Gumbs was a bit young to have so much responsibility. He was in his early thirties, and Kameron was perhaps two years younger. But the cruise line was lucky to have them both.

"Thanks for giving Kameron the night off," she said.

"Sure thing," He tapped a stack of papers into a pile and slid them inside a file folder. "How did the babysitting go?" He swiveled his chair to face her, and she noted the way his knees poked upward like a teenager sitting in an elementary school chair. Now that she had a bit of sway, she should talk to Roberta about getting Paul a chair that fit him properly.

"Oh, Kameron was great! Clara was conked out when we got there, but apparently, they were doing karate all night. I'm sure that won't come back to haunt us." Ellie chuckled. "And Clara told her all about The Bossy Bee, her favorite television show."

Paul looked pleased. "I'm glad. Between you and me, I worry that we're going to lose Kameron before long. She's fully capable of doing *my job*, and on such a small ship we have little room for advancement." He frowned, but then he seemed to shake off his worry. "But never mind that. How was your dinner? You look stressed."

Ellie crossed her legs and felt her plastic chair squeak in protest beneath her. "Do I? Dinner went well. But there was a small incident at Karaoke Crush." She winced.

"And what did Violet do this time?"

She told him. He didn't seem too surprised.

"I see. And how did Mr. Nickles take it?"

Ellie thought back. “Murray? He seemed fine. He even stuck around afterward and did some magic tricks for the guests.” Was it just her, or did Paul look guilty about something? “What is it?” she asked.

He rubbed his forehead. “I *may* have given Violet some bad news earlier.”

“What news?”

“When I questioned Ms. Young and Mr. Nickles last night, they confirmed that they are indeed romantically involved. And I *accidentally* let that slip to Violet before her show. She didn’t take it very well.”

“Wait. If those two are together-together, why did she tell me he was her employer?” Ellie uncrossed and recrossed her legs. “Is she hiding something?”

“Yes, but it’s not what you might expect. Apparently, Mr. Nickles is separating from his wife and there’s a prenuptial agreement that penalizes any adultery. While he swears that he didn’t start dating Ms. Young until he and his wife were already separated, they’re keeping their relationship a secret until the divorce is finalized.” Paul frowned. “The magician might be an adulterer, but that’s not my business. I’m only concerned with who murdered our victim.”

He pulled his notebook out of his shirt pocket and flipped to a page crammed with handwritten notes. “And I have an update for you. According to my background checks, our guests in 1289 are both who they appear to be. Melanie Young, age 52, an actress and tour guide from Hollywood, California. And Mr. Murray Nickels, stage name Murray the Magnificent, a professional magician with clients up and down both coasts. In fact, they're traveling for business. Mr. Magnificent," Paul's eyebrows twitched at the name, "has a corporate event scheduled at the Double Diamond Casino in Nassau in two days' time. He and Ms. Young intend to disembark in Nassau and stay for one week."

"They're leaving the cruise early? That's weird. Why didn't they fly to Nassau?"

"Apparently Mr. Nickles has a fear of flying. I called the Casino and verified the event; it's on their schedule."

"And have you learned anything about the victim?"

He flipped to a different page. "I have. Our victim's name is Samantha Rawlings, age twenty-eight, a lifelong resident of Los Angeles. She's crew." Paul let out a heavy sigh. "She was one of ours. At least, she was going to be. Wynona hired her as a backup dancer for *Pirates of Peking*. And she didn't show up for work."

"That explains why she looked so fit," Ellie said. "She was a professional performer."

"Well, there's more to that story. Wynona said that Samantha had worked as a stuntwoman in Hollywood. She sent over a copy of her resume." He reached over and took a file folder off his desk, then pulled out a stapled packet of paper for her to look at.

Ellie scanned down the page. Samantha's headshot showed a beautiful young woman with dark hair and green eyes. And she had several dozen stunt credits. "Interesting. But if that's true, why was she taking a job as a backup dancer? I presume stunt work pays better than backup dancing."

"I wondered the same thing. According to Wynona, actors, including stunt performers, like to fill up their resumes with specialized skills. If you know how to dance, you can double for a dancer more easily — that sort of thing. It was a temporary assignment. Samantha was set to fill in for a dancer with a twisted ankle. Now that we've identified our victim, I have a call into the Los Angeles county police department. They'll contact her family and see if there's any pertinent information there."

"So, we have three Los Angeles connections," Ellie mused aloud. "Murray, Melanie, and now the dead stuntwoman, Samantha. That hardly seems like a coincidence."

"It's too early to say for sure," Paul said. "But it may suggest a connection. Oh, and we have some insight into cause of death. We knew she was strangled, that much was clear from the mark around her neck, but Strunk says there was a pattern to the ligature marks. She was strangled by something like a heavy chain; it left a pattern behind on her skin. The links were just shy of a centimeter long. If we find the chain, we may find the killer."

"How terrible," Ellie said, feeling a pang of grief for the poor woman whose life had been cut short so unfairly. "I suppose there was no sign of a chain in the suitcase?"

"I'm afraid not. But we have footage of her checking in at PortMiami. And the suitcase we found her in? It was hers. She carried it on. The port authority has footage of her standing in line at the terminal, checking in, and pulling her suitcase toward the ship. But that's where we lost her, in between the terminal and the *Spirit*. There's no record of her checking in on our end. It's like she disappeared during the walk across the gangway."

Ellie thought back to the configuration of PortMiami. After passing through the boxy terminal building, guests went through a gangway, an intermediate structure with zig-zagging ramps that brought them up to the height of the promenade deck. That walk took ten minutes, tops. Had the victim been killed during that short interval, just prior to boarding? She looked at Paul. "Do you have footage of Murray and Melanie coming on board?"

He nodded. "Yes. Apparently, they raised quite the stink over that parrot. The port employees had to call in a supervisor, and everyone remembered them. Murray and Melanie passed through security approximately forty minutes before our victim."

"And did they board the ship promptly?"

"Yes, that was the next thing I checked. Eight minutes after they left the terminal, their badges were logged at the security station."

They sat quietly for a few minutes. Ellie ran through a mental picture of what she'd been told, forward and backward. Paul tented his fingers in his lap, and he seemed to be doing the same. After thinking it through, Ellie asked, "What do you think happened to the rest of Samantha's belongings?"

"She only had the one suitcase," Paul said.

"Sure. But whoever put her body in that suitcase made room inside it. No one travels with a gigantic suitcase only to keep the thing half-empty. That meant the killer had to dump some of her belongings out. You didn't find her purse or ID, right? If you find what the killer removed, you might find more clues."

Paul smiled at her. "I didn't even think about that. I'll call the port again and have them sweep every inch of ground between the terminal and the ship."

"And what do you think about the luggage tag the victim was holding?" Ellie asked, keeping her voice even.

"I'm not sure what it means. Ms. Young recognized the luggage tag. It was hers. She said it tore when she pulled her bag out of the trunk of the taxi, so she threw it away outside the terminal building and wrote a fresh one out at the counter. I don't have video of her doing so, but it seems plausible."

"So, assuming she's not lying, someone fished Melanie's luggage tag out of the trash. Why?"

Paul shrugged. "I wish I knew. They were both adamant that they'd never seen her before. But the tag had her name and room number on it. Perhaps she was being followed?"

Ellie thought back to the discovery of the body. "Maybe."

"They say they didn't recognize the dead woman," Paul said. "Do you believe them?"

"Probably. I know people can lie, but they both looked *so* surprised. They were as shocked and horrified as anyone would be. And poor Murray turned as white as a ghost."

"Like he was afraid of getting caught?"

"No. It was more like he'd never seen a dead body before, and he was about to wet his pants." She smiled at Paul. "You're doing a great job, by the way. Tell me, is there anything I can do to help?"

Paul's brown eyes looked at her as if he were considering something tricky. But he only said, "You've got company."

"Well, yes, but I'm not with them twenty-four seven. What do you need?"

When he spoke, he didn't quite meet her eyes. "There's something you can do to help. But I don't think you're going to like it. You should have a chat with Violet."

"About what?"

"About her behavior." He winced. "Look, she's causing scenes in public, arguing with guests, and now this business with the karaoke show? Think it over. What do you think Roberta would do if she were here?"

"I have no idea."

"Roberta would suspend her," Paul said firmly. "Violet would be confined to quarters until Roberta had either fired her or Violet had convinced her that the reign of terror was over."

"She wouldn't!"

"Listen. The only reason Violet is acting this way is because Roberta isn't here. The captain won't intervene unless he must, and by the time he jumps in, we're talking about a formal reprimand, which is something that will follow her around for years. But you are—"

"Me?" Ellie held up her hands. "Nope. I am *not* Violet's boss."

"But you're filling in for her boss. And what do you think that means?" Paul raised an eyebrow.

Ellie thought back to all she'd seen. The fight in the atrium was bad enough. But now there had been a second incident. And if she'd been a guest aboard the ship, she wouldn't have found it acceptable, at all. Her heart sank. "I'll talk to her."

"Good."

Ellie stemmed her unease by clenching and unclenching her hands. "But what should I say?"

"That's above my paygrade. But hopefully she'll listen to you. Because otherwise…" He bit his lip.

"What?"

"I'd hate to have to gag her and store her in a supply closet until we get back to Miami."

Chapter Fourteen

SHE FOUND VIOLET JUST BEFORE midnight, sitting at the wooden bar at the back of the Moonlight Lounge. The jazz quartet was up on stage, playing a slow song while a half-dozen couples slow danced at the front of the room. Most of the booths were empty, and the party had moved upstairs, where the DJs were throwing an EDM dance party for the stay-up-late crowd.

Violet's tumbler contained nothing but ice, and she was stirring it with a pink plastic swizzle stick, looking down into the wet cubes like they might contain answers to her deepest questions.

"I know what you're going to say," Violet didn't look up from her glass.

"You do? And what's that?" Ellie hopped up on the stool next to Violet. The bartender shot her a look that was a question, and Ellie shook her head.

"You're going to say the song I sang tonight was really mean."

"Would I be wrong, if I said that?"

"I needed to know, Ellie. And now I do." Violet's mouth had curled up in a triumphant smile.

Violet was proud of herself for what she'd done? Ellie kept her voice even as she said, "Okay. What do you know now?"

"That horrible man? Murray? He doesn't actually care about Melanie. If he had, he would have refused to sing the song with me. Either he's the biggest moron on the planet — a theory I haven't abandoned, by the way — or he simply doesn't care enough about her to defend her honor. And did you see the way he stuck around, promoting himself, long after she'd stormed off? He cares more about his ego than his girlfriend. And now, she knows exactly what kind of man he is." Violet nodded to herself.

"Oh, because you showed her? Because you humiliated her in front of dozens of strangers?"

"You don't get it," Violet snapped. "He doesn't *care* about her. All that stuff about the secret love affair? It's bogus. She just wants me to be jealous. And she figured that weird little man is the perfect patsy."

"Violet, hon, you're not making any sense. Is Melanie a fool, needing your protection from this guy, or is she just using him to get back at you? Those aren't remotely the same thing. And why now? After all this time. Besides, none of this makes what you did—"

"I don't want to talk about this," Violet said.

"Look, Melanie hurt you, badly. You're furious at her. And you're also a bit jealous. That's—"

"I am *not* jealous."

"Fine. You're not jealous." Ellie felt her patience wearing thin. "So why are you getting up in their business then? What exactly are you trying to accomplish here? Other than ruining your career." She tried to keep her tone gentle, but exasperation bled through and stained the words.

"Excuse me?" Violet's voice flared with anger and surprise. "When did you get so high and mighty?"

Ellie took a breath to steady herself. "Look. I don't want to fight. But I need you to get yourself back under control. You can't roam through the ship harassing our guests to satisfy a personal vendetta. I know you still love Melanie—"

"Oh! You know what I'm *feeling*, do you?" Violet scoffed and pushed her glass away. "I can't believe you're talking to me like this. After all we've been through. When have I *not* had your back, Ellie Tappet? Never. That's when. And the *one time* I have an outburst, the *one time* I'm not little Miss Perfect, you—"

The tirade had gone on long enough. "Hey! This *is* me having your back. You shouted at a guest. You caused a scene in front of everyone. And then, as if that weren't enough, you used your music, your *gift*, to cut someone down, right in front of everyone. You *know* that's not acceptable. Besides, we're not talking about a one-time mistake. We're talking about you letting your personal feelings get in the way of everything you stand for. If Roberta was here, you'd be—"

"Well, she isn't," Violet said flatly. "And you're not the captain. If you have a problem with what I'm doing, maybe you should take it up with *your* boyfriend. I'm sure he'll salute and do whatever you say."

Ellie stood up. "This isn't about Ben. I represent the owners, Violet. And I won't let you ruin this cruise, attack our guests, or make things harder on the crew. You're a leader. Act like one. I came to you to give you one more chance. Because I care about you."

Violet's nostrils flared but she didn't respond.

"But let me be clear," Ellie said, pitching her voice low. "If you harass our guests again, in *any way*, I'll suspend you pending a formal review. You'll be confined to quarters until Roberta gets back, and I'll let her decide what to do with you."

Violet's mouth twisted, but she didn't speak. She just stared, her green eyes burning like twin flames.

"Violet," Ellie said in a softer tone. "You know I want to help. And I wouldn't be saying this if—"

When Violet spoke, it was in a clipped voice, devoid of all emotion. "I don't need your help. You've said your piece, Ellie. Can I go now?"

"Violet—"

"Is this performance review over? Is there some document you need me to sign? Or can I leave?"

Ellie felt her shoulders slump. Her body felt heavy, like she might drop right through the carpet and crash into the level below. She nodded once. "I said what I needed to say."

"Good." Violet hopped off the bar stool and it wobbled with the force of her departure. She stormed out the door and left it swinging behind her. At the far end of the bar, the bartender used a clean white towel to wipe down his wares, his expression as blank as a fresh sheet of paper.

Chapter Fifteen

THE NEXT DAY, ELLIE GUIDED her family through the bustling port town of Charlotte Amelie on the island of St. Thomas. The sun blasted down with angry force, and her scalp was baking like a pie, even through her white summer hat. As they walked, she pointed out sights of interest in her best tour guide voice. "Do you see that pretty church over there? That's Dutch colonial architecture. The island of St. Thomas was colonized by the Dutch before it became a US territory about a hundred years ago."

She couldn't help but smile at Marcie and Junior, who were looking up and around as if their eyes couldn't quite take in all that they were seeing. It was good to see them enjoying themselves, even if she felt as bitter as old tea leaves at the bottom of the pot. Playing tour guide might keep her mind off the fight she'd had with Violet. Thinking about it made her heart ache, so it was best to think of something else. Anything else, really.

Across the two-lane street, a tour group from the ship was listening to a local guide talk about Blackbeard the Pirate, whose real name was Edward, apparently. Ellie felt a prickle of amusement. *Edward the Pirate* didn't have quite the same ring to it. No wonder he'd gone with something else!

"What are you thinking about, Ma?" Marcie had caught her smiling. Clara was on her hip, and for the moment the little girl seemed placid, taking in the sights along with the rest of them. Marcie shifted her higher and adjusted the position of her arms.

"Pirates," Ellie said. "Are you sure you don't want to let her walk? We can go as slow as we need to. The ferry to St. John runs every twenty minutes, so we're not in a rush."

Marcie considered this, then shook her head. "No. There's too much traffic on this street."

Ellie's mind went to a bike rental shop three blocks to their right. If memory served, they rented beach strollers. "I have a better idea," she said. "Come on."

They procured a stroller for the day, and Clara didn't object to being pushed through the charming streets, her legs kicking up and down as they went. They spent two hours visiting shops selling jewelry, clothing, and souvenirs. It wasn't until nearly lunchtime that they got on the ferry to St. John. Junior folded up Clara's stroller and carried her on board, his free arm laden with square paper shopping bags from the morning's bounty. The 'ferry' was a low metal boat made of shiny metal; it reflected the bright sunlight like a mirror. The inside of the boat had hard vinyl benches to sit on. Thick orange vests were stowed below like hardback books on a shelf. Junior sat down and put Clara on the floor in front of him. "Are you sure this is safe?" he asked.

"Safe as houses. And just wait till we get going." Ellie said. She felt a flutter of anticipation as the ferryboat captain started the motor and told everyone to hang on tight. The boat backed out of the harbor, slowly at first, then they zoomed straight through the water and toward the bright blue sea. The wind blew Ellie's silver hair back and she faced forward, smelling the salt air, feeling the warmth of the sun on her knees and shoulders. They were moving fast! In the distance, rising out of the water like the humped back of some Paleolithic creature, vegetation-furred islands beckoned adventurers forward. Many of the smaller islands in the area were uninhabited, as they had no services. She noticed Junior looking at her with a surprised expression.

"What?"

He put one arm around the back of her shoulders. "It's good to see you so happy, Ma. I don't think I've seen you smile like that, since..."

"Since your dad died? Yeah." She leaned on his shoulder for a moment. "I miss him, every day. You know that, right?"

He nodded. "I do." Then he shielded his eyes with one hand and looked out to sea.

Watching her son, Ellie felt a pang of something like sadness. The echo of an old memory, perhaps. She brushed it away. "So, if you thought St. Thomas was lovely, wait until you see St. John. They have beautiful beaches." She winked at Marcie. "And *fantastic* shopping."

"Ma," Junior groaned.

Marcie laughed. "Come on. How long has it been since we've been on one of Ma's over-the-top shopping sprees?"

"Over the top?" Ellie put one hand to her chest. "As if! I just like a bargain, that's all. And now that I'm headed home for a week, I can do some proper shopping. You've seen my stateroom, right? I could *really* use more closet space."

Junior looked like he was going to object, but Marcie put her hand on his knee. "Ma has plenty of closet space at home, right? We can store some of her stuff, and then she'll just have to come home regularly to swap things out."

He nodded. "Fine. But all I want right now is a nice beach, a big lunch, and a palm tree to sit under. That's *my* idea of heaven."

Ellie shot Marcie a devilish look. "Shall we drop Junior off at the beach? He looks like he could use some me-time. I think we've been running him ragged."

Marcie nodded sagely. "Yes. But let's eat first. He gets as cranky as Clara when his blood sugar gets low."

"I'm not cranky," Clara insisted. She tugged her hat off and looked up, grinning beneath her tiny purple sunglasses.

Junior dropped a kiss on top of her head. "Of course you're not. And neither am I. Your Ma is being silly."

"Mama is silly," Clara agreed.

Ellie looked at Marcie. "You two are doing a great job with her."

Marcie looked pleased. "Well, she makes it easy. Most days, that is." She tickled Clara, and Clara ducked between her father's knees, hiding. Junior kept one hand on her shoulder and one eye on the water surrounding the boat. Before long, St. John came into view. The island was a green jewel bordered by pristine white beaches, completely covered in vegetation, although here and there a colorful roof peeped out from the trees. The ship turned and Cruz Bay came into view, a pristine blue harbor in which a dozen or more brilliant white sailboats bobbed gently, their sails tied tightly to their masts. The heavy mass of trees, vines, and bushes thinned out near the beaches, and the tall wooden structures of beachfront hotels stood proudly along one arm of the harbor.

"Wow," Junior said, his voice soft with awe. "It's so green. And blue! It's exactly like a postcard, except it's real."

When they arrived in Cruz Bay, the ferryboat captain offered his hand to each passenger as they made the transition from ship to shore. As the family walked down the dock, Marcie asked, "Where are we headed?"

Ellie made a mental itinerary, shuffled a few items around in consideration of sightseeing with a toddler, then led her family to a restaurant several of her prior guests had raved about. Once they were seated on the patio beneath a bright green umbrella, and lunch had been served, Ellie heard someone calling her name from across the low wooden fence that separated the patio from the sidewalk beyond. She stood up to get a better look.

"Excuse me? Ellie? That's your name, isn't it?" The guy who spoke was heavyset; he wore dark jeans, a t-shirt, and a black leather vest embossed with flaming skulls. Three rows of pointy silver studs jutted out from his belt, and he'd attached his belt to his wallet. As if someone might steal from such an imposing guy! She recognized the man's easygoing smile at once.

"Dick, it's nice to see you! Are you enjoying the island?" She turned to her kids and pointed over toward the sidewalk. "Marcie, Junior, that's Dick, one of my guests from *The Lofts*." She walked over to the edge of the low wooden fence so they could talk without shouting over the other diners. "Who's your friend?" she asked.

The man standing beside Dick was also in his forties, but he was so unlike his companion that they may as well have been two different species. The man was shorter and slimmer, for one thing, and his dark blue shorts, bright white polo shirt, and the cardigan sweater tied around his narrow shoulders made him look like a college professor headed to the links for eighteen holes. He had a large pair of binoculars hanging around his neck, and a small notebook tucked in his front shorts pocket. *Ah,* she thought. *Not a golfer. A birder.*

"This is Jules," Dick said. "We met at the meet and greet last night, and he let me tag along with him today." Dick grinned. "Anyway, we're looking for the nature preserve. Can you point us in the right direction?"

His companion smiled, but the corners of his mouth barely lifted, as if the smile were something he offered only begrudgingly. "They've got forty species of tropical birds here," Jules said. His precise diction and lofty vowels immediately marked him as an Englishman. "And I hope to see all of them before returning to port."

There was a Julian on her roster for *The Lofts*; this must be him. It was good that the guests were making friends! She took a spare map out of her purse and made some notations with her fountain pen. "Most of the island is a nature preserve, but you'll need a car to get around." She held the map out and pointed at one of the places she'd marked. "You can rent a car here. Or you can hire a taxi over here." She pointed again. "Just be sure to schedule a pickup time because cell coverage is spotty. And this long road here? That goes straight through the preserve. The staff there can point you to the best birding spots."

The British gentleman nodded. "Thank you. And apologies for disturbing your meal." He shot a sidelong glance at Dick, as if to say it had been all his idea.

Dick took the map back, oblivious to his companion's disapproval. "You said your family was visiting. Is that them?" He shaded his eyes from the sun to get a better look.

She smiled proudly. "Yes, we're headed to the beach. Have fun you two! And I'll see you on the ship later."

When she returned to the table, Junior had demolished his lunch down to the garnish and he was eying his wife's meal with an envious expression. Ellie waved at a nearby waiter, a young guy with blonde surfer hair and eyes the color of potting soil. "Can we order more food for my bottomless pit of a son?" The man nodded and deftly picked up a stack of dirty plates from a nearby table, promising to return quickly. The patio was getting louder; every table was full now, and conversations were lively.

Marcie helped Clara with her drink and turned back to Ellie. "Those two were an odd pair."

"What do you mean?"

"A biker and a birdwatcher? Did they come on the cruise together?" Marcie looked in the direction they'd gone.

"No, they're both solo travelers. I met Dick before breakfast the other morning; he was looking for the newspaper. And I always set up a meet and greet so people can find activity partners." She shrugged. "We're all just people, hon. And it can be lonely to travel alone."

Marcie nodded. "I can see that. You seem to know a lot about the island. Do you spend a lot of time here?" She looked out over the patio at the blooming bushes beyond. The flowers were pinker than candy hearts and shaped like exploding stars. "It's so vibrant."

Ellie nodded. "The excursions desk gives us maps. They teach us the transportation system, and tell us what to watch out for. And when I hear recommendations from other guests, and it all stays in here." Ellie touched her right temple.

"Listen to her, talking like a businesswoman," Junior teased.

"I *am* a businesswoman, kiddo," Ellie said with warmth. "Besides, it isn't all that different from teaching school. You've got people who need help, and you've got difficult personalities, and…." She thought back to her fight with Violet at the bar, and her heart sank. She'd promised herself that she wouldn't let the fight ruin her time with the kids, but it was hard not to worry. Perhaps she'd been too hard on Violet.

"Ma. Are you okay?" Junior frowned.

She nodded. "I am. I'm sorry. It's just that I got into a fight with my friend last night, and it stings a little."

"You're worried about her," Marcie said.

Ellie shrugged. Violet was an adult, and she was going to make her own choices. "Have you ever had a friend who was so determined to do the *wrong* thing that all you wanted to do is lock them in a box until they wise up?"

Junior looked over the rim of his glass. "You mean like when your retired mother runs off, gets embroiled in murder investigations, and starts dating some guy you've never met?"

"Junior!" Marcie looked appalled.

He held up a hand. "Now, now. Don't jump down my throat. I like Ben. He seems like a good guy, and I approve. We all know Dad didn't want Ma to be lonely. So that's that. But I can't pretend to be happy about the other stuff she's gotten mixed up in."

Ellie shot him a sharp look.

He nodded. "Don't pretend to be surprised. Remember when you ran off to break up a fight the other night? It was irresponsible for the crew to get you involved in a security matter. You're not trained, and—"

"My friend was arguing with her ex," Ellie said, trying to keep the exasperation out of her voice. "It's not like I was taking down an armed gang of drug dealers, guns a blazing." She glanced at Marcie. "Do guns blaze? I've never been clear on how that works."

"Ha ha," Junior said without humor. "And don't think I didn't notice your little distraction last night when Ben brought up that murder. *You* found a murderer? Are you some kind of private investigator now? Is that why you don't want to come home? Because you think you're Sherlock Holmes?"

"Don't be ridiculous," Ellie said, amused at the mental picture of her wandering around the ship with a Sherlock hat and a magnifying glass. "So, I figured out who killed Morgan. Paul and I make a good team. Does that honestly surprise you?" She knew Junior meant well, but his attitude was more than a little hurtful. Was it so unbelievable that she might put a few facts together?

"I don't like it," he said.

"Why? Because I should be doing something more age-appropriate? Shall I procure some doilies and a rocking chair? Or start a book club?" She tapped her chin. A book club sounded fun. She filed that notion away for later.

"Yes. Start a book club. Learn to knit. Do more ziplining for all I care. Just leave security matters to the professionals." Junior's eyes met hers with full sincerity. "And I don't see why my opinion is so controversial. Back me up, Marce."

Marcie reached over to help Clara color the cartoon dog on her placemat. Clara's lunch looked like it had exploded on her plate, but hopefully some of it had ended up inside her body. "You're out on a limb," Marcie said, not looking up. "But you just keep on sawing, honey. I'm sure it will go *just* fine."

Junior shook his head, his jaw clenching. "Ma. You're a smart woman. That's not in question. And I know you like sticking your nose in wherever you see a problem, but—"

"Ron," Marcie said quietly.

"*But*," Ron repeated, raising his voice to speak over his wife. "I know what's going on here. Mom's their boss now. The crew doesn't want to tell her no. So of course, when she butts in, they're going to humor her. But it's not responsible. And it's not *safe*. And frankly, you should know better, Ma. Dad wouldn't like it." Junior thanked the waitress as she dropped off a basket of fries, hot and glistening with traces of oil. He dipped a fry in ketchup, then chewed it in one bite. He looked up, "Anyway, let's change the subject. It's such a nice day outside. What's first? Beach or shopping?"

Marcie looked at Ellie, and an understanding passed between them. She could have it out with Junior, right here, in the middle of the restaurant, and the Lord knew he had it coming! Where was this patronizing attitude coming from? And she could tell from the way Marcie was looking at her that her daughter-in-law would have her back.

Ellie's shoulder muscles felt like heavy knots. She took a slow breath, willing her body to relax. A fight wouldn't be the best use of their rare and precious day together. Besides, the patio was packed, and some of the diners were almost certainly from the ship. It was bad enough that the bartender had witnessed her fight with Violet. Did she want everyone talking about her argument with her son too?

Ellie sipped her drink and set it back down. With effort, she said, "I'll think about what you said, kiddo." She smiled at Marcie. "What do you say, beach first?"

Marcie nodded. "Yeah. The beach sounds great."

AFTER A LAZY AFTERNOON OF relaxation, fruity drinks, and building sandcastles with Clara, they headed back toward Cruz Bay to catch the return ferry. They walked, Clara riding piggyback on the adults, demanding a new steed every so often, yelling 'Giddy-Up' into their ears when she wasn't pleased with the pace. Junior hadn't favored her with any more of his 'concerns' during the beach trip, but Ellie felt his words buzzing around her head like mosquitoes, stinging her, bringing itchy irritation that flared up, again and again.

If only there were an anti-itch spray for emotional wounds! She'd sell it by the bottle and end up richer than Roberta Crowley.

The walking trail branched off to the left, and Ellie had a thought. "Hey, can we make one more stop?" They'd split the shopping bags between them, but even so, Junior was giving her a weary look. "More shopping? Ma, I think we cleaned the islands out. At this rate we'll need to buy an empty suitcase."

"I just need some refills for my fountain pen," she explained. "It won't take but a minute." She guided them down the dirt path and toward a blue lamppost in front of a ramshackle wooden house. A hand-painted sign read: *Madame Tiffany's Collectibles.* Behind the lace curtains in the window a glowing neon sign shaped like a hand flickered as they approached.

She opened the creaky door and stepped inside. Madame Tiffany's one-eyed cat was nowhere to be seen, but the shop was as neat as a pin and as quaint as an old-fashioned English teahouse. Marcie walked toward a table that held a dozen small music boxes. "Oh, these are exquisite. Clara, sweetie. Look, but don't touch."

Junior had spotted the small table in one corner, the one that held a large crystal ball. A heavy lace curtain had been half-pulled shut and it concealed one seat. The visible chair was made of carved wood with motifs of tropical birds and flowers, and there was a fat orange cushion on it. Junior glanced back at the neon sign, taking in the glowing hand and the diamond-shaped eye embedded at the center. He leaned closer to whisper, "Ma. What *is* this place?"

"Welcome to my store, young man." Madame Tiffany pushed through the beaded curtain behind the sales counter. Her long, gray-frosted dreadlocks hung almost down to her waist, and she wore a midnight blue caftan interwoven with silver threads. "I am Madame Tiffany. Merchant of the Islands. Seer of the unseen. Knower of the—" She snapped her mouth shut. "Ellie Tappet? Girl! Is that you? Come over here and give me a hug! How's that handsome man of yours?" She stepped forward and enveloped Ellie in a sandalwood scented embrace.

"Ben is well, thank you," Ellie said, releasing her with a smile. "This is my son, Ron. His wife, Marcie. And my —"

"Oh! You must be Clara." She stepped over and held out her hand. Clara reached out and shook Madame Tiffany's hand like they were old acquaintances. Tiffany beamed at Marcie. "Oh, she's a sharp little thing, isn't she?" She turned her attention back to Clara. "You keep talking, young lady. Trust me, you'll be heard." She stepped back and swept her arms out wide. "So, what can I do for you? I am at your service."

"Um..." Junior shot Ellie a confused look. It was cute, and she worked hard not to laugh, lest he take it the wrong way.

"Fountain pen refills," Ellie said. "I used up all of my cartridges writing my romance novel."

Tiffany nodded and began rummaging in the drawers of a wooden hutch along one wall. The windowed shelves were laden with jars of herbs, thick, scented candles, and assorted oddities, including a broken-looking mantle clock. She came back with a dozen small boxes.

"Take your pick. And how is the writing going?" She smiled at Ellie and her eyes flashed with amusement, as if she were silently saying that she already knew the answer. But that was just her style. Madame Tiffany was quite the salesperson!

"I gave the book to a friend to read. When she gets back from vacation, I'll get her input, and then I'll take it from there." She lowered her voice. "I already have an idea for another book."

"Excellent," the shopkeeper said. "Now, is there anything I can get for the rest of you?"

"How much for this music box?" Marcie asked, pointing to an enameled wooden box no longer than her hand. It had a tiny window in the top, and an engraved pattern of roses.

Madame Tiffany picked up the box and turned it over. "Hmm. I seem to have lost a price tag." She shot Junior a stern look. "Young man, I need to reach something on a high shelf in my supply room. Will you assist me?"

Junior looked surprised, but he nodded. They went through the beaded curtains and were gone for nearly five minutes. When they returned, neither one of them looked happy. "Sorry about that," she said. "We looked high and low, but we didn't find what we were looking for." She shot Junior a sidelong look and quoted Marcie a price for the box.

"Sold," Marcie said happily.

Madame Tiffany boxed up their purchases and smiled at Ellie. "Tell that man of yours I said hello, okay? And come see me the next time you're on the island." Her mouth compressed. "I have some new stock coming in that I think you'll like. Bring Benjamin with you. Tell him it's important, will you?"

"Will do!" Ellie gave her a wave as they headed out the door. They continued walking toward the ferry dock. "She's such an interesting person, isn't she?"

Marcie nodded, and Junior made a small "hmpf."

"What's that, kiddo?" Ellie asked. "She didn't try to give you furniture, did she?"

He shook his head. "No. Everything is fine." Clara was tugging at his hand, so he picked her up with a big swooping motion, lifting her high in the air. She laughed, and he smiled up at her. "Come on, Ma. Let's get back to the ship. I know you won't be happy until you've made up with Violet."

Chapter Sixteen

KAMERON WAS MANNING THE SECURITY desk when they got back to the *Spirit*. Junior put all the shopping bags on the belt for the X-ray machine. Ellie handed Kameron her ID badge, which she scanned and handed right back. Kameron smiled and waved at Clara with her fingers. "How was your day, Clara?"

Clara screwed up her face, made a fist, and shot it out in the air. "Ki-yah! I saw a blue fish."

"Ki-yah indeed." Kameron looked pleased. "Hey, Ellie. Paul wants to see you right away. He says there's been a development in the," she glanced at Ellie's kids, "the thing you were discussing."

"Okay," Ellie said, ignoring the way Junior was looking over at her. She'd promised to think about his words, and she would. That didn't mean she'd agreed with him. "I'll go see him as soon as I drop off my stuff."

Kameron blew a kiss at Clara as they walked toward the elevators. "Clara," Ellie asked, pushing the elevator button. "What did Kameron teach you about karate?"

“Only punch bad guys,” Clara said. “And run.”

“Run?”

She nodded. “Run away *fast*. Hide. Punch the bad guys.”

“Do you run away first, or punch first?” Junior asked, crouching down to her eye level.

“Run away first,” Clara said firmly. Her arm shot up, punching the air. “Then pow!”

Junior looked back in the direction of the security crew. He didn’t seem upset, only thoughtful. “That’s right. Run and hide when you see a bad guy. Or ask a grown up for help.”

“Pow!” Clara shouted, loud enough that a few passengers coming up the ramp outside looked in her direction.

Ellie chuckled. No doubt Kameron had done her best to try and instill good ethics in little Clara, but when you were two and a half years old and feisty, the allure of *pow* might be too hard to resist. May God help any rude little boys and girls in Clara’s daycare when she got home! It wasn’t always so easy to tell a good guy (or gal) from a bad one. Sometimes the good guys had a mean right hook. She glanced at Junior.

After she reached Marcie and Junior’s stateroom, she hesitated. “What did you want to do next? We could ”

Marcie smiled at her. “Go. Take care of things and check on Violet. We’re going to have a rest, and maybe we’ll get room service tonight. It’s been a fun day, but I think Clara is beat.” Junior was already inside the room, and Ellie heard Clara’s voice calling “Pow Pow Pow!”

"That was my shin, kid," Junior replied quietly. "Are you ready for a nap?"

Ellie picked up her shopping bags from the ground. "Thanks. I'll check in on you in the morning if we don't talk sooner." She waved to Marcie, then hurried toward her room. Paul must have learned something new about the case.

⚓⚓⚓

PAUL WAS WAITING FOR HER. "We've had a break in the case. And I wanted to run it by you before I take any action."

That was flattering, but maybe Junior was right. Maybe Paul was just humoring her. Besides, she'd practically ordered him to keep her updated. So she asked, "Do you need me to call our attorney or something?"

He pointed at a chair opposite his own. "No, although if you think that's wise, feel free. Mostly, I want your opinion."

Pride flooded Ellie's body, starting in the center of her torso and rushing out into her fingers and toes. "Aha! You're saying that I'm *not* just a nosy old broad that you're humoring because you have no choice in the matter?" She scoffed. "I knew it!" Paul was staring at her like she was a lunatic, so she snapped her mouth shut. "You were saying?"

"Wait. Did someone say that I said that?" Paul leaned forward. "Because I didn't! I wouldn't! I—"

"That's good," Ellie interrupted. "But just to be clear, you wouldn't say such a thing because it's incorrect? Or you wouldn't say it because I own part of the cruise line and you're secretly afraid of me?"

Paul leaned forward; his brown eyes were full of concern. "Ellie, did you buy a packet of 'special herbs' from a man in a Rasta hat while you were at port? Because the special ingredient isn't tea; it's paranoia."

She crossed her arms and fixed him with a hard stare.

Paul's eyelids lowered to half mast, as if he were trying to decide if she were friend or foe. "Fine. If it will make you feel better, I'll answer." He ticked off statements on his fingers as he went. "Yes, you are a very 'nosy' woman. No, you are not an 'old broad.' And yes, I value your opinion very much. If I didn't, you wouldn't be in here. Owner or no, it doesn't matter to me. I keep my own counsel, and I choose my own friends. And no, I'm not afraid of you." He raised an eyebrow. "Can we talk about the case now? Please?"

She laughed a little. She couldn't help it! He was so painfully earnest. "Paul, I'm sorry. You've always been honest with me; I know that." She sighed. "It's just that my son dressed me down at lunch for 'interfering where I'm not wanted' and now I'm carrying around a can of whoop-butt with no place to set it down."

"Whoop-butt? Do you mean a can of whoop-a—"

"Hush," she smirked at him. "We have work to do. You said we had a break in the case?" She crossed one ankle over the other and waited.

Paul leaned back in his chair. "This afternoon, I spoke to the police officer who broke the news to our victim's family. And it turns out that Samantha Rawlings isn't who we thought she was."

"So, she's not a dancer?"

"Well, she might be able to dance; I don't know. And she did work as a stuntwoman for a while. But for the last three years she's been working in an entirely different profession."

"Well, don't leave me hanging."

"Samantha Rawlings was a bounty hunter."

Ellie felt her breath whoosh into her lungs. "Truly? That young woman in the suitcase was a bounty hunter? Like the shaggy man with the sunglasses on television?"

"Yes. She was a licensed bounty hunter in the state of California. And according to the local PD, her sister said she was chasing a wanted criminal. And get this: The bounty was *eighty thousand dollars*."

"Who would pay so much for a bail skipper? Does she have a lead on D.B. Cooper or something?" Paul looked perplexed, so she quickly added, "Forget about it. He was a famous fugitive back when dinosaurs roamed the Earth. Did the victim's sister know who her sister was chasing?"

Paul frowned. "Unfortunately, no. Samantha kept the details to herself. But she said the bounty was private pay, meaning that the reward didn't come from the state, as part of a bail bond. The reward would be paid by the victim or their family."

Ellie thought through what they'd learned so far. "Okay. We have a woman, Samantha, a *bounty hunter*, who supposedly came aboard as a backup dancer, but she was actually a bounty hunter. And she was found dead. With Melanie's luggage tag in her pocket."

"And she'd been strangled by some sort of chain," Paul said.

A memory flashed in Ellie's mind. An image of the first time she'd met Melanie Young, inside her stateroom. "Oh no." She thought it through again, and the image didn't fade. "Please tell me I'm wrong. Because if I'm not, it's going to break Violet's heart right in half."

"What is it?"

"Remind me. What do we know about the garrote that was used to strangle our victim?"

"The doc said the marks on her neck were about a centimeter wide. Why?"

"When I — er — introduced myself to Melanie in her stateroom the first night of the cruise, I—"

"When you snooped," Paul said.

She ignored him. "When I *kindly* offered her some extra towels, Melanie was wearing a long pearl necklace. They were big pearls too. The necklace went down to her belly button and it looped twice. I noticed it right away because it was so unusual. Later, she'd switched to a different necklace, a gaudy-looking zirconia one with a big red stone in the center. Was it possible that..." She shook her head. "No, I don't think that would work. I *must* be wrong. Violet was so sure that Melanie isn't the murdering type. And this would devastate her." She glanced at Paul. "Violet still loves her, you know? That's why she's acting so strangely."

Paul thought for a moment. "Imagine a bounty hunter pursuing a criminal for a large reward. She's murdered, but she's got a luggage tag gripped in her hand when she dies. *The very same luggage tag that she fished out of the trash.*" He made a circling motion with his fingers. "And why would she have that particular tag?"

"Because she was tracking Melanie!" Ellie said. "Or Murray. They were both in the same room."

He nodded. "So, the criminal, either Melanie or Murray or both, realizes that they're being hunted. And they kill Samantha and shove her in a suitcase. Maybe they even call for a porter, to have the bag taken away. Possibly they didn't notice the paper she had in her hand?"

"If so, that wasn't very detail-oriented of them," Ellie said.

"Well, if we arrest them for murder, I'll be sure to let them know. Next time, we'll demand they remove the evidence of their crime more thoroughly."

"It tracks," Ellie said, ignoring his last comment. "Except that you completed background checks on both of them. Are they fugitives?"

"Nothing came up, but criminal background checks don't always show arrests or pending charges. I searched the *L.A. Times* too, but there was nothing in there under their names. And I asked the detective I reached in L.A. to see if he could track down who that bounty was for.

He's busy, but he said he'll let me know if he hears anything." He thought for a moment. "Wouldn't a strand of pearls snap under pressure?"

"They might," Ellie said. "It depends on the strength of the cord. Did Strunk say how many lines were on the ligature mark?"

Paul nodded. "Just one line. How big were the pearls?"

Ellie winced. "A bit less than a centimeter? I don't know. They were large. Could they have left that pattern? I might be grasping at straws here. And like I said, I do hope I'm wrong."

Paul reached for one of the portable radios sitting in the rack nearby, flipped it to the correct channel, and clipped it onto his belt. "Well, we should keep our minds open. But I want to question Ms. Young and Mr. Nickles one more time. Maybe we can get them to crack? And we can ask Doctor Strunk to examine those pearls. If we rule them out, we rule them out."

"Can he check them for DNA?" Ellie leaned forward.

"We don't have that kind of equipment," Paul admitted. "But he can see if the size is a match. And I want to search their stateroom again. Maybe there was something else that could have been used as a murder weapon."

"Do you really think one of them is a killer? Maybe whoever killed that girl shoved that luggage tag in there to throw us off their scent. I mean, the bag *was* delivered right to room 1289. It could be someone trying to draw our attention to the wrong people."

"It's possible," Paul said. "But at the moment those two are our only leads. Do you want to join me for the interview? Maybe you can chat them up while I take a look around."

She nodded. "I wouldn't miss it. But Paul..."

"Yes?"

"Let's keep Violet far, far away from this. If Melanie is the killer, she's going to take it hard. We can't let her be alone when that happens."

Paul stood up with a weary sigh. "I guess that's the thing about love. When you love someone, you're giving them everything they need to hurt you."

"Paul, have you ever been in love?" she asked.

"Once," he said, turning toward the door. "But it was a very long time ago."

Chapter Seventeen

MURRAY OPENED HIS STATEROOM DOOR just a crack. He peered through the opening, and when he saw who was waiting, he flung the door open wide with a sunny smile. "Mr. Gumbs! Always a pleasure. I take it that you've received my complaint? Please, come inside." He swept his hand back as he stepped backward, revealing the living area as if it were a stage of his own design.

Paul glanced at Ellie as they stepped inside, and his expression seemed to say that any complaint was news to him. Murray went into the kitchenette where he reached into his mini fridge, his bottom sticking out as he felt around inside the cold compartment. Something clinked, and he stood up, holding a tiny bottle of cognac. He unscrewed the top and sniffed it before lifting it up. "Would you like a drink?"

"No thank you," Ellie said. Melanie was nowhere in sight, but her bedroom door was shut tight, and it sounded like someone was running her shower. "We have news about that body in the suitcase, and we wanted to ask you a few questions," she said.

Murray came back with the tiny bottle of booze and a clean glass. He poured the brown liquid into the tumbler and eyed it disapprovingly before downing it in one gulp. "I see." He addressed Paul. "As you've brought a representative from guest services, perhaps she could note down a suggestion. For what we're paying for this room, I should be able to enjoy a drink of adult size." He shot Paul a mild glance. "So, the woman in the luggage? Well, I'm not sure what any of this has to do with me but share away!" He put the empty bottle on the table and sat back in an upholstered chair.

"You know, I'm right here," Ellie said, sitting on the couch, adjusting the cushion behind her back for maximum comfort.

"Excuse me?" Murray looked over, his expression blank.

"You suggested to Officer Gumbs that I note down your suggestion." She smiled sweetly at him. "But you can speak to me directly. I'm right here. In front of you. With eyes and ears of my own."

He looked surprised, only that she'd challenged him, she suspected. Where was this attitude of his coming from? And what complaint was he referring to? Murray had been reasonably charming at karaoke night, and she'd felt badly for him at the time. But his stock was dropping fast.

Paul was still standing. "Sir, the victim had your room number clutched in her hand. You can't blame us for inquiring."

"Actually, I can." Murray swirled the last few drops of brown liquid in his glass. "Here's how I see it. First, I was *harassed* by your port staff. They wouldn't allow my emotional support animal on board. That was unacceptable, but is Murray the Magnificent petty? No. He is not. I let it pass. But then there was that nasty business with a dead body outside my suite. And that suitcase was just sitting there, where anyone could trip over it." He rubbed the back of his head. "When I fell, which was *your fault*, by the way," he glared at Ellie, "I got a concussion. And what does that joke of a doctor of yours prescribe? *Rest?* That's negligence." He pointed at Paul with one finger.

"Sir, if you require medical attention beyond the scope of our onboard care, you can either call for a medical evacuation or—"

"Negligent is what it is," Murray interrupted. "Think about what the media will say when they hear my story. The harassment! The murder that *you* insisted that we hush up. And my injury." He rubbed his neck again and squinted his eyes. "I didn't want to go there, I really didn't, but I'm afraid you leave me no choice."

Ellie folded her hands in her lap and watched him blather. This little performance wasn't at all convincing. She tried to imagine how Roberta would respond, and all she came up with was a mental image of the distinguished lady glaring at Murray until he burst into flames. "We left you no choice except to do what?" she said at last.

"Well, I'll be taking legal action, *obviously*!" Murray said this as if she was the stupidest woman on Earth. "Enough is enough! I'm entitled to compensation. Pain and suffering for all I've been through."

"Because you fainted," Ellie said. "And you wet your pants a little."

Murray pointed at her and smiled wickedly. "See? That right there. My attorneys are going to *love* her on the stand. And we haven't even talked about how that horrid woman attacked my beloved in front of everyone. You thought I didn't notice that, did you? How many witnesses do you think were in there, eh? Fifty? Seventy?" He folded his arms across his chest. "I'll subpoena all of them."

Ellie glanced at Paul. He stood still, his expression fixed, as if he'd turned to stone. *That's new*, she thought. When Paul didn't speak, she sighed and crossed her legs at the ankle. "Mr. Nickles, if you have a complaint, I'll be happy to take your statement and elevate it to our board of directors. But at the moment—"

"I'd be amenable to a settlement," Murray said. "You can tell your board I'm not going to be unreasonable. Murray the Magnificent is eminently reasonable, even when provoked. But I am prepared to litigate if necessary."

"Excuse me?" Paul said, his voice an octave higher than usual. He turned to Ellie. "Is he seriously trying to—"

Ellie held up a hand. "Like I said, we'll be happy to take his statement. But first, let's attend to the matter at hand. Unless that is, Mr. Nickles is unwilling to discuss the matter? We could always turn our murder investigation over to the local authorities in Nassau. That would slow matters down, and he might not make his business engagement, but it remains an option." She smiled primly at Murray, and in the back of her mind, she heard a whispered suggestion in Roberta's voice. That was just her imagination, of course, but it gave her strength regardless. "I'm sure his client won't mind," she added. "We'll just tell them that their magician is being questioned in a murder inquiry."

Murray cackled. He tipped back his head and laughed! "I like her," he said to Paul. Then, as if the previous conversation had never happened, he shrugged. "Go ahead. Ask me what you want to ask. Or should we wait for Melanie? Oh! There she is."

Melanie had opened her bedroom door, and she stood on the threshold, barefoot. She wore an *Adventurous Cruises* bathrobe and her hair was swept up in a clean white towel. "We have company?"

"They have news about that poor woman in the suitcase," Murray said.

"Oh." Melanie's gaze went from Murray, to Paul, and back. "Give me a second to get dressed. I'll be right back." She shut the door.

Ellie glanced at Paul to see if he wanted to ask any questions before Melanie returned, but he was still regarding Murray with simmering distaste in his eyes. She was almost impressed! It took a lot to get under Paul's skin.

"Where's Sal?" Ellie asked. "I've gotten used to seeing him on your shoulder."

Murray went back to the mini fridge for a second drink. "He's in his cage sleeping. That's one of the best things about birds, you know. When it's time for bed you just drape a dark cloth over their cage, and it's lights out! So much easier than kids."

"Do you have kids?" Ellie asked. *Because if you do, I pity them.*

"Ah," Murray's cheeks darkened. "I'm afraid not. My ex wanted them, but I didn't. Got the snip, you know, to put the matter to bed once and for all." He glanced at Paul. "I assume that Officer Gumbs told you about my — um — relationship with my assistant. Your discretion on the matter of my divorce is much appreciated."

Ellie imagined Murray's wife back home in California. And although she'd never met the woman, it wasn't hard to imagine her lifting a glass of wine to celebrate the loss of Mr. Magnificent. She noticed Murray was looking at her expectantly, and she shrugged at him. "Why not? After all, you've been perfectly gracious to us."

Murray's nostrils flared.

Before long, Melanie came out of her room. She'd put on shorts and a T-shirt and her hair was damp. "Sorry to keep you waiting." She sat down next to Murray and reached over to hold his hand. "You said you had news?"

Paul cleared his throat. "We do. We've identified the woman in the suitcase as Samantha Rawlings of Los Angeles. I need to ask: does that name mean anything to either of you?"

They both denied it with shakes of their heads.

"Well, this is where things get awkward," Paul said. "Ms. Rawlings was scheduled to come on board to do a trial run as a backup dancer in our new musical. But it seems she came aboard under false pretenses. She was a licensed bounty hunter in California, and according to her sister, she was chasing a large bounty when she made arrangements to come aboard our ship."

The effect on the pair was immediate. Murray stood up, spilling his drink on his slacks, and said, "That's terrible. Just terrible. Who would do such a thing?" He turned to Melanie, his eyes wild, reaching for her. Melanie watched him rant and ramble with a faint air of disappointment. Sighing quietly, she said, "Sit down, Murray. It's going to be fine. Let me get you another drink."

Ellie looked at Paul. He watched Melanie go over to the mini bar, pour a drink, and bring it over to Murray. He took it and thanked her. His hands were unsteady. How many drinks had the man had? Perhaps he'd already been three sheets to the wind when he'd threatened to sue. Murray turned to Paul. "As I said, that's awful. But I'm not sure what it has to do with us."

"Well, sir, the bounty hunter came on board, and she had Melanie's luggage tag held in her hand. One logical conclusion would be that Samantha Rawlings was coming on board to take one of you into custody."

"And you think we killed her?" Melanie's voice was as mild as a Florida winter. "I assure you, we didn't know that woman. And even if we had murdered her, why leave the body where it could only cast a shadow of suspicion over us?" She leaned forward and looked into Paul's eyes, and then Ellie's, as if trying to impress the truth of her words. "I swear, on God in heaven, I've never met a Samantha Rawlings in my life. And I had nothing to do with her death."

"Me either," Murray said. "Check my references! You'll hear that I'm a class act. A complete professional. Murray the Magnificent is known for—"

Unable to listen to the man talk about himself in the third person any longer, Ellie held up a hand. "You understand, we have to ask these questions. We have a responsibility to the victim and her family."

Melanie nodded. "I do. You said she has a sister? What a horrible thing, to lose a relative like that." She frowned. "What else do you need from us?"

Paul pulled out his notepad and pencil. "At risk of being blunt, have either of you fled bail?"

"No," Melanie said placidly.

Murray swallowed.

"Mr. Nickles?"

"Certainly not," he said.

"And are either of you fugitives from the law?"

"No," Melanie said.

Murray echoed her words.

Paul stared at Murray. The magician's cheeks were flushed and his forehead was damp. Murray was wearing his black suit with the red vest, even inside his own suite. Why? He looked every bit as uncomfortable as he'd been holding that microphone on stage. Worse, maybe. She waited for one of them to say something, but they sat there, looking at one another. It went on long enough that Ellie felt the tension surrounding her like wads of cotton batting, making it hard to breathe.

"Paul, I think Murray is lying through his teeth," she said at last.

Paul didn't take his eyes away from the man. "Sir? Are you *sure* there's nothing you want to tell us?"

Murray's moist forehead shone harder and released drops of sweat down both temples. "Oh, there's no need. I mean, *no*, I have nothing else to say. Not that I'm hiding anything. Because I'm not." He sat up straighter on the couch. "In fact, I demand that you leave my stateroom. I have rights, and I won't be bullied, and—"

"Murray," Melanie's voice was exasperated. "Stop. Please. Let's just tell them the truth."

He turned to her. "Are you sure? Because—"

She squeezed his hand. "I am. Listen. You've been a good friend, but this ruse has gone on long enough." She turned toward Paul. "The woman in the suitcase was looking for me. I'm the one she wanted. But I didn't kill her. I swear."

Chapter Eighteen

"I MET MURRAY AT A cafe on Hollywood Boulevard about six months ago," Melanie spoke so quietly that Ellie could hear the hum of the air flowing through the HVAC system. Paul had joined them on the couch, and Melanie sat between her and him, her damp hair forming curly tendrils on her T-shirt.

"I was waitressing during the low season — we don't get as many tourists in the winter — and Murray and I became friends. Good friends." She gave the magician a fond smile. "One night, I had two martinis after work. It had rained. The streets were wet. On my way home, I slammed my car into a red Lamborghini outside the Diplomat Beach Resort."

She took a shaky breath. "The car was idling at the curb, and I didn't see anyone in the front seat. I figured the valet must have just pulled it around for the owner, and I knew I'd fail a sobriety test, so I went home. I needed to drive to get to my job. And losing my license wasn't an option."

She lifted her head and shot Paul a rueful look. "I couldn't afford to pay for the damage to that car. And worst of all, I had let my insurance lapse. I figured that whoever owned that car was rich, and I was broke, so why not let their insurance cover it?" She winced at the memory. "But the next day, I learned there was someone in the car. The woman was injured, but thankfully it sounded like she was going to be okay. The next night I took a cab to work, my car needed a new front end, and I saw the surveillance cams right outside the resort. And the man who owned the car, well, I hear he has a lot of connections. He's a movie producer."

"You were going to be arrested," Ellie said.

"I was so stupid." A single tear rolled down Melanie's cheek. "They were going to pick up my license plate, no problem. And I was freaking out. I told Murray that I had to get out of town, fast, and he said he was headed to the Caribbean for work. Did I want to come along as his assistant? I said yes." Her shoulders slumped. "I knew if they arrested me, I was going to prison for a long time. So why not go to paradise for a while? I figured if I was lucky, maybe I'd pick up some jobs under the table, chill on the beach, that sort of thing."

Paul spoke softly. "Mr. Nickles, are you aware that aiding and abetting a fugitive is a crime?"

Murray opened his mouth to speak but Melanie stilled him with a hand on his leg. "No. Stop. He didn't know why I needed to leave. I told him I was in trouble and running away from some scary people. He offered to help me without hesitation. He is responsible for *none* of this." She laughed weakly. "Although, the first time you questioned us, he was so nervous that he basically threw himself at me and insisted we were a couple." She patted him on the knee. "You're a terrible liar, Murray. That's one of the things I love most about you."

She hung her head. "I'll stay on board the ship, Officer Gumbs. Lock me up, or whatever; you can deliver me back to the authorities in Miami. But please don't penalize Murray. His business may not recover if he loses this gig. It's been a while since he got a job like this one."

Murray looked like he was about to argue, but the energy ran out of him and he seemed to deflate like a leaky balloon. He looked at Melanie, and his chin trembled. "Thank you," he said, softly. "Truly. I'm sorry I couldn't protect you."

They hugged, and Melanie pulled away first, wiping her eye. Then she held out her hands, wrists up, and looked at Paul. "Okay. I'm ready."

Despite the seriousness of the moment, Paul's mouth quirked up on one corner. Melanie had seen too many police procedurals, and it showed in the way she held out her arms to get cuffed.

After a moment, he spoke. "There's no need to make you uncomfortable, Ms. Young. Although I will be confiscating your key card and confining you to quarters for the remainder of the cruise. You can make use of room service, and if you require escort to the medical office, call the security desk and we'll arrange it. We check every guest badge at port, so if you think you can slip away unnoticed, be aware that you can't. My officers will know to watch for you."

"I won't give you any trouble."

"Good. Well, in that case, I see no reason to prevent Mr. Nickles from disembarking the ship, so long as he doesn't get any bright ideas, like thinking that he can aid your escape from justice."

He shook his head. "I won't. But Melanie, if you need any assistance, I can recommend a lawyer to you. I want you to have good representation. You made a mistake, yes, but there's no reason why it should ruin your life."

Her face flushed. "You've already done so much; I feel like I should say no. But the truth is, I'll take all the help I can get."

"Very well," Paul said. "We have just one more question. It concerns a pearl necklace."

Ellie studied their faces closely, but neither one of them seemed to react.

"Melanie, I understand you were wearing a long pearl necklace when you came aboard," Paul said.

She thought for a moment. "Yes, I was. When Murray suggested I pose as his assistant, I bought some dresses and costume jewelry to fit the part."

"Where is that necklace now?"

"I put it in the safe," Murray said.

"You put costume jewelry in the safe?" Ellie asked.

Murray shrugged. "I didn't know the pearls were fake. I thought they looked quite pretty."

"I need you to open that safe," Paul stood up.

Murray hesitated. "I think you're taking this all a bit far. We *told* you the truth. And now you want to rifle through our belongings?"

Paul's voice was bland. "Sir, your terms of passage give us authorization to search. If you won't open it, I will."

Melanie went over to the small safe located inside the kitchenette. "Murray, it's no big deal. Let's just get them what they need so we can put this behind us." Five faint beeps rang out as she pressed the combination code on the safe, followed by a soft pop as the metal door swung open. She peered inside the compartment, her face disappearing behind the small door. "Oh! That's strange."

"What's strange?" Murray went over to join her.

"The pearls aren't in here. Did you move them?"

"Of course not. Let me see."

"No, let *me* see." Paul strode over to the safe and stepped between them. A moment later he stepped back, his expression impatient. "Hold out your arms please, both of you."

They exchanged a surprised look but obeyed. Paul quickly patted them down and gave Murray's cuffs a shake. Then he stepped back. "Nothing up their sleeves," he quipped, glancing back at Ellie. Then he stepped back further. "My apologies. I had to be sure."

"Why do the pearls interest you?" Melanie asked. "Like I said, I don't think they were worth much."

"They may match the murder weapon," Ellie said quietly.

Melanie's face went white. "Wait. If you think someone killed her with that necklace, then you must think..." She pressed her lips together. "No. I *did not* kill her! You have to believe me. I've never seen her before. In fact, I think I should—"

Murray stepped between Melanie and Paul. "The contents of our safe were stolen! No doubt stolen by the same person who murdered that unfortunate girl." He crossed his arms. "Clearly, this room isn't safe. I demand you move me to a more secure room. And I want an investigation!" His voice trembled. "I am Murray the Magnificent, and I will *not* be intimidated. I had other valuables in that safe. Valuables that are missing!" He pointed at Paul, "Your security is a joke! First, a woman was murdered on our doorstep. Now, a theft! I don't know what kind of operation you're running, but this is unacceptable. I have rights! I—"

Melanie reached for him. "It'll be okay. You just need to calm down. Here, sit down."

"Don't talk to me like I'm a child," he countered. "I need to check on Sal. He hasn't eaten. I keep feeding him, but he won't eat. I never should have taken this cruise. You know how much Sal hates to travel. It's not good for him." Murray stalked off into his bedroom and a moment later he shouted for help.

Inside his stateroom, Murray stood next to an empty birdcage. He held a black satin cloth loosely in one hand. "Sal's gone!" His face crumpled, and he put his hands over his face, letting the cloth drop to the ground. It collapsed flat onto the floor.

Paul moved closer. He peered into the cage. He lifted the metal bar that opened the large door, and he reached inside. Down on the bottom, atop the folded newspaper at the base of the cage, someone had left a torn scrap of white paper. Paul took the paper out, opened it, turned it, and frowned.

He looked up, his eyes round with worry. "It says, give me what I want, or else."

"Or else what?" Melanie asked.

He held out the paper. "That's it. *Or else.*"

That's when Murray the Magnificent burst into tears and demanded that they all leave him alone. Paul put a hand on his shoulder and marched him into the living room. He left Murray on the couch and told Melanie to keep an eye on him. Then he glanced over and said, "Ellie, help me search this place, will you?"

"What are we looking for?"

"Everything."

Chapter Nineteen

SHORTLY AFTER SEVEN THE NEXT morning, Ellie smacked her blaring alarm clock with one palm. Her head ached like it might split in half, and her tiny room was pitch black except for the faint glow from the numbers on the clock. Her body demanded more sleep! She rolled over in bed and felt herself drifting back off. Sleep was a cozy black hole and she wanted nothing more than to let the gravity drag her back down into slumber. But she'd promised her kids she'd meet them for breakfast, and that's what she was going to do. After tearing a brush through her tangled hair and pulling on some clothes, she headed upstairs to the Seabreeze Bar. Clean salt-tinged air blew past her face as she stepped outside onto the lido deck, and the morning haze filtered the light that landed on her hands and arms.

Behind the lacquered wooden bar, Manny poured small glasses of orange juice and set them on a round tray. She walked over to an empty table and peered over the railing. Down below, the wake from the ship's massive engines churned beneath the water, and a long white trail followed the *Spirit* like a frothy tail.

The ocean was relatively calm today, and the itinerary was *at sea*, meaning that there would be no ports to visit. Already, the tables inside the large buffet were filling up. She could see the crowd inside, through the big glass windows that surrounded the rectangular space. There was food in there, if only she found the energy to get up and wait in line.

Manny came over with a silver carafe and set it on the table. "Here's your tea." He halted and looked her up and down. "You look like you slept in a dumpster. What happened?"

She rubbed her eyes. "Thanks for that. And what *happened* is I was up half the night searching the ship for a stolen parrot."

Manny picked up the carafe. "Ah. I'll bring you coffee."

"Leave the tea, please." She dropped into a chair. "I gave up drinking lighter fluid in college."

He snorted and set the carafe back down. "I take it you didn't find the bird?"

"No. Sal remains at large. Paul has the security staff doing sweeps every half hour. At one point he was wandering the halls calling 'Polly want a cracker' and I think that's when I went to bed. Or maybe I dreamed it?" She eyed the silver carafe with anticipation, but she didn't pick it up. It looked so heavy! And the cups were on the far end of the table. The other end of the table was another country. Paraguay, possibly.

"The bird's probably in someone's stateroom," Manny said. "Did that magician guy leave him unattended? I doubt he strayed too far." He glanced over the railing, and she knew what he was thinking. If Sal had flown (or been tossed) over the railing he likely wouldn't have survived. As a domesticated bird, he likely didn't have the wing strength to make it far, and they were many miles from shore.

Ellie shook her head. "No, he was stolen. The bird-napper left a note, and the magician is freaking out. That guy is a piece of work, by the way, but he was genuinely distraught about that bird. I think Strunk gave him a sedative to shut him up." She yawned. Her mouth opened as if on an oiled hinge, threatening to split her head in two. Manny took pity on her and poured her tea.

"Drink that," he said. "I'll bring you a waffle."

"You are a saint among men. Can I have strawberries too?"

"What's this about a birdnapping?" Marcie came over, carrying Clara. Clara had a banana in one hand, and she was waving it around like a tiny yellow sword. Junior held two plates of food from the buffet. He set one down in front of his wife, and one in front of himself. Ellie told them about the missing bird, and the fruitless hunt to find him.

Manny came back shortly, carrying a waffle and fruit for Ellie. Under one arm, he'd brought a coloring book for Clara. He set it down and placed a tiny cellophane packet of crayons on top.

"You must be the Tappets. I am Emmanuel Napole Estrada, at your service." He gave a slight bow, and reached out to shake Marcie's hand, then Junior's. "But you can call me Manny."

"Oh! You're Manny the bartender! Mom has told us all about you." Marcie smiled up at him. "It's so nice to meet you. Were you also in on the bird search last night?"

He shook his head solemnly. "No. I prefer to leave investigating to the professionals."

"That's what I tried to tell her," Junior said, nodding appreciatively at Manny. "But she's so stubborn."

Manny cleared his throat gently and adjusted his black half-apron. "Ah. Well... I meant I leave it to the professionals like Paul and your Mother." He ran one tan palm along the surface of his black hair, which stood straight up like a freshly manicured lawn. "Besides, I require eight hours of beauty sleep, every night." He reached down and opened the packet of crayons. "Now, if you need anything, on the menu or off, I am here for you." He hesitated. "Although, now that you're here, Ellie, I was hoping to have a word. Is it true that I have you to blame for this coconut crocodile craze?"

Ellie chuckled. "That drink hasn't become a *thing*, has it?"

Manny threw up his hands and addressed Marcie. "Is this how she is at home? Causing trouble then pretending she had nothing to do with it?"

"Never," Marcie said loyally.

Junior cut a piece of his waffle and held it up on the end of a fork. "No comment," he said, before plunging it into his mouth. Marcie laughed as she moved some of her breakfast onto a small plate for Clara.

"I have gotten approximately three *hundred* requests for the coconut crocodile," Manny said, raising an eyebrow. "Several gentlemen wanted the original formulation, the one with fish sauce. And thus I had to improvise."

"Do I want to know?" Ellie asked.

"You most certainly do not. But let me just say, I've never had people so enthusiastic about such a disgusting concoction. Last night during the dance party, I sold sixty of your drinks; fifteen were the 'original' formulation. Also, do you know how hard it is to find gummy crocodiles in the US Virgin Islands? I've been making do with sharks and frogs, and our guests are demanding crocodiles. They're *adamant* that only crocodiles will do. There was this one intoxicated gentleman, very insistent, and I managed to convince him that a gummy *worm* was a crocodile species native to the Philippines. And you know how it pains me to mislead our guests." He put one hand on his chest and lowered his gaze mournfully.

Ellie laughed! Still, she strove to look chastened when she said, "Well, I'm sorry for springing that on you. Next time I have to invent a drink, I'll come up with something with fewer strange ingredients."

He waved her off. "All is forgiven. But lest you get too self-satisfied, you basically invented a caribeño with candy in it. Thankfully, I'm well versed in Puerto Rican cocktails. Oh, and how is Violet?" He frowned to himself. "She hasn't been by."

"We aren't speaking at the moment," Ellie admitted.

"Why not?"

"Well, she was harassing a guest, and—"

"Her ex, you mean."

"Yes, but she can't just—"

Manny shook his head. "You weren't here when it happened. And you probably can't imagine the sight of Violet walking this ship like a ghost, for *months*, hardly talking, never singing." He sighed. "Don't judge her too harshly."

"I don't. And I'm worried about her."

Clara's blue crayon rolled out of reach. Manny swiftly plucked it up and set it at the little girl's elbow. "It wouldn't surprise me if Violet's old flame has a few enemies among the crew. I'm not saying that one of us is responsible for the crime, but it's no secret that this is the woman who snapped Violet's heart in half like a twig."

Marcie looked up at Manny. "You guys are like a big family, aren't you?"

Manny nodded. "Yes. And usually that's positive." He shrugged. "I hope the crew is not involved. But I've learned to tell your mother all my theories. Or else she'll come by and drag them out of me at an inopportune moment."

"You think someone might have taken the bird to get back at Violet's ex? It wasn't even her bird. It belongs to the magician," Ellie said.

Manny shrugged. "It would be wrong if they did so. But we have long memories aboard the *Spirit*. Keep your eyes open. And I'll let you know if I hear anything. Have you identified the body in the luggage?"

Ellie nodded. "Yes. We're on it."

The tables in the bar were starting to fill up with breakfasters. Manny went to check on the other tables. Ellie glanced down at her plate. She hadn't considered the crew angle. But even if someone had been cruel enough to steal the parrot as a prank, why would they leave that threatening note? It didn't add up. Was the theft of the bird and the pearls related to the murder? Or were they unrelated events?

Ellie looked up at her kids. "Manny was the first friend I ever made on the ship. He's..." Her voice trailed off when she saw their faces. Junior looked frosty. Marcie had the expression of a woman who'd just had a shock, but who was trying to play it cool. Clara, oblivious, had her mouth full of banana.

"There was a body?" Marcie asked, her voice quiet. She shot a look at Ron, and his mouth became a thin white line. "Like, here. On *this* cruise?"

"Yes." Ellie cut the largest bite of waffle that she could manage and shoved it in her mouth. She'd forgotten the syrup, and it was a bit dry, but there was no such thing as a bad waffle.

Junior's voice was surprisingly calm as he asked. "And you're *helping*?"

She nodded, still chewing. "Mmm-mmm."

Junior took a breath, as if to calm himself. "And were you going to mention this at any point?"

Ellie finished chewing and swallowed. "I wasn't sure. After your little lecture at the restaurant, I figured maybe you'd rather not know."

"Hang on." Junior seemed to be thinking hard. He glanced at Clara. "How many M-U-R-D-E-R-S have you had?"

"Since I've been here?" Ellie pretended to adjust the napkin on her lap. "On *this* ship? Specifically?"

"Yes," Junior's eyes were boring into hers like lasers.

She considered the question. They still didn't know *where* the young woman in the luggage had been murdered, exactly. And he hadn't asked about crimes at port, or crimes that had been foiled, or victims that had recovered. She looked up with a big smile and said, "One! We've had one other," she smiled at Clara, "M-U-R-D-E-R aboard the ship. Prior to this one." She glanced at Marcie, who was looking at her like she knew exactly the kind of math her mother-in-law was doing.

"I can spell," Clara said proudly. She beckoned Ellie closer. Ellie leaned over and listened. Clara whispered a bunch of letters, slurring them together in her sweet voice.

"You *can* spell," Ellie said in a delighted tone. "Before too long you'll break our code and then you'll be unstoppable."

"I don't stop," Clara said breezily, before reaching for the salt shaker at the center of the table. Marcie distracted her with a tickle and used her other hand to snatch the shaker away.

Ellie looked over at Junior, daring him to insult her again. He swallowed, once, and glanced down at his hands. Before he could say anything, Marcie burst in. "Well, I'm not surprised that mom has taken on crime fighting as a hobby."

Junior looked over. "You're not?"

"Well, I thought about it last night, after we got back to our room. And when Dad was alive, those two were always going on and on about his investigations. He'd come home with stories about a case they were working on, and she'd barrage him with questions the whole time. Did he talk to this person, and had he considered that person's motive, and so on." Marcie smiled at Ellie. "You two were like – I don't know – Watson and Holmes." Marcie speared a piece of watermelon with her fork and let it dangle in the air for a moment. Clara reached for it with her little fingers, and Marcie let her have it.

"I remember that too," Junior said, his expression softening. "I just wish..."

"What do you wish?" Ellie asked.

"I wish someone was here to keep an eye on you. I told Dad I'd keep you safe, and..." he squeezed his eyes shut and sat still. When he opened them, they were bright with unshed tears.

Oh, my sweet boy. Ellie reached over and squeezed his hand. "I'm never alone around here. Surely you've seen that."

"I still don't like it," Junior said, pulling his hand back. "Advising Dad was one thing. It wasn't like you were out interviewing witnesses in the middle of the night." His expression darkened. "Police work is dangerous, Ma. And I don't want you getting hurt."

Ellie held out her hands, "Look at me, kiddo. Do I seem hurt?" She smiled at him but he just glowered at her. A flutter of worry burst in her belly. You couldn't raise a child to adulthood without knowing who they were, inside and out. Had her boy changed, or was something else going on? She caught Marcie's anxious glance and gave her a smile in return.

"Well, so long as you're being safe." Marcie said, as if the matter were decided.

They finished their breakfasts, and Manny made his rounds, checking in with guests seated around the bar area. "So, we have the whole day at sea," Ellie said. "What would you like to do today?"

Marcie shielded her eyes from the sun and looked up and around. "Well, tonight we should see that musical. It's family friendly, right? And I figured maybe today Clara and I could have some girl time."

"Girl time," Clara agreed, picking up a crayon and sniffing it.

Ellie shot Marcie a look that was a question. Marcie looked from her to Junior, then lifted her eyebrows slightly. Ellie said, "Ah. Yes. And while you and Clara are having girl time, Junior and I can... Well, we'll find something to do."

"Take him along on your investigation," Marcie suggested.

"What?" Ellie and Ron replied simultaneously.

"I'm sure you have people to talk to, right, Mom? And that poor parrot is still missing." Marcie made shooing motions with her hands. "Ron's a cop. And you know the territory. Go. Solve something!" She smiled. "After you've done your work, you can meet us at the big pool before dinner."

Ellie nodded. She *had* hoped to talk to Wynona today. She was the only one who'd actually spoken to the victim. And in all the hubbub about the parrot, she'd forgotten to ask Paul about interviewing the porters. Maybe one of them remembered where they'd found that big suitcase? And how did they know where to deliver it, without a luggage tag on the outside? It seemed more and more likely that the killer had left it there. And that meant someone may have seen them. Should they canvass the suites for witnesses?

Marcie was waiting for an answer. "Oh, I doubt Junior wants to come," Ellie said, "He's made his feelings clear."

"I'll go with you," he said, sitting his fork down atop his plate. "I never said that I wouldn't."

"Good. It's all settled!" Marcie packed Clara's coloring book away. She picked her daughter up and set her on the ground, holding out her hand. "What do you say we go play? Girl time?"

Clara waved at them both until they were out of sight. Ellie finished her tea, and Junior finished his orange juice. After a silence that stretched on too long, Ellie muttered, "Last time I checked, I'm a girl too."

Junior laughed at that, and she glanced over, risking a smile of her own. "Yeah, I think Marce wants us to work our stuff out." He added, "Not that there's anything to work out."

"Of course not," Ellie replied. "She's imagining things."

"So, who did you want to talk to first?"

"You don't have to come. I won't be mad."

"I know. But I want to spend the day with my Mom." He shrugged. "How's this? You pick the activity today, and I'll pick the activity tomorrow. That's only fair."

Her heart lifted. Junior might be unhappy about her choices, but once he saw what she did (she only talked to people!) he'd simmer right down. A demonstration was in order, and it was time to put this matter to bed once and for all. And whoever had killed Samantha Rawlings was in a boatload of trouble. Paul Gumbs was on the case, and so was she, and now they'd be dealing with not just one Tappet, but two. Surely their powers of deduction would be magnified!

"Okay then," She stood up. "Let's go talk to Wynona. And I'll fill you in on the case on our way over."

Chapter Twenty

INSIDE THE SHIP'S LARGE THEATER, a dress rehearsal was underway. On the high stage, a woman in an old-fashioned dress with a tight bodice and voluminous skirts wielded a slender sword. She pointed it at a man in a naval uniform. His artfully torn jacket had shiny brass buttons running down the center. "Sir, it is *you* who shall yield, not I!" she shouted.

Her enemy reached out to her tenderly, and he grasped the blade of her sword, pressing the point against his chest. "I'd sooner die than lose you. If my death is your wish, bring your wish to bear upon the end of your sword. It matters not. I shall renew my chase inside the iron gates of heaven!" Orchestral music swelled and fell like ocean waves. All around them, the 'crew' stood frozen, watching the moment in awe.

Wynona strode out on stage. She wore capri pants and chunky wooden heels, and her skinny legs were like two toothpicks holding up her ample torso and masses of curling brown hair. The stage lights bounced off her golden belt and matching bracelet, and for a moment she looked like Wonder Woman wrapped up in the Lasso of Truth.

I wish I had one of those, Ellie thought. *That would be a real time saver.*

Wynona held up her hands. "Cut! Marie, that was excellent. Josef, you had me on tenterhooks! Keep up the good work." She pointed up to an actor in a scruffy blue uniform. He was high on the prop-ship's mast, hanging off by one hand, his body supported by one arm as if he weighed nothing. "Raul, don't forget your cue. We've got enemy pirates coming, people! Never forget. These are dangerous, blood-thirsty fighters, and the audience needs to see the fear on your faces *before* the crescendo hits." She pointed at the empty seats beyond the stage. "They should feel the pirates coming *before* the words come out." She beamed at the cast as if they were her own children before turning around to retreat into the wings. Upon catching sight of Ellie and Junior, she flicked a curious glance outward and yelled, "Everyone, take five! We'll reset from the end of the last song."

Wynona stepped gingerly down the staircase that connected the stage to the carpet. "Ellie! What can I do for you? Oh, and is this the handsome son I've been hearing about?" She stuck out a hand, but left it palm down, as if she expected Junior to kiss it. He squeezed her hand briefly and let go and she dipped slightly as if he'd pressed his lips to her skin.

"Ron Tappet." He smiled politely. "I'm spending the day with my Mom, and she wanted to talk to you. I'm just along for the ride."

He sounds like a bored teenager, Ellie thought, before turning her full attention to Wynona. "I'm sorry to interrupt rehearsal. This won't take long. I'm helping Paul sort out our little mystery, and I understand that you knew the woman found in the suitcase? I'm sorry for your loss."

Wynona's pale brown eyes were full of sympathy. "Oh, thank you, darlin', but I'd only spoken to the poor girl on the phone. But it's so frightening what happened! Samantha was a delightful dancer. I saw her audition tapes. Now we're down a dancing pirate, and..." She snapped her mouth shut. "Well, that's not what's important, is it?"

"What can you tell me about her?" Ellie asked.

"Not much, I'm afraid. The girl told me that she was a stunt performer, and she said she wanted to add a dance credit to her resume. I was leery of bringing someone on for such a short stint, but she promised to make it worth my while."

"How so?" Junior asked.

Wynona grimaced. "Well, she said she'd owe me a favor if I ever came back to Hollywood." Two pink spots appeared on the apples of her cheeks. "That sounds dreadfully selfish, I know, but that's how our industry works. And as much as I hope things work out for me here on the *Spirit*, it's never a bad idea to earn a favor or two.

Samantha seemed well-connected in the indie film world, and I figured it wouldn't hurt to bring her on board for a week. Her tape was good."

Ellie smiled to put her at ease. "Well, don't worry about any of that. Mostly, I'm interested in the woman herself. Can you tell me what she was like, as a person?"

Wynona put her weight on one hip and touched her chin. "Well, we only spoke twice. But she struck me as very assertive. She told me up front what she wanted, what she was offering, and why I should hire her. She was a very businesslike woman."

"Most performers butter you up first, you know. They flatter you by describing everything you've done, and they call you a genius, and it's all quite tiresome. Samantha wasn't like that. My preference was for someone who could stay longer than a week, she was filling in for Esther, and there was a chance Esther might need more time, but Samantha said no, she'd already accepted another gig that put her back in L.A. after the sailing. I decided to take a risk on her." Wynona shrugged. "Fat lot of good it did me. Now I'm out a backup dancer *and* I hear the poor girl was killed and stuffed in a suitcase?"

Wynona shot Junior a worried look. "I've *heard* things about this ship. It has quite the reputation. But I decided not to listen to gossip." She crossed her arms and looked at Ellie as if she were at fault. "This is what I get for leaving Los Angeles. Back home, they might stab you in the back, but they won't *actually* stab you in the back." She frowned to herself, then embarrassment flashed across her face. "Sorry! Don't get me wrong. I'm happy to be here doing entertainment on a cruise ship. Super happy!" Her smile faltered. "You won't tell Roberta what I said, will you? About the favor. Because I can't afford to lose this job."

Ellie hid a smile. Wynona struck her as one of those people who let every stray thought in her head pop right out of her mouth, even when it didn't reflect favorably on her. She didn't mind. Wynona might not have a filter, but it meant she was probably telling the truth. "I won't. I'm curious though, how did you get Samantha's name?"

Wynona scratched her ear. She snagged her earring on accident and winced when her earlobe tugged down. "Now, that *was* unusual. I usually go through an agency for temps. But Samantha came to me directly. She called my number, and she said she'd been following my work for years. In fact, she knew my whole resume. A genuinely nice girl. And she accepted entry level rates too." Wynona's face fell. "*Please* tell me she wasn't some kind of secret criminal. Because I'd feel terrible if I let her manipulate me into coming on this ship."

"Quite the opposite," Ellie said. "Samantha was a licensed bounty hunter. We think she came on board to catch someone."

Wynona gasped and lifted her hand to her mouth. Her nails were painted bubble-gum pink. "Just like in the movies. Well, isn't that wild?"

Junior, who had been watching, unfolded his arms. In a serious voice, he asked, "Wynona, was Samantha coming aboard to arrest you?"

The effect on Wynona was immediate. She burst out laughing like this was the funniest thing she'd ever heard. "Oh! Me? No, young man, I'm not fleeing anything except a run of bad luck back home. Unless they go after retired actresses with no retirement savings and too much credit card debt, I doubt she was much interested in me."

Junior smiled warmly at her, turning on the charm. "Well, did Samantha mention an interest in anyone else on board? Did she mention anyone she knew, or make any friends here, or make any requests?"

Wynona seemed to be thinking hard. "No, sweet thing. She seemed excited. She said this was a huge opportunity. I presumed she meant the dancing, but she had another job to do, I guess."

Ellie hesitated. Sometimes sharing information helped a witness make new connections. Would this be one of those times? "Apparently the bounty she was chasing would bring her eighty thousand dollars."

Wynona's fake eyelashes sprung apart, and she goggled at Ellie. "That much! Oh my. Maybe I'll look into becoming a bounty hunter myself!" She frowned and shook her head. "No. I'll keep my nice, *safe*, job thank you very much. Do you know who she was chasing?" Her voice lowered and she took a half-step closer. "Are they dangerous?"

"We don't know," Ellie said. "Paul's looking into it. But don't worry. Even if the person she was chasing is on board, I doubt someone with that kind of price on their head would want to stand out. If they're here, they're probably staying out of sight."

Wynona glanced back at the stage with a faint frown. The actors were talking, and some of the women had taken their wigs off. "I should get back. Have you ever worked with actors? They're wonderful people. So creative! But you take your eye off them for five minutes and they're scattered to the five winds like a herd of house cats at a mouse jamboree."

"Paul said that you asked the performers if they knew Samantha?" Ellie prompted.

"I did. None of them had worked with her before. Granted, that's probably a good thing. I can't have my performers off their game so close to opening night." She leaned closer and whispered, even though the stage was twenty feet away. "They're an excellent troupe. But there's *so much* drama. One of the backup dancers moved Marie's wig and she went *full* Kardashian."

"Which one?" Junior asked, tilting his head.

Wynona leaned forward and whispered, "Khloé. With hints of Kanye."

"Yikes," Junior said.

"I know, right?" Wynona nodded appreciatively. "Ellie, if I hear anything, I'll let you know. And please come see the show tonight! They've been working so hard; they deserve a full audience."

"We'll be there," Ellie promised. Once Wynona was out of earshot, Ellie turned to Junior and asked, "Who was she referring to?"

Junior's mouth quirked up in one corner. "I have no idea."

Chapter Twenty-One

WHEN THEY GOT BACK TO *The Lofts* the lounge was empty and there was a pile of dirty dishes in the kitchen sink. "Have a seat, kiddo," Ellie said. "Let's talk through the case while I clean up a little." She glanced around the room to see if there were any other dishes left about. Someone had drawn a parrot on the communal white-board in the living room. Beneath the doodle, the artist had printed the words: *Have You Seen This Bird?* along with the extension for the security office. Whomever had done the doodle had drawn it in the style of a wanted poster. That was cute. Had Kameron drawn it, or Paul? They'd both seemed rather taken with that bird.

She put some coffee on to brew for Junior and steeped some tea for herself, then busied herself washing the dishes. "So, what do you think of the investigation so far?"

Junior drummed his fingers on the kitchen counter. "Well, I arrived in the middle of things, so it's hard to say." He glanced down at his hands. "Although, I'm confused about one thing."

Ellie glanced up. "What's that?"

"You've got two good suspects, Murray and Melanie. Why don't you just detain them and hand them over to the cops when we get back to Miami? Let the police sort it out."

Ellie lifted the sink handle. Warm water ran over her hands, and she added a squirt of soap to her clean yellow sponge. "We don't have that authority, hon. Paul's a security officer, and our terms of passage give us some latitude, but we can't just detain people because they're suspicious. Can you imagine?" She spread her soapy hands out in the air as if she were framing a headline. "Cruise line detains innocent man against his will." She shot him a small smile. "Our investigation ends the moment our suspects disembark the ship. Everyone gets in cars or on a plane and they're gone! We can turn over evidence to any relevant law enforcement body, but it's difficult for them to make it a priority. They weren't here. And they usually have their own cases to deal with."

She turned the last clean cup upside-down on the drying rack and carried their beverages over to the counter. "I'm feeling stuck. And I hate it! Without our help, that young woman's family may never learn what happened to her, and the person who did it may get away."

"Well, what would Dad do?" Junior asked, drumming his hands on the table. "He'd say we should go back to the beginning. Let's recap. The victim was a bounty hunter, and she came aboard the ship under false pretenses in pursuit of a criminal. One of your suspects, Melanie, says that she may have been the target, as she fled a hit and run. The victim had Melanie's luggage tag in her hand when she died, and her body was inside a suitcase, delivered to Melanie's room."

Ellie nodded. "And then on top of that, Melanie's friend, the magician, had his parrot stolen last night, along with jewelry and other valuables. And it just so happens that one of the necklaces may have been our murder weapon."

Junior shrugged. "You don't have to be a genius to put it together. Melanie was fleeing justice, the victim confronted her, she kills the girl, stuffs the body in the bag, and leaves it to be collected. The magician, who is already covering for her, covers for her even harder. He tosses the murder jewelry overboard along with some other bits and bobs and says someone else did it."

"Okay. But then why steal the parrot? Why leave a note making vague demands? Also, how did the victim get on the ship? We still don't know. And would Melanie have left her room number in the victim's hand?"

"Criminals aren't smart people," Junior said. "If they were, they wouldn't choose such a dangerous line of work."

"Melanie isn't a career criminal. She's an actress." Ellie thought back to the moment when Melanie had held her hands out to be cuffed. "Maybe not a great one."

"So you *do* think Melanie did it," Junior said.

"No. I don't."

He looked at her over the rim of his coffee mug. "You don't think she did it, or you don't want to believe it, because your friend asked you not to?"

Ellie sipped her tea. The mug warmed her hands, and she considered all that she knew so far. Was she just humoring Violet? No. There was more to it than that. "Let's cast a wide net," she said. "Let's say that Melanie didn't kill the bounty hunter. Who are our other suspects?"

"Here's another question, first: Why did the victim go to such pains to get a one-week assignment. Wouldn't it have been easier to buy a ticket? If I were a bounty hunter, that's what I'd do."

It was a good question. "Maybe she wanted access to the crew levels. Guests can't access the private parts of the ship." Her eyes widened. "Wait! Do you think she intended to smuggle her target out in that suitcase? Maybe her target fought back? And maybe *she* ended up in the suitcase after the scuffle."

"Ma," Junior was shaking his head.

Ellie continued, gesturing as she went. "It must have been a relatively small person, like her. And—" She felt the air burst into her lungs as the idea hit her. "Maybe the victim planned to shove Murray in the suitcase! He'd fit."

Junior was shaking his head. "You're trying too hard to make your theories fit the evidence, but it doesn't work that way. You need to follow the evidence and keep asking open-ended questions: Who? When? Why? Where? and How?" He rubbed his neck. "This mystery feels a lot like a messed-up Sudoku puzzle, Ma. When you're three-quarters of the way in, and your numbers won't add up, you can't change the math. You need to go back, retrace your steps, and figure out what you missed."

"Since when do you do puzzles?"

"I've had some free time on my hands," he glanced down at his cup. "Don't change the subject. Give me your questions. What don't you know?"

She composed her thoughts. "Well, there are the big questions: Who killed the victim? Where, and why? We already know the how."

He nodded. "What else?"

"Who took Sal? Why? What did that note in the cage mean? Who wrote it? When was Sal taken? And who stole the contents of Murray's safe?"

"What was in the safe?" Junior asked.

"The pearl necklace and some other costume jewelry. A few hundred dollars cash." She paused, considering the list. "But *not* their passports."

"Is that unusual?"

She nodded. "Most guests store their passports in their safes. If you lose them, it's a real hassle to get through security back home."

"Seems worth asking about, doesn't it? Now, what does your gut tell you about those two? We've considered the evidence, and you've got your questions. Now, your gut will tell you what's most important."

She thought for a moment. "My gut says that Melanie and Murray have been lying their faces off the whole time. I don't trust them, and I certainly don't like them. But they were horrified when we found the body. I don't think they killed her."

"And what bit of evidence is bothering you the most?" Junior asked.

"The note in the cage," she replied automatically. "Give me what I want, or else? What good is a vague threat like that? Either it's totally bogus, or the bird-napper is a moron, or Murray was lying, and he knows *exactly* what the birdnapper wanted."

"See? You have many promising lines of inquiry," Junior said teasingly. "There's no need to invent any wild theories. Just follow the questions. They'll lead you where you want to go."

Gratitude welled up in her body like fresh water after a drought. Since the beginning, this crime had felt like a knotted-up string, impossible to untangle. But now, she felt hopeful. "You're a lot like your Dad, you know."

"I'm not," Junior's chin lowered. "I wish I was, but..."

Where was his sudden sadness coming from? She reached over and brushed a lock of hair off his forehead. "Are you ready to tell me what's going on with you and Marcie?" she asked.

"What do you mean?"

He sounded so surprised that she was taken aback. Surely he couldn't be *that* clueless? "I'm referring to the fight you've been having with Marcie. You're bottling something up. She's worried. You're sending her calls to voicemail. She's walking on eggshells as to not make you even more upset. You've noticed that, right?"

"She thinks I'm upset with *her*? No! It's just—" He shook his head. "It's no big deal. I'll talk to her." He looked troubled, and her heart went out to him. She wanted to ask what was on his mind, but it seemed only fair that he talk to Marcie first.

"Good," she said, patting his hand again. "I hate seeing you two so stressed out. Speaking of which, if you *weren't* running around the ship with me today, if you had the whole day to yourself, what would you do?"

The furrow on his brow melted away. "I'd probably watch the game. Have a beer. Take a nap on one of those big chairs on the sun deck. Maybe get more of that chocolate cake from the buffet."

She pointed at the big U-shaped couch on the other side of the room. "There you go. The TV has all the sports channels, and I want to go talk to Paul before I meet you and Marcie for dinner."

"I'm not leaving your side. Where you go, I go." But as he said the words, his gaze drifted to the couch longingly, as if it were an oasis in the desert.

She beamed at him. "Kiddo, I'm just going to go ask Paul a few questions. There's nothing to be alarmed about. Are you still so convinced that I'm rushing off into the face of danger?"

He shot her a guilty look. "Maybe not. But please promise me that you'll be careful. And no heroics."

She held up two fingers. "Scout's honor." Then she dumped the dregs of her tea into the sink. "Enjoy your game. I'll see you in a few hours."

Chapter Twenty-Two

PAUL'S DOOR WAS OPEN. SHE knocked on the frame and stuck her head inside. "Hey. Any luck finding our feathered friend?"

Paul looked up from his computer. It was open to the official website of Murray the Magnificent. From an oversized photo on the front page, Murray beamed into the camera, holding out a bouquet of red plastic roses. His other hand held a single white egg, and his black top hat had playing cards stuck into the band. "I'm afraid not. Although Murray has called me twice this morning to 'remind' me that he has friends in the media." His expression soured. "But when I find Sal, I may run away and look for a safe place to set him free. No one should be forced to spend time with that insufferable man."

"Then why are you looking at his website?"

Paul shrugged. "You saw how quickly he turned on us once Melanie wasn't in the room. I don't trust him. That's why I'm redoing his background check."

"Smart." Ellie said. "Any luck?"

"No." Paul locked his computer screen with a quick keyboard command and the *Adventurous Cruises* mermaid logo danced across the screen in a zig-zag pattern. He rubbed his short brown hair with one hand. "At this point, I'm tempted to walk up and down the halls calling Sal's name. If he's still alive, he can talk, and if he can talk, maybe we can find him."

"We tried that last night," she reminded him. "Can I see the note? I just had a chat with Junior about the case, and it gave me an idea."

Paul went to the far side of the room and opened the man-sized safe. Inside, she caught a glimpse of two long rifles resting against the metal backing. He took out a plastic bag with a scrap of paper in it and handed it over. "Have at it. I tried pulling prints, but all I got were smudges," he said.

Ellie looked closely at the note. The paper was thick and ivory, four inches by six inches. The page had been torn from one of the complimentary pads of paper that housekeeping left in every stateroom. "Give me what I want, or else..." she read aloud, twirling her hand in a continuing gesture.

"Or else what?"

"Exactly! There are too many coincidences here. Murray and Melanie are from L.A. and the bounty hunter was from L.A. too. The bounty hunter was killed, and her body was left outside *their* room. Now there's a note like this, and they *swear* they don't know what the birdnapper wants? What if one of them wrote this note, and they were just trying to get us out of their room. Murray was cracking under our questioning, the man has *no* poker face, and the missing bird was a mighty fine distraction, wasn't it?"

Paul's nostrils flared. "I'd trust those two about as far as I could throw them. One-handed, with the ship's anchor tied to their ankles. But I can't do much without evidence. And on that score, I've got nothing. Besides, if they killed our victim, I still can't see how. And Melanie's already turned herself in for the hit-and-run. What's left to do?"

Ellie handed the note back to him. "I was thinking about what happened last night. Remember how Murray stormed off into his bedroom? It's as if he *wanted* to find that note while we were still there."

Paul thought for a moment. "It does seem that way. But that doesn't tell us who killed Samantha."

"I know. But let's start with the questions we can answer." She pointed at the paper and smiled. "If Melanie or Murray wrote that note, we can prove it."

⚓⚓⚓

THEY CLIMBED THE STAIRCASE THAT connected the crew level to *The Suites* and headed toward Melanie and Murray's room. On the way, they passed the owner's suite, and Paul shot Ellie a sidelong glance. "Have you spoken to Roberta lately?"

"I left her a message. And I told her that the investigation is in good hands." Paul seemed to stand even taller under that small bit of praise, and she smiled. "I wish she were here and running the show. We're running out of time and Violet hates my guts. And I can't stand the thought of going home until I've made things right, but I don't know how."

"It was easier when you weren't responsible for things, wasn't it," Paul's voice was gently teasing. "Don't worry. Violet's got a temper, but you two will make up. She's not the type to hold grudges."

Ellie thought back to the way Violet had unloaded on Melanie in front of everyone in the atrium. "I hope you're right. I feel like the world's worst friend right now." She took longer steps to keep pace with Paul. Despite the lack of natural light, the warm glow from the glass wall sconces on the left and right provided plenty of illumination. An opening on the right led to an alcove containing an ice machine. Out of the corner of her eye, a flash of black and red caught her attention. Dark hair. Scarlet lipstick? It had been just a flash, but she knew. She stopped in her tracks. "Hold up."

Paul was at Murray and Melanie's stateroom, just ahead of her, one hand poised to knock.

Ellie jerked her head to one side, toward the alcove. She cleared her throat and waited. When nothing happened, she did it again, with more force.

"Do you need a lozenge, Ellie?" Violet's voice was dryly amused. "They stock them in the gift shop right between the condoms and the aspirin."

"Violet," she whispered, moving closer to the opening. "What are you doing?"

Paul came over to look. From the hallway, the alcove appeared empty. "I told you to stay away from your ex! Why are you here?"

"There's no Violet here," Violet said breezily. "Just the ghost of the ice machine." Something opened inside the alcove, and something slammed shut. Three cubes of ice pitched out through the opening, one at a time, landing on the carpet near Ellie's sneakers. "OOOOOOOooooo haunted ice machine!"

Ellie put her hands on her hips but all she wanted to do was laugh. "Violet! Come out. Right now."

There was a faint creak of something being slid across linoleum, and Violet stepped out into the alcove, brushing dust off her jeans. A dark smudge of dirt ran down her otherwise spotless white T-shirt from where she'd rubbed against something.

"Are you spying on your ex?" Paul asked, his voice incredulous.

"And were you wedged behind the ice machine?" Ellie added.

Violet rolled her eyes. "Why would I *spy* on Melanie? To *spy* implies that I want information. And I don't. I'm just here to make sure no one comes and offs her before the police haul her away to jail as she so richly deserves." Violet's voice was falsely cheery, but she couldn't hide the worry in her voice.

"You're guarding her!" Ellie exclaimed.

Violet scoffed. "Let's not make a bigger deal out of this than it needs to be. Mel has gotten herself mixed up in something awful, as usual, and she's way over her head. And I had some vacation time, so I decided to keep an eye out for any *problems*. That's all."

Ellie stepped forward. "I'm not judging. And I'm not here to boss you around. I'm sorry that—"

Violet shut her up with a sad smile. "I know. But you two have been so busy trying to figure out who killed that woman that it's never even occurred to you to ask if anyone else is in danger."

"I've considered it," Paul said defensively.

"Have you? A woman is strangled and delivered to Mel's doorstep, with Mel's name in her hand. That sounds like a message to me. How do you know she's not the next target?"

Ellie felt her shoulders tense. She hadn't considered that angle. And how would she feel if a murderer might be going after someone *she* loved? She had to admit, it might make her act a little crazy

Paul looked skeptical. "No more dramatics."

Violet's right shoulder dropped and she glanced skyward, rolling her eyes like a teenager. "Paul, I'm just getting some *ice*." She held up her hands. "Sue me."

"And let's say someone *did* go after Melanie," Paul said. "What was your plan? Crack them in the head with frosty cubes of water?"

Violet stepped back into the alcove. When she came back, she was holding an enormous bottle of vodka in her hand. The glass looked thick, and she gripped it by the stem, swinging it like a baseball bat. "Just in case," she said.

Paul looked at Ellie with a question in his eyes. He was leaving the next move up to her. She reached for the walkie talkie at her waist and handed it over to Violet. "If you see something, use this, not that." She pointed at the vodka bottle. "And no heroics. Or I'll let Paul tie you up and stow you in his safe until we get back to Miami."

"Can I have a few air holes?" Violet fluttered her eyelashes at Ellie before ducking back inside the alcove.

Paul paused again outside room 1289. "Are you sure that was a good idea?" he asked quietly.

"No, but I trust her." Ellie said. "Just like I trust you."

Chapter Twenty-Three

MELANIE OPENED THE DOOR. HER hair was pulled back in a loose ponytail, and she wore casual shorts and a striped tank top with tiny gold stars on it. She looked ready to relax by the pool, except of course that she'd been barred from leaving her stateroom. The sliding door leading to the balcony was partially open, and the sun cast a yellow block of light on the carpet. "Please, come in. Have you found Sal? Murray hardly slept last night."

Ellie glanced around the suite. There was an empty room service tray on the kitchenette counter, and a stack of dirty dishes atop the tray. Food for two? It looked like it, but the magician was nowhere in sight. "Where's Murray?" she asked.

"He was getting antsy, so I sent him out for a walk. I think he intended to stay in the room with me for the rest of the cruise — he feels bad that I got caught — but he hates being cooped up. Just because I'm stuck indoors, it doesn't mean he has to be."

Paul walked over to the desk. It sat in a small nook off the living room; the surface was bare except for a Tiffany-style lamp and two leatherette portfolios holding room service menus. He pulled open the desk drawer and lifted away the stack of magazines inside. When he found what he was looking for, he stuck it in his pocket.

"What's he doing?" Melanie asked, turning her head.

"There's a possibility that the birdnapper left something behind," Ellie said. She walked over to the small blue couch and sat down. "Come, sit with me. How have you been holding up? Is the crew taking good care of you?"

Melanie came over and sat across from her in an upholstered armchair. She stroked the patterned fabric with one hand. "They've been quite kind to me, all things considered."

"Well, we all make mistakes in life," Ellie said, keeping one eye on Paul. He'd moved into Murray's room, and although she couldn't see him, she heard doors opening and closing. It shouldn't take long to complete the search, but she didn't want Melanie to know exactly what they were up to. She smiled at Melanie and held out her hands. "I speak from experience, having made a lot of mistakes myself."

But Melanie didn't seem interested in chatting. She stood up and walked toward Murray's open door. "Officer Gumbs, do you need a hand in there?"

Ellie moved to intercept her. "While I'm here, I wanted to apologize for the way Violet treated you during karaoke. I spoke to her about it, and I can assure you that it won't happen again."

Melanie looked surprised. "Oh, that? I don't care. Violet's determined to see me as the villain of the piece, and I don't have the energy to argue with her."

"If you don't mind me asking..." Ellie began tentatively.

"I do mind," Melanie said, returning to the living room and dropping into one of the upholstered chairs with more force than necessary. "So let's not."

Paul came out of the room and glanced at the women. He said, "Excuse me, I have just a few more places to check." Then he stepped past them and walked right into Melanie's room.

Melanie's sharp glance at Paul melted away as soon as she caught Ellie watching her. She interlaced her fingers atop her bare knee. "I wish you guys would spend less time searching our belongings and more time keeping an eye on Murray."

"Why? Do you think he's in trouble?" Ellie asked.

She shook her head. "No. That's not what I meant. But I'm worried about him. He's freaked out about Sal, of course. And he lost his lucky poker chip in the theft, so he's angry about that too. And to top it all off, there was that horrible man who shouted at him in front of everyone." She shot Ellie an irritated look. "I expect Violet has turned the crew against me, and that's fine, but there's no reason to take it out on Murray. He didn't do anything wrong."

Someone had been shouting at Murray? He hadn't mentioned it the previous evening. Ellie waited for Paul to come back out into the living room. When he did, he gave her a small nod. He'd collected what she'd asked him to.

"Melanie," Ellie said, "Who was shouting at Murray?"

"I don't know who. But it happened yesterday morning. He went to the buffet to pick us up some cinnamon rolls, and I was here doing my hair. When he came back, he said that a man had screamed in his face and that the staff had done nothing. He said they just stood there and watched it happen."

"What was the argument about?" Paul asked.

"He didn't say. But he was pretty shaken up." She crossed her arms around her waist. "You know, I wish I'd never come on this stupid cruise. The whole thing was a bad idea from the start."

"Did Murray say what the man looked like?" Ellie asked.

Melanie's eyes narrowed. "Why?"

She shrugged. "Well, if Murray made an enemy onboard the ship, it's possible that they took Sal," she said with a shrug. She turned to Paul. "I think we should try to find the guy."

Melanie considered this for a moment. "No, he didn't describe him. But you're welcome to ask Murray yourself. He should be back any minute. And you really should be tracking down the thief. I don't care about the jewelry, but that poker chip had a lot of sentimental value. And the thief probably has Sal." The corners of her mouth tugged down, and she sighed. "I'd help you search myself, except, well, you know."

"Tell us about the poker chip," Paul said. "Murray didn't mention it last night when he gave us the contents of the safe." He glanced at Ellie.

Melanie thought for a moment. "It was blue and white. I'm not sure that it was worth much. I suppose it could have been. Murray carries a lot of poker chips; he uses them in his act. That one was special because it belonged to his best friend."

"What's the friend's name?" Paul asked.

"Tom something. Murray mentioned him once, and he was *so sad* when he said his name. I assume he's dead, but Murray didn't want to talk about it." She looked up at Paul. "He's been through a lot, you know. There's the divorce, and his business hasn't been doing well, and now with Sal taken..." She sighed and picked at a stray thread on her shorts. "He could use some luck." She looked up at them. "You two could help him, you know, instead of judging him. Don't think I can't see it."

"I don't know what happened with Sal," Ellie said quietly. "Or with that woman in the suitcase. But I can tell you're a good friend, Melanie. Murray is lucky to know you."

Melanie smiled a little at that. "He should be back soon."

"Was anything else stolen last night?" Ellie asked. "Your passports, for instance?"

Melanie shook her head. "No, I keep my passport in my purse, thank goodness."

Twenty minutes later, Murray hadn't returned. They left, promising to check back in. As soon as they were outside *The Suites*, and far away from Violet's prying ears, Ellie stepped into a crew stairwell and turned to Paul. "How many did you get?"

"I found four," Paul said, reaching into his shirt pocket to produce four *Adventurous Cruises* notepads. Ellie studied them. Only two had been used, the other two were smooth and unblemished. Whoever had written that birdnapping note had done so on a notepad just like these. She handed those two back to Paul and rummaged in her handbag.

"I learned this trick from a mystery novel," she said. "Let's just hope that our suspects press down hard when they use a pen."

Ellie took a pencil out of her purse, put on her readers, and tore off the first unused sheet on both notepads. She turned the pages, studying them, moving closer to the light fixture on the wall. There were divots on the page, hard to see given the uniform cream color of the paper, but they were there. Some were long squiggly lines, and others were shorter marks.

"Hold some of this, will you? Just don't touch the center of the page." She hung onto one notepad and page and gave Paul the rest. Flipping the notepad over to reveal the smooth cardboard backing, she turned the page upside-down and used the flat edge of the pencil lead to carefully shade in the page. When she was done, she picked it up and looked at it beneath the light. The places where pressure marks had dented the page were easier to read now, as the pencil had darkened them more than the background. But the words were backward and hard to read. She handed the page to Paul. "Can you make sense of this?"

He scrutinized the page, his forehead furrowing. "Two club. One large." He considered this. "The words kind of trail off, I think there's a section missing. Oh! Here's another part. It says: 'Hold May'." He frowned. "Who's May?"

Ellie was already shading the back of the other page. "That's a lunch order, hon. Two club sandwiches and a large something, hold the mayo."

Paul looked faintly embarrassed. "Ah, well at least we've cracked the case of what they had for lunch." He pulled a plastic zipper bag out of his pocket and bagged the sheet, as if it were evidence. Paul was nothing if not methodical.

She handed him the other sheet. "This one looks odd. Are those numbers?"

Paul held it up in the light. "Huh. It's a long number, separated by dashes." His lips moved silently. "I see fifteen numbers. Three groups of four, and one group of three." He frowned. "I'm not sure if this is complete."

"A phone number?" Ellie put her pencil away.

"No. It's too long."

The other two notepads were smooth and unused. She checked the rest of the pages on the used pads to make sure they hadn't missed anything. "Well, I suppose we learned *something*." Ellie said. "I was fairly certain that Murray had written that birdnapping note. But now I don't think so. He could have been smart enough to throw the entire notepad away. But I doubt it."

Paul shrugged. "We can't blame a person for a crime they didn't commit. No matter how irritating they are." He put the other sheet of paper in its own Ziploc bag and sealed the top with diligent care. "I'll do a search on these numbers when I get back to the office. Maybe they mean something."

"Well, it was an idea," Ellie said. "And speaking of ideas, did you know there's only one place on the ship that offers cinnamon rolls for breakfast? If we find the mystery man who yelled at Murray, maybe we'll find Sal."

Paul nodded. "Is it terrible that I'm more worried about Sal than I am about our murder victim? I know that sounds horrible," he winced, "but—"

"It's not horrible. We have two victims here: Samantha and Sal. One murder, and one kidnapping. And Sal might still be *alive*." She reached up and patted him on the shoulder, rising slightly on tiptoe to do so. "Let's go find him."

Chapter Twenty-Four

"YEAH, I WAS WORKING THE pastry bar yesterday." The man who spoke was in his early thirties, and his casual stance and disinterested tone were at odds with his spotless white kitchen jacket and the precise setup of his workstation. Sharp knives were organized by size on the wall, attached to a magnetic strip. On the counter nearby heaps of freshly cut vegetables formed pyramids of green, red, and yellow on a long cutting board. "It was a wild ride. We ran out of fig danishes, *twice*. You don't want to get between a hungry horde of breakfasters and their pastries! Trust me. That's a good way to lose a finger."

Paul and Ellie glanced at each other, and the man laughed out loud. "I'm kidding! Sorry, that's what passes for humor here in the buffet. Anyway, what can I do for you two? It's rare to get a visit from security." He chewed on the toothpick in the corner of his mouth and looked Ellie up and down. "And you're the new owner, right? I'm

Kevin." He stood up straighter and plucked the toothpick out of his mouth, sticking it in his pocket as if it might offend.

Ellie nodded. "It's nice to meet you. We heard there was an altercation with a guest near the pastry station yesterday." She held up her hand at forehead height. "One of the guests was a man about my height. He was probably wearing a black suit, and you might have noticed his—"

His face lit up in recognition. "Oh! The guy with the parrot? Yeah, you can't miss him walking down the street, can ya? Sure, I remember him. He's a regular. He comes here a few times a day to get food to go. Never sticks around to eat. He seemed like a nice enough dude. The first time we met, he offered to pull an egg out from behind my ear, but I said no thanks. I wouldn't want My Tam — she's our omelet chef — getting touchy about her supplies." He spread out his hands in the air and rolled his eyes. "She likes everything *just so*, and—"

"Did you see him fighting with someone?" Paul asked quickly, before Kevin went off on another anecdote.

"Kind of? There was this other guy. British. One of those yachting types. Tweed pants. Sweater vest. The whole nine yards. He's up here a lot too, but he likes to sit over by the big window with his binoculars. Anyway, they were both in line, waiting for eggs, you can order any kind of omelet you want, and the waiting area is over by the pastries. It's horrible for the dieters, you know. They're standing there waiting for their egg white omelet, and *pow*, the cinnamon rolls just punch them in the nose."

He grinned. "Anyway, the next thing I know the British guy is wagging his finger at the parrot guy. He called the parrot guy a bunch of names I didn't understand. They sounded like insults, though. And the parrot guy shouted at him and told him to mind his own business. Then the parrot guy stormed off without his omelet." He shrugged. "I wouldn't call it a fight. I've *seen* buffet fights, and let's just say, you don't want to be cleaning strawberry puree out of the carpet at two in the morning. That stuff gets nasty." He shrugged. "This was just two dudes fronting. And the whole thing lasted like twenty seconds."

Ellie turned to Paul. "I think I know who the British man is. His name is Jules and he's staying in *The Lofts*. We should go look for him."

"Or you could talk to him right now," Kevin said. He pointed at the far side of the buffet, near the big windows that faced the side of the ship. "He's over there with his fancy binoculars. Just like usual. Maybe you can get him off his butt for an hour or two." He shook his head, apparently mystified. "Why spring for a nice cruise just to spend the whole time sitting on your muffin? I don't get it!"

"Thanks Kevin," Ellie said with a smile. "You've been a huge help."

He shot her a gratified smile. "Thanks, boss. I don't suppose you could mention it to My Tam? She's still peeved I was late on Monday." He jerked his chin toward a petite woman with a dark apron over her white kitchen uniform. She was inspecting the pasta station with an expression usually reserved for military parade lines.

Ellie nodded. "Sure thing. But be on time, okay? She's your boss, not me."

Kevin ducked his head and stammered that he would be on time from here on out. As they moved toward the far side of the buffet, Paul shot her an amused look but said nothing.

Jules was peering through his binoculars when they arrived at his table. Paul moved to speak, but she stilled him with one hand. According to the birders she'd met on board, the hobby required great patience, and she didn't want to distract him if he'd found something wonderful. After a moment he put his binoculars down with a sigh. He reached for the teacup at his elbow and that's when he saw them standing there. His eyes flicked open wide and he cleared his throat. "Ah. Ellie. It's a pleasure to see you again. And this must be..." He peered through his glasses at Paul's name tag. "Officer Paul Gumbs." He smiled up at them. "I'm Julian King. It's a pleasure." When they didn't move, he eyed Paul warily. "I take it this isn't a social call?"

"I'm afraid not," Paul said in a soft voice. "We were hoping that you could assist us on a rather delicate matter, Sir. It won't take but a moment."

"Of course. Please, join me. Quite sorry about the mess." He stacked his dirty dishes on top of his buffet tray to make room. Despite the warmth of the day, he was wearing dark slacks beneath his polo shirt, and he'd draped a thick woolen sweater over the back of his chair. There was a stack of books next to his binoculars on the table, and all the books were dedicated to sea birds. A heavy silver pen sat diagonally on top of the books, ready to capture what he saw. His sandy-brown hair was combed over his head in a smooth curve.

Ellie sat next to Paul. She hadn't missed the way Paul had sized the man up and shifted his tone accordingly. With Kevin, he'd hung back and let her lead the conversation. And with Julian he'd been deferential but direct, treating him more like a consultant than a suspect. Paul Gumbs had come a long way since she'd met him! Back then, he hadn't been half so good at considering his audience.

"We're sorry to interrupt your meal," she said, breaking the ice. "You go by Julian? I thought—"

He offered a small smile. "My new acquaintance Dick insists on calling me Jules, and I saw no benefit in correcting him." He shrugged. "You know how it is when meeting Americans abroad. They bring a certain enthusiasm to the table, and it's invigorating, but they're—" Julian's eyes froze on Ellie's crew badge, no doubt noticing the old Stars and Stripes displayed proudly next to her name. "Ah..."

"We're an informal bunch; that's true." She smiled to show no offense was taken.

"Indeed. In any case, I could use a distraction. I'd hoped to catch sight of roseate spoonbill today but we're a bit too far from shore, I'm afraid. Still, I'm eager to arrive in Nassau. I've arranged for a private tour, and I have a dozen species I hope to spot." He patted his leather-bound journal.

"You're an ornithologist?"

Julian smiled. "Oh, I can't claim any credentials. But yes, I'm partial to our feathered friends. With their habitats in retreat, it's essential that we advocate for them. As God's creatures go, so will we, in time."

Ellie nodded her agreement then turned to Paul. "You had a few questions?"

"Yes. We were hoping to ask you about a man named Murray Nickles. He wears a parrot on his shoulder."

Julian's pleasant expression melted away like a snow cone on a blistering hot day. His eyes went to the corded epaulets on Paul's shoulders. "Ah, has that odious man filed a complaint against me?" His expression hardened. "You should know that I never laid a finger on him."

Paul nodded. "We're well acquainted with the gentleman's..." he searched for the right word, "personality. And there's no complaint against you. But we were hoping you could help us. Sal has been taken."

"Who?" Julian asked.

"The parrot. He's been taken."

Julian's expression hardened. "I seriously doubt *that*. If anything happened to that bird, it's due to his ill-tempered owner. I have no doubt you'll find that he's responsible, although via design or sheer negligence I couldn't say."

"Why do you say that?" Ellie asked.

Julian frowned. "I can only tell you what I saw. First, you should know that this ship isn't a safe environment for an African rainbow parrot. Domesticated birds have their flight feathers clipped. It's an unfortunate necessity for birds who are unable to fend for themselves in the wild. But even with his feathers trimmed, that bird could easily make it past the ship's outer rail and fall into the sea. Or he could become prey for a wild bird with sharper instincts. There's a species of hawk out here that's quite notorious. Only the most careless bird owner would bring such a fine creature here, to what is essentially a floating amusement park full of strangers." He sniffed. "No offense."

"None taken," Paul said. "When you two spoke, what happened?"

"I was waiting for my breakfast. And that man was there with his bird. And he — the bird, that is — bit him on the earlobe. Now, right there, that's another sign of neglect. Parrots are intelligent, playful, and devilishly charming animals. But without proper stimulation they'll adopt destructive behaviors. In fact, Birding Magazine reported that—"

Paul cleared his throat gently.

"Quite right," Julian said, his cheeks reddening slightly. "Anyway, the parrot bit the man's ear, and the man shoved him!"

"He shoved the bird?" Paul's eyebrows lifted.

Julian nodded. "He pushed him with two fingers, rather hard. The parrot vocalized his distress and sunk his talons in more deeply, as any bird would do when trying not to fall, and the man called him a very foul name, and he raised his fist, and the poor thing ducked like it was afraid of being hit.

"Obviously, I couldn't stand by," Julian continued. "I marched right over and gave him a piece of my mind. It's bad enough to take a beautiful wild animal and domesticate it. But I try not to judge. Perhaps the bird was injured as a fledgling. He may have been a rescue bird. These things happen. But even still, I cannot countenance animal abuse. I told him that he didn't deserve such an animal, and I threatened to report him to the authorities. I may have," his cheeks flushed, "made some indelicate insinuations about his parentage. He practically turned tail and ran. That's what bullies do, as I'm sure you know. You confront them, and they run away like the cowards they are."

"And I don't suppose you took it upon yourself to remove the bird from his custody?" Ellie said gently.

Julian frowned. "Alas, no. I haven't seen either of them since then. Although you say his name is Murray Nickles? I'm going to jot that down in my notebook right now. And if I can figure out where he lives, you can bet the local animal welfare council is going to receive a phone call when I get home. I mean — abusing a parrot! What kind of monster would do such a thing?"

"He seemed very distraught about the loss of his bird," Paul said. "He wept."

Julian seemed surprised. "I can't explain *that*. But whatever he was feeling, it certainly wasn't respect for his bird. The man is a hack. He wears that parrot like an accessory, as if it were nothing more than a colorful scarf he'd picked up on sale. And did you see him doing tricks for the audience after karaoke the other night? He pulled that business card out from behind six different ears. Any well-trained eight-year-old could learn that trick given ten minutes of practice and a YouTube video. When you find that bird, and I pray you do, I beg you: don't put it back in his custody. It wouldn't be right."

"You were at karaoke?" Ellie smiled at him. "I didn't see you there."

Julian smiled faintly. "I attended with some other residents of *The Lofts*." He glanced at his binoculars mournfully. "My night vision is poor, I'm afraid. Evenings are so *dull*, and I hoped the entertainments aboard might serve as a distraction. The singers did their best, but they're hardly professionals. Well, except for that one woman dressed like a disco ball. Appalling outfit! But her voice was quite lovely."

Ellie hid a smile. "Thanks for your help. We've searched the ship from top to bottom, and I'm starting to fear Sal is gone. It's been nearly a day, and we're all worried."

"Have you tried using a call?" Julian asked.

"What kind of a call?" Paul asked.

Julian's expression brightened, and he reached for something in his pants pocket. "Parrots are incredibly sociable, and when given an opportunity, they prefer to live among their own kind. If you play a call he'll recognize, the fellow won't be able to resist a response." He turned on his phone and brought up an app, swiping through dozens of photos of bird species. His thumb stopped moving when a colorful parrot showed on the screen. "Here. This might do the trick nicely." He glanced up at Ellie. "What's your email address?"

Chapter Twenty-Five

FORTY-FIVE MINUTES LATER, PAUL, BEN, and Ellie stood on the bridge. At the front of the large room, two bridge officers stood watchfully, their eyes on the sophisticated control panels below. The window was a bright horizontal strip of blue that stood in contrast to the relative darkness of the room. Paul was reviewing the script he'd written, for the third time.

Ellie stepped closer to Ben and resisted the urge to slip her arm around the back of his waist. It seemed wrong to be canoodling on the bridge. Still, she stood right next to him, her hip touching his leg. "I love it in here," she said. "It's like being in the cockpit of an airplane, if the cockpit was big enough for a dozen people."

As the ship sped forward, the water ran directly beneath them, under the ship and below their feet as if the ocean itself had become a massive treadmill. Looking straight forward, she felt like a dolphin bounding through the water.

Ben smiled at her. "It's the best room on the ship. We have *all* the toys in here. ARPA, RADAR, GPS, ROTI, and here, look at this." He pointed at a small display screen. "That's the RAI, or rudder angle indicator. Very high-tech."

One of the bridge officers glanced over from a nearby terminal. "We could use a coffee pot, if there's room in the budget," she said.

Ellie turned to Ben. "You can spot a big school of fish from ten miles away, but you don't have a coffee pot?"

He shrugged. "We have hundreds of coffee pots on the ship. Do we really need another one?"

"Yes," two of the bridge officers said simultaneously.

Ben laughed. "They may have a point." He glanced at Paul. "Are you ready?"

Paul nodded. "I've got staff stationed all around the ship. Victor has the hotel crew helping us out too."

Ben gestured at a thick metal microphone on his desk. "The Com is yours."

Paul cleared his throat and pressed a round red button on the control panel. All around the ship, two chimes rang out, one high and one low. The microphone stuck out from the panel like a fat, silver thumb. Paul bent down closer to it. "Good evening. My name is Paul Gumbs, and I'm your security officer. On behalf of Captain Spark and the entire crew, we hope you're enjoying your stay aboard the *Adventurous Spirit*. We need your help with an important matter. Sal, an African rainbow parrot, has escaped from his cage, and in just a moment, we'll be playing a parrot call over the ship's speakers."

"Here's where you come in," he continued. "After we play the bird call, we'd like you to listen carefully. If Sal is in your area, he may respond. Can you help us find the missing parrot? If you hear him, please contact a member of the crew immediately. We thank you for your assistance. The call will follow in five seconds, and again fifteen seconds later."

He held up his phone and silently counted down. Then he pressed a button on his phone while holding it up to the microphone. A series of eager squawks followed. He waited, then repeated the process. Then he hit the red button on the console again, and his shoulders relaxed.

Ellie nodded at him. "That was well done. Come on. We may as well join the search party." She blew a kiss at Ben and headed out the door.

They walked down the wide hallway on the crew level, listening intently. But all she heard was the hum of the industrial-sized washing machines in rooms off to her left. They headed back upstairs. She looked down the long hallway and caught sight of the housekeeping staff walking through the residential areas, pausing from time to time, listening.

She pulled her new walkie talkie off her waist and waited. Paul was working his way toward her from the opposite end of the ship. Two minutes went by. Then two more. Her heart sank. It had been a good idea, but perhaps Sal was gone. Wouldn't he be calling back if he could?

A burst of static on the radio made her jump! "Songbird here. I found him. He's in *The Suites* in a supply closet. I can hear him, but I need a key."

Up ahead, one housekeeper turned to another with a smile on her face. They fist-bumped.

The radio flared to life in Ellie's hands, the tiny display lighting up like a celebration. "Gumbs here. What's his condition? Should I send the doctor?"

Privately, Ellie wasn't sure what Doctor Strunk would make of a parrot, dead or alive. But Violet responded, "Songbird here. He sounds okay. He's asking for Murray."

"Gumbs here. To everyone listening, well done. Very well done!" Paul's happiness was plain even through the staticky interference of the handheld radios. Ellie headed toward *The Suites.*

Over the ship's speakers, two tones rang out. "This is your Captain speaking. I'm pleased to announce that the parrot in question has been located. We're grateful for your kind assistance, and thanks for making this a happy ending! Enjoy your evening."

She met up with Paul at the entrance to *The Suites.* "Did you hear that?" she asked. "I heard everyone cheering in the atrium as we went by." She smiled at him, but he didn't smile back.

"I wish the Captain hadn't announced that we'd found him," Paul said, almost to himself. Was he worried that the birdnapper knew what they were up to? No, Paul sounded sad, and that meant he was worried about Sal.

"We can't steal Murray's bird. No matter how much we want to."

"I know," Paul said with a heavy sigh. "But Sal deserves better."

⚓⚓⚓

"HE'S DOWN HERE!" VIOLET WAVED from the end of the hallway. Ellie glanced at Murray's stateroom door as they passed it. No doubt he'd heard Ben's announcement. So why hadn't he gotten in touch with security? If he was as distraught as he'd claimed to be, wouldn't he want to check on his bird straight away? Of course, given what Julian said, Murray's anxiety may have simply been an act. Or guilt?

She checked her watch. It was nearly five, and she was due to meet the kids for dinner shortly. At least she'd have some good news to share! And when this was all over, she'd need to buy Julian a coconut crocodile. Without his help, they might not have found Sal before it was too late.

Violet pointed at the door. "Do you hear him?"

She didn't, at first. But when she focused, she heard the squawking inside, faint but audible. "Paul, get him out of there." She jiggled the handle.

"Like I didn't try the door," Violet said, rolling her eyes.

Paul pulled a set of keys out of his slacks pocket and flipped through them until he found one that he wanted. "Skeleton key," he said, sticking the metal key in the hole. He turned the round knob and opened the door. The closet was full of cardboard boxes, and there was no light inside. On the ground behind a low stack of boxes like a mini retaining wall, there was a clear spot the size of three sheets of paper laid side-by-side. Sal was down there, bobbing his head excitedly and dancing from side to side. "Murray! Murray the Moron! Murray!"

"Aww, he wants his moron," Violet said. She tilted her head to one side and pointed at the ground. "What's that?"

"Here, let me." Paul moved some of the boxes away, creating an opening.

Ellie kneeled, ignoring the brief flare of pain in her hip. On the linoleum, next to a splattering of bird droppings, there were pieces of what appeared to be breakfast cereal. She saw crescent moon shapes and circles. She picked up a piece and sniffed it. It smelled like dusty corn. "I think it's bird food. And look. There's a dish of water shoved back there."

"This must be where the birdnapper was keeping him," Violet said, looking down at Ellie. "Is he okay?"

Paul got down on his knees and Ellie backed up to make room for him. Paul put one hand on the dirty ground next to the parrot. He made a soft clicking sound and spoke too quietly to hear. After a moment of eying Paul warily, Sal hopped onto Paul's hand. Paul lifted his hand to his shoulder and settled the bird there. Sal made a low cooing noise. "There you go, big guy," Paul said, lifting his other hand to the bird. Sal scratched his head against Paul's index finger. "Come on. Let's get you somewhere safe," Paul said quietly. He walked slowly toward the crew exit. They followed him.

Once they were inside the security office, Paul set Sal down on top of his large safe and asked Ellie to get him some fresh water. By the time she came back, Sal had hopped over to one of the computer monitors and was standing atop it, his talons curled over the edge, and his eyes half-shut. She put the water down and turned to Violet, who was speaking to Paul in a low voice.

"I'm just saying it could work," Violet was saying.

"I'm *not* using Sal as bait. Even if we manage to get the birdnapper to come back after him, the bird is traumatized. How would you feel after being locked in a dark room for a whole day, alone, with no prospect of rescue?"

"We'd give him food and water, obviously. I'm just saying that we could wait for someone to steal him again. Then - bam - we've caught the birdnapper. All we need to do is let it slip where we're keeping him, and—"

"He's been through enough," Paul said, crossing his arms over his chest. "My answer is no."

Ellie held up her hand. "Guys, there's no reason to think the birdnapper will come after him again." She reached into her pocket and held up one of the pieces of food she'd found in the closet. "If this is bird food, and I think it is, we need to have another conversation with Murray. Do we really believe the birdnapper came prepared with bird food and a water dish? Was there some master bird-stealing plan that ended up with poor Sal shoved in a closet just down the hall from where Murray was staying? Come on."

"The birdnapper could have taken those things when they took Sal," Violet said.

"Maybe," Paul said. "But I'd like a word with Murray anyway. Why hasn't he contacted us? And where was he earlier today? We've been running around this ship all night and all day, and he's conveniently never around. Violet, did you see him come back to the room at all?"

She shook her head. "No. I walked up and down the hall after I heard your announcement. And it's lucky I did. With all those boxes in the way, and with that heavy door, I don't think anyone would have found Sal unless they were listening really carefully."

"Let's go," Ellie said. "If we hurry—" She glanced at her watch and winced. "I'm already running late. I'm supposed to go meet the kids for dinner and a show."

"Go," Paul said. "I can handle the interrogation. I'll bring Kameron with me in case he gets feisty."

She hesitated. "Maybe I can—"

He shot her a withering look. "Ellie. Your family came all this way to see you. You can't blow them off."

She held up her hands. "I know. You're right. But I'm coming to see you right after the show. And I'm counting on you to get to the bottom of this, Paul. I want an update as soon as I get back."

Violet crossed her arms and leaned against the door. "Wow. She sounds more and more like Roberta by the day. We should get them matching shirts or something. Something to coordinate with those bossy pants."

Ellie turned to insist that she was only trying to help, but then she saw Violet's wicked smile. "You had that coming," she said with a saucy lilt to her voice. "You've had it coming all week." She made a lip zipping motion. "But I said it, and now we're good." She shot Ellie a worried look. "We *are* good, right? I'm sorry I stormed off the other night."

Ellie's heart lifted. She didn't mind being teased, so long as Violet wasn't angry at her any longer. "Maybe I had it coming. And maybe I didn't. But yes, we're good." She shrugged. "Besides, Roberta has many fine qualities! Like her ability to delegate." After organizing her thoughts, she turned to Paul. "Figure out what's going on around here. Use whatever resources you need. We're running out of time." She pointed at Violet. "You can help if Paul says it's okay. But no brawling. I mean it!"

Sal was resting on top of the monitor, his eyes closed tight. She considered her options. Roberta had left numbers for the corporate lawyers. It was their job to keep the cruise line out of trouble, wasn't it? And now they worked for her. "That bird is evidence," she said, finally. "Paul, I'd like you to log him as evidence, and get his cage and toys. *After* we figure out who stole him, and who killed Samantha Rawlings, we'll consider returning him to Mr. Nickles. *After* a consultation with an animal welfare expert."

"Is that legal?" Paul sounded skeptical, but he was already getting up from his chair. "Murray's going to throw a fit."

"Let me worry about that," she said. "Now, if you'll excuse me, I have a prior engagement." She swept out of the room and strode down the hall toward the elevator. As much as she wanted to continue running down leads with Paul, it was physically impossible to be in two places at once. And in the tussle between work and family, sometimes you were forced to choose just one.

Junior, Marcie, and Clara were waiting. The thought made her smile, and she hurried her steps to meet them.

Chapter Twenty-Six

AFTER A SATISFYING MEAL IN the main dining room, along with an enthusiastic retelling of the capture of Sal the parrot, Ellie, Marcie, Junior and Clara went to the theater to enjoy the ship's new musical. And *The Pirates of Peking* started with a bang. Literally! The deep red curtains opened to the boom of a cannon and a plume of smoke that rolled out into the front few rows of the audience. And at the same time, a spray of water from hidden nozzles made the left and right sides of the audience gasp out loud.

Actors spilled across the stage, forming rows that shifted left and right like human waves, singing a cheerful ditty about the happiness of life at sea. From the delighted expression of the guests filling the theater, it was obvious that Wynona had a hit on her hands! Ellie leaned forward to watch, admiring all the small details on the stage. The costumes were colorful without being gaudy, and the sets were impressive without detracting the eye from the action. When the canon boomed a second time, Clara said "Wow!" in a tiny voice full of such wonder that those sitting in the row ahead of them turned around to smile at her. Marcie shushed the little girl gently and pointed at an actress in long, full skirts half-hanging off the mast that sprung up from the boat on the right side of the stage. She swung a silver sword as she sang, and the chorus below echoed her words. Ellie imagined Wynona backstage, watching her people with an intent expression, making sure everyone hit their cues, one at a time. There were few things as inspiring as seeing a hard-working crew come together to achieve something spectacular.

For a split second, she imagined that she saw Samantha Rawlings dancing among the chorus line, and her heart ached in sympathy. *I wish we'd figured out what happened to you,* she thought upward, as if her words might reach heaven.

Tomorrow they'd arrive in Nassau, and the investigation would continue. But she couldn't escape the feeling that she'd already failed. Sal was resting safely in Paul's stateroom, and Melanie would be returned to the authorities in Miami to face justice for her hit-and-run. But who had killed Samantha? After everything they'd gone through, she was no closer to the answer than she'd been the moment they'd found that suitcase in the hallway.

They were sitting near the back of the theater, on the lower level. Above them, the balcony formed a partial ceiling. Marcie was at the aisle seat, close to the theater's left exit. Clara might be a sweet child but sitting still for a ninety-minute show was a bit much to ask of any two-and-a-half-year-old. Shortly after the first act, Marcie took Clara outside the theater for a walk. Just after they returned, Ellie heard a familiar section of music. This was the scene she'd seen them rehearsing earlier! Junior must have remembered it too, as he nudged her gently and leaned forward. Marie, the lead actress, looking beautiful in her long dress, pressed her sword point against her lover's chest. Up on the crow's nest, a man looked out back into the theater with a shocked expression, his mouth dropping open. His sharp intake of breath was picked up on the microphone, and Ellie felt a small surge of triumph on behalf of the actors. It worked! The audience was on the edge of their seats now. Several of them turned around to look. So did she, even though she knew nothing was back there. The audience looked excited! The man in the crow's nest pointed forward, "Pirates, Captain! They approach at great speed!" The 'captain' bellowed orders, and the crew sprang into action, hoisting cannon balls and pulling heavy ropes. They hummed an ominous tune as they worked.

Something pricked at the back of Ellie's mind. A reminder. Something she was supposed to do? No, it was something she'd seen. She turned around again and that's when she spotted it. A middle-aged couple, very handsome in their evening wear, sitting two rows back and toward the center of the theater. The man wore a double-breasted suit and he'd styled his gray hair into stiff peaks, almost like cupcake frosting. She'd seen him at karaoke, along with his wife. And his wife was wearing a long pearl necklace! She'd looped it an extra time to shorten it, but it bore a remarkable resemblance to the one Melanie had worn! Ellie's heart leapt into her throat!

She quickly turned around. Junior was watching the show, and she wanted to get his attention. But would talking to him spook her quarry? She didn't want to appear suspicious. She pulled out her cell phone and checked for a Wi-Fi signal. *Thank goodness Roberta sprung for the internet package*, she thought. She quickly opened the ship's messaging app and sent Junior a message.

THERE'S A WOMAN SITTING BEHIND ME WEARING THE MISSING PEARLS!!!!

She hit send and tucked the phone down in her lap beneath her folded hands. She waited, but Junior didn't so much as twitch. She nudged him, and when he looked over, she wiggled her phone and pointed at his pocket.

He looked surprised, but he pulled his phone out and turned it on. Marcie smacked his shoulder gently and mouthed "Put that away."

He glanced at his wife, then at Ellie, then his wife. Ellie shot him an insistent look (would she be interrupting if it weren't important?). At last, he sighed and unlocked his phone. After he read the message, he turned to look at the couple. Ellie mouthed 'no!' and he stopped. Did the man have no subtlety? Junior shrugged and gestured vaguely with his hands. He typed something.

Okay. What do you want me to do about it?

Ellie's phone pinged loudly when the message arrived, and the woman on her right shot her a dirty look. She winced and put the phone on silent. "Sorry," she whispered. She messaged back. *Don't let her escape. When the show is over, let's follow her.*

He peeked at his phone and shot her a look that said he wanted to argue, but she glared at him and his shoulders fell. He nodded at her once, and she relaxed.

Up on stage, the battle was fought, the pirates were vanquished, and the lovers sailed away on their honeymoon in a tiny boat while their crew sang their hearts out and swayed to the music. The lights went up, the crowd applauded, and everyone seemed to get to their feet at the same time. Ellie got up quickly and leaned to whisper in Junior's ear. "I'm going to follow the woman and her husband out the far door. You take the other side. I don't want to spook them."

He frowned. Clara was tugging on his arm. "Hang on, kiddo." He lowered his voice. "Ma. Wait. I don't want you —"

But the couple was already moving toward the exit, and she waved Junior off. He didn't need to come if he didn't want to. Either way, she was going to find out who those people were. She'd taken another peek when the lights went up. More than ever, she was sure it was the same necklace Melanie had worn.

She walked as quickly as she could without bumping into the people in front of her. The aisles along the seats were narrow, and for a while, they moved in lockstep, the couple in question just two people ahead of her, a few aisles over. But the line bunched as it merged into the central walkway, and she lost sight of them in the crowd. In front of her, a couple stood, blocking her path, talking about their dinner plans.

"Excuse me," she said loudly, turning sideways and sliding through them. The woman's behind brushed against Ellie's top, and she made an unhappy noise. As Ellie stepped forward into the mass of people, she heard Junior calling her name from behind, asking her to stop and wait for him.

And she would stop. As soon as she caught up with the thief.

Chapter Twenty-Seven

ELLIE TURNED SIDEWAYS AND SQUEEZED herself through a cluster of theater goers who were bunched up near the exit like a herd of cows waiting for the dinner bell. One of them muttered something about patience, and she sent back a look of apology, but she didn't stop moving. She spotted dark blue satin. The woman's dress! She hurried forward, closing the gap. The husband glanced back at her with an irritated expression and looped his wife's arm through his own. He quickened his pace, dragging her forward like an older child drags a much younger sibling. She felt a grim sort of satisfaction. If the guy was running, he knew he'd been made. And that meant he had something to hide. Was he the one who'd strangled that poor girl? If so, she'd wring that information out of him like soapy water from a wet rag. She darted forward through the crowd, moving left and right to get through the bodies, reaching forward, muttering "excuse me, sorry" as she burst through a family of six taking their sweet time moving out of the aisle.

The couple was almost within arms' reach! "Excuse me," she called. "Ma'am?"

The woman turned around, jerking her arm out from her husband's grasp. "Yes?"

Ellie walked up, smiling brightly. "I'm *so* sorry to interrupt. I just *had* to ask you about that necklace," she gushed. "I love pearls, and I've never seen a strand that long and thick."

The woman's expression went from confusion to pleasure. "Oh! Thank you. They are something special, aren't they?" She patted her husband's arm. "Robert got them for me for our eighth wedding anniversary. Well, this cruise was supposed to be my present, and then he surprised me with these." She shot a fond look at her husband, who was standing still. His face looked oddly flat, as if he had gone from flesh-and-blood human to a cardboard cutout.

"Well, you're a very lucky woman," Ellie said enviously. "Sir, if you don't mind my asking, where did you find them? I'd love to get a similar necklace for my daughter-in-law. She's over there." Ellie waved at Marcie, who was approaching with Junior and Clara. Marcie looked concerned, and Junior held up one hand, signaling that Marcie should stand back. He stormed forward, his face awash in frustration. At six foot two, Junior was by no means a small man. The man she was questioning watched Junior coming, and his left eye twitched.

"Hon?" The woman tapped her husband's shoulder. He tore his eyes away from Junior and looked at his wife. "What?"

"She wants to know where you got the necklace. Did you hear her? She's going to get one for her daughter."

The man (Robert, his wife had said) glanced at Ellie and looked her up and down. She imagined him sizing her up, taking in her rounded figure, her smile, and the fine lines around her eyes. She beamed at him with her most grandmotherly smile. *Don't mind me. I'm just a nosy woman looking for shopping tips.*

He seemed to force himself to smile. "Oh, at the gift shop."

"The gift shop here?"

"Yes," he said. "If you'll excuse us, we have a reservation."

"We do?" His wife started to say, and he hooked her arm again as if to drag her off. Ellie held up a hand to stop them. Junior had stopped at her side, and she could practically feel him glowering. What was up with him? Whatever it was, she couldn't afford the distraction. "On the ship? Which gift shop was it?" She asked. "The one with the watches, or the one with the engagement rings?"

"Ah, the one with the rings." He said. Robert's hair was silvery gray like hers, but he'd styled it into smooth waves atop his head, and not a single hair was out of place. It was too perfect. She smiled at him. "Oh, I know where I remember you from! You two were at the karaoke show, weren't you? You spoke to Murray afterward. He's such an interesting guy, isn't he?"

Junior spoke low. "Hey, Ma. Is everything okay?"

She nodded. "Of course. I was just telling Robert here that I remember seeing him at karaoke. Of course, that was before he stole the pearl necklace from Murray's safe."

"What?" Robert's eyes went wide. "I didn't *steal* anything."

"You didn't?" Ellie asked, too sweetly. "But then why did you give your wife stolen pearls? We don't sell pearls aboard the *Spirit*, by the way. I'm well acquainted with our onboard shopping. It's excellent. But you're lying about that necklace. Were you aware that same necklace was used to strangle a young woman on the first day of the cruise?"

All color drained from Robert's face. "Wait. It's not what you think. I just—"

Before he could continue his explanation, his wife slugged him with her sequined handbag. It must have been heavier than it looked because it made a solid *thump* when it connected with his shoulder. "You *lied to me*!" she shouted, her eyes flashing. "Again! After all the counseling we did? You *swore* to me, Robert. You *swore on your mother's grave that* that you were done with your lying, cheating, idiotic—" She lifted her handbag and whapped him with it twice more.

"If you'll just wait a second," Ellie said, holding out her hands. "Let's just calm down and—"

But before she could get through to either of them, Robert took off at a run down the hallway, knocking aside two women in the process and pounding up the carpeted stairs. His wife shouted profanities after him and burst into tears.

Ellie rushed forward and helped one of the prone women to her feet. "Are you okay?" she asked. The woman nodded. "I'm fine. But can you tell that guy not to run in the halls?" Over at her side, Junior was helping the other woman up. And Marcie was there too, checking her over.

"Well?" She demanded, looking at Junior.

"Well what?" He stepped forward. "Are you okay? Should we call someone?"

She pointed up the stairs. "Go! Get him! Quick! Before we lose him. His wife has the murder weapon! And he was talking to the magician. Those two have to be in cahoots!"

Next to her, the woman Ellie had just helped up backed away slowly, looking at her as if she might be insane. *Right. Let's use the inside voice.* She jerked her head toward the stairs and beckoned Junior forward. "I'll grab the elevator. You need to see what floor he took."

"Ma. I have no authority here. I'm just a—"

"I grant you all the authority you need. Come on." She turned toward the stairs. She looked back. Junior still wasn't moving. "You're not coming?"

Clara broke free from her mother's grip and ran toward Ellie. She arrived and reached for her hand. Ellie took it automatically. It was warm and small. Clara lifted her other hand straight up in the air. "Bad guy. Pow! Run away!" She pulled Ellie away from the stairs. "Let's gooooo!" she whined, bopping up and down, her bottom lip trembling like she might cry. Ellie looked down at her granddaughter, sighed, and picked her up. "Yes, my love, when we see a bad guy, we run away." She opened her purse and took out a handheld radio. "And then we call the good guys." She depressed the button on the side. "Paul. I found the pearls. And I'm on my way."

Junior strode forward. "I'm going with you."

"You are?" Ellie asked. "I thought you had no authority here?"

Junior groaned. "I'm helping. I'm a helper! I'm just not going to chase some old guy across the ship like a crazy person."

"Old!" Ellie said.

Marcie came up and took Clara from Ellie. "Come on. Let's go find your security guy. He can find all the Roberts on the ship, right? And he has photos? Let's hurry, before he hurts someone else."

"Marce," Junior began.

Marcie put one hand on Ellie's shoulder and steered her toward the elevator. She shot her husband a look over her shoulder. "We're going with Mom. Are you coming?"

Chapter Twenty-Eight

ELLIE POUNDED ON PAUL'S OFFICE door with her fist. "It's Ellie! Open up."

Paul opened the door. "Patience! There's no need to shout."

"Well, I happen to be chasing a wanted criminal. I assume you'd be interested." She put her hands on her hips. Next to her, in Marcie's arms, Clara mirrored the move.

"Bad guy. We ran!" Clara giggled.

"I see you brought backup," Paul said, taking in the sight of them all.

"I found Melanie's pearls," Ellie said. "A woman was wearing them. And when I asked her husband where he got them, he lied. Then he took off running."

"His name is Robert," Marcie said excitedly. "We know that because his wife yelled at him before she started hitting him with her purse."

Paul stared at them. "I see. And now you want to do what, exactly?"

"Let's go find him!" Ellie said. "There can't be too many Roberts on the ship. You look him up, and we'll go get him, and then we'll question him. I bet he's the one who took Sal. And he may have strangled Samantha. Either way, this is the lucky break we've been waiting for. But we should go now. Who knows what will happen now that he knows we're onto him?"

"No," Junior said.

"What?" Ellie turned to look at him.

"I mean, no, Ma, you're not chasing a criminal through the ship. It's unacceptable." He pointed at Paul. "And you should know better than to take her along. I know she's your boss, or something, but you can't just go along with whatever she says."

"Ron," Marcie said sternly. "You shouldn't talk to your mother like that."

He shrugged. "I can't stop you from feeling that way. Oh, and you're not going either. I don't know what kind of crazy pills you women have been taking, but this is a job for professionals, not for amateurs." He picked up Clara and swung her up in the air. She giggled at the upward motion. "Now, you go with your mother and grandma, kiddo. I'll catch up with you in a bit." He looked at Paul. "I saw the guy. I can help you identify him from his ID photo if you like."

Ellie felt a slow-burning heat rising from her belly to her throat. Junior had never spoken to her this way before, and she didn't like it, one bit. "Excuse me. You aren't the boss here. I am. And if you think—"

Junior wheeled to face her. "Mother! For all that's holy, will you for *once in your life* listen to someone who loves you? Please. Just this once. I'll never ask you for anything again. Do it as a personal favor to me. Go back to your room. Take Marcie and my child and go sit somewhere safe until this guy is apprehended. Do this *one thing* for me."

Ellie crossed her arms. She wouldn't tolerate this kind of attitude from a partner, and she wasn't going to accept it from her son either. "Why? Because I'm too old? Because you say so? Well, maybe I should head home right now and get back in my rocking chair and play the dutiful grandmother until I'm as old as Moses. Is that what you want? For me to stay in my place so you never have a worry in the world?"

Marcie took Clara from Junior. "What's up with you lately? You've been as grumpy as a bear in winter. For weeks! It's bad enough you've been snapping at me and dodging my calls, but now you're bossing Mom around? Hon, please, tell me what's happening here. Because I think we all know Mom isn't the problem."

Paul was edging back into his office, one slow step at a time, as if he might be able to disappear. Ellie shot him a look that said *don't even think about it* and he stopped moving. He plucked a clipboard off the wall and pretended to study it as if it were the most fascinating thing in the world.

"Yes, I've been stressed," Junior said. "But that has nothing to do with this."

"Why should I believe you?" Marcie asked. She noted the way Clara was watching the back and forth and she softened her tone. "All I want is the truth, Ron."

"This has *nothing* to do with that."

"Nothing to do with what?" Ellie asked, stepping closer to Marcie. Now they were in a small line, all the girls together. A united front! Whatever this nonsense was, it was best to get it out of the way now. Before Junior found a way to avoid the topic, yet again.

Junior's face was turning red. "Fine. I was going to tell you when we got home, so I didn't ruin our vacation. But since you're both *hounding* me, you may as well know. I quit my job last month." His eyes went to the floor. "I'm not a cop any longer. And now you know. You've been officially informed."

"You quit the force?" Marcie's shock was plain. "But why? And why didn't you tell me?"

Paul had managed to partially shut the door during the melee. The door squeaked as he moved it, and everyone turned to stare. Paul's gaze flicked from one person to the other. At last he looked at Junior. "Sir, perhaps you'll help me with our search for the man in question?"

"Paul," Ellie said. "Don't you even—"

But Junior darted into the office and Paul slammed the door, enclosing him and Junior inside. The lock turned with a dull metallic click. Ellie pounded the door with the side of her fist, twice. "Traitor!"

Inside the security office, the men were silent.

Marcie had fallen silent as well. Ellie turned to her. "Are you okay, hon?"

"I just… I can't believe he didn't *tell* me. I could tell he was struggling at work. But why would he keep something like that from me?"

Ellie put a hand on Marcie's upper back and guided her down the hallway and toward the elevator. Her frustration, having splashed out, quickly faded away. She wanted to be upset with Junior, but hadn't she kept her own secrets? "He was afraid of what we'd say," she said simply. "It's hard to let people down. Especially when you love them so much."

"I don't care if he's a cop, Ma. I just want him to be honest with me."

"I know." Ellie sighed. "Come on. I could use a cup of tea. And Clara's well past her bedtime."

Chapter Twenty-Nine

INSIDE *THE LOFTS*, ELLIE BUSIED herself making tea in the kitchen while Marcie settled Clara into Ellie's bed. Her stateroom was a short distance from the lounge, and before long, Marcie came back out.

"She fell asleep right away," she said. "And she was happy to see her SammyJack again."

Ellie smiled. Samuel L. Jackson (also known as SammyJack) was a stuffed pink Octopus that Clara had given her to take on vacation when she'd first come aboard the *Spirit* as a passenger. "Well, she's welcome to have him back if she wants," Ellie said. "Although I've gotten used to him hanging out on my dresser."

Over on the big couch on the far side of the room, four guests were enjoying a pre-recorded football game. Something must have happened, because one of the guys was making whooping noises and pumping his fist. She glanced over, and recognized Julian and Dick right away, along with two fifty-something women she'd only met in passing. Dick was the one whooping, and Julian was next to him, holding a tall glass of beer and watching the antics with a bemused expression.

She smiled to herself and carried two cups of tea across the kitchen and set them on the counter near the high stools. *The Lofts* were working their magic once again, and this time without her assistance. Four former strangers were enjoying an evening together, talking and laughing. The women were slightly sunburnt, and probably they'd spent too much time on the upper decks enjoying the view. Julian, still prim and proper, had a genuine smile on his face for once, and Dick still looked like an extra in a biker movie. His leather jacket was emblazoned with scary looking skulls and flames. But there too was another truism. It was foolish to judge a book by its cover.

Well, you could learn a lot about a book by the cover. But it didn't work the same way with people. Most people wanted the same things, she thought. They wanted to be respected, and they wanted to be loved and to love, and they wanted to have a sense of purpose and to believe that what they did mattered, not only to themselves but to others. Junior was respected on the force, she could tell by the way he described his work, and he was loved by his family. So why had he left the career he'd worked so hard to attain?

Junior had been a sensitive child, always in tune with the feelings of the people around him. In a way, it had been a surprise that Cole had gone into teaching, not his older brother. But Junior had idolized his father, and he'd gone straight into the academy after two years of college. He couldn't wait to be just like his Dad.

And then Ronnie died, she thought.

Marcie's mouth tugged down. She looked into the deep brown tea in her cup like it might contain an answer to the question she was holding. Ellie hopped up onto the seat next to her and sipped her own tea. It was dark and rich with a hint of Bergamot, and the flowery scent rose into her nostrils like the steam from a hot bath. "What are you thinking, hon?" she asked.

"Men!" Marcie said, picking up her teacup and slamming it back down on the counter. "That's what I'm thinking. I'm thinking that life would be a lot easier without men." She glanced at Ellie. "Like, where does that Paul guy get off? Doesn't he work for you?"

"Yes, but—"

"Yes," Marcie said acidly, "but he listened to Junior and ran off. And why? Because Junior's a man? Because he gets to make all the decisions without consulting anyone. Like me, his *wife*? Am I supposed to just shut up and like it? Men! I'm done with the lot of them."

"Hey," Dick called over from his position on the couch. He had a bowl of popcorn in his lap, and the remains of a beer in front of him on the coffee table. "We're not *all* bad."

Ellie shot him a small smile. "Sorry. We didn't mean to disturb you."

Julian's beer was almost full. He lifted it up in salute. "Would you ladies like to join us? Dick has been teaching me about American football. What a dreadful spectacle it is." He smiled at Marcie. "But it's a good distraction. And we could all use a distraction now and again."

Marcie nodded. "Thanks for the offer. It's very kind. But I think I'll sit here and complain about my husband for another twenty minutes or so." She laughed a little, and Julian nodded politely, his gaze slipping back to the television.

Ellie raised her voice to be heard over the sound of the game. "Thanks for the parrot call. It worked, just like you said it would."

Julian looked gratified, and he got up from the couch to come closer. He set his drink on the high counter. "I'm pleased to hear that! And was the feathered chap okay? He wasn't harmed?"

"He's safe and sound. Whoever stole him left him food and water, so thankfully there was no physical harm done. Thanks to you."

Julian's face turned a rather unattractive shade of pink. "Ah. Well. It was my pleasure. Do you know who took him?"

Ellie shook her head. "Not yet. Our head of security is looking into it, but before I could ask him for the latest news, he had to take care of something else." As she spoke, she realized that she wasn't *too* annoyed with Paul. Yes, she was miffed that he'd run off without her, but Junior had needed an ally, and Paul had stepped right into the gap. That's who Paul was.

Julian sipped his beer and winced like it was the most disgusting thing he'd ever tasted. But then he caught her watching and he forced himself to smile. "American beer. Very – um – light and refreshing."

"Did you enjoy your day at sea?" Ellie asked.

Julian looked pleased. "I did. After we spoke, I found that roseate spoonbill I was looking for. He was nestled along one of the smaller islands we passed." He blinked his eyes dreamily. "He was stunning. And there will be more to see tomorrow in the Bahamas. I am *quite* content, and you can expect an enthusiastic recommendation on your website when I return."

"I'm happy to hear that," Ellie said.

Julian leaned forward and spoke low. "Could I trouble you for a favor?"

She nodded.

"Dick keeps hinting that he'll be joining me tomorrow on my birdwatching excursion. He's a nice enough chap, but very *loud*, and birds don't like noise. They prefer to make the noise themselves." He shot her a guilty look. "Perhaps you could find him an alternate activity for tomorrow? Something more suited to his temperament?"

Ellie chuckled. "Sure. I'll drop a few hints before I go to bed. There's a food and wine tour I think he'd like."

Julian looked pleased. "Wonderful." He glanced at Marcie. "And on behalf of the male half of the species, my apologies. We may be showy in our plumage," he adjusted his pristine blue polo shirt, "but we do make mistakes." Marcie nodded and laughed, and Julian went back to the couch and sat carefully between Dick and the women. The sportscaster gleefully announced a touchdown and Dick stood up quickly, shouting in victory. Julian quickly gripped his beer with two hands, holding it steady so it wouldn't spill.

"I'm sure Junior will explain when he gets back," Ellie said, once they were alone again. "He's probably—"

Before she could finish the thought, the double doors nearby burst open. Violet came through, half-dragging Melanie in her wake. Melanie's steps were uneven, but she didn't seem to be resisting. It was more like she was unsteady on her feet. "Ellie, you need to hear this." She pulled Melanie to the kitchen and released her. Melanie gripped the edge of the counter and glared at Violet.

"Tell them what you told me," Violet said.

Melanie had almost stumbled as Violet released her arm, and at first Ellie was concerned that Violet had been too rough. But Melanie's eyes were slightly unfocused, and her mouth was a sloppily drawn line. Where was the prickly woman she'd met earlier? The woman with the proud spine and the hard eyes? Melanie stood taller with painful dignity, but then her shoulders slumped, and her spine rounded. "This isn't *fair*," she whined, pointing at Violet. "She made me come. I was supposed to stay in my room."

Marcie got up from her chair. "She could use some water. And a strong cup of coffee. Violet, sit her down, please, before she falls." Her tone said that this wasn't a request.

Violet looked at Marcie in surprise, then turned to Ellie with a grin. "Do they manufacture Tappet women in Florida? Because she sounds *exactly* like you."

"Hush," Ellie said, helping Violet maneuver the intoxicated woman into a chair, keeping one hand on her shoulders until she was safely seated. She shot Violet a disapproving look. "What did you do to her?"

"Me? Nothing." Violet's green eyes were bright, and her voice was triumphant. "I got tired of waiting around, so I decided to have a friendly grown-up chat with Melanie here. The kind with martinis. *Lots* of martinis. And after a certain amount of yelling, and an unnecessary amount of name-calling, and the fourth martini, Miss *I-have-terrible-taste-in-friends* finally started talking."

Melanie rolled her eyes. "It doesn't matter anyway. They can't do anything. He's leaving *tomorrow*."

"Who's leaving tomorrow?" Ellie asked.

"Murray. Michael. What*ever*. He's outta here. And then I can go home and get away from *her*." Melanie pointed at Violet, and her hand slapped down on the counter as if she weren't fully in control of her limbs. She turned to Marcie, who was hitting buttons on the coffee maker. "Did you know I used to *date* her? Ugh."

Ellie slid a big tumbler of water in front of Melanie. "Drink that."

"She never could hold her booze," Violet said, her expression smug. Then her mouth tightened. "The bounty hunter wasn't after Melanie. She was after Murray. And apparently Murray isn't Murray. He's Michael."

"But Paul looked into his background. Very thoroughly. Murray the Magnificent has a website and everything. The reviews for his magic shows go back *years*. Are you saying that was all fake?"

Melanie scoffed. "I thought she was supposed to be super-smart or something."

The sports fans on the couch were looking over now, curiosity plain on their faces. Julian stood and took a step in their direction. "Does she need a doctor? If it's alcohol poisoning—"

"Pipe down, Jeeves," Melanie shot back. "Go eat a scone. I'm *fine*." Marcie brought over a cup of coffee and Melanie drank it, ignoring the water at her elbow.

Ellie shot Julian a grateful look. "I'll take her in for a checkup." She spoke to Violet in a low voice. "Let's get her into my room, shall we?"

"Clara's in there," Marcie reminded her.

"Right." Ellie frowned. They could take Melanie downstairs to the crew level, but she didn't seem too steady on her feet. And out here, they had an audience. That might be okay, but she didn't want to discuss a murder in front of the guests.

"Tell you what," Marcie said. "I'll take Clara back to our room."

"Are you sure? I could—"

Marcie smiled. "It's okay, Mom. You have responsibilities. And so do I. But you'll tell me all about it later, right?"

Ellie nodded. "I will. I promise." She turned to Violet. "Get her up on her feet. I'll call Paul."

Chapter Thirty

THEY FIT INSIDE THE ONE-PERSON stateroom, barely. Violet sat next to Melanie on the twin-sized bed, and Ellie leaned against the modular storage wall opposite. Paul had promised to come when he could, but he didn't say when that would be. He was in the middle of something important.

"How much vodka did you give her?" Ellie asked.

"I didn't force it on her, if that's what you're worried about," Violet said. "Murray never came back to the room, and after you and Paul left, I waited for almost two hours. I was hungry and tired of waiting, so I invited myself in for a chat." She smiled arrogantly. "And you were right. I was wrong to take my feelings out on Melanie in front of everyone. I needed to take them out on her privately. It was the right thing to do."

"You're a jerk," Melanie said. She sounded slightly more coherent now, and she had finished drinking her water. "It's not *my* fault you were never home." She turned to Ellie. "I mean — what did she expect? That I'd live my life, alone, and then pretend to be a couple when she deigned to visit me? Three weeks a year isn't a relationship. It's a joke."

"So, we got to talking," Violet said.

"And drinking," Melanie said, rubbing her head with one hand.

"And drinking," Violet agreed, "and I finally got Mel tipsy enough to loosen that stubborn tongue of hers." She glanced at her watch. "I'm tired of waiting for Paul. That story she spun about Murray protecting her? The car crash thing? It was an act. He paid her to say those things. She's been lying the whole time."

"It was a performance," Melanie insisted, stifling a yawn. "And a very good one, if you ask me."

"Her *employer* is fleeing his creditors in California. He was a finance guy. A stockbroker of some kind? And he stole their money."

"He was a wealth manager" Melanie said defensively. "And he didn't *steal* anything. It was all a big misunderstanding, but they wouldn't listen. Stocks can lose their value. Anyone with half a brain knows that."

"Anyway, Murray," she held up air quotes, "*managed* his clients' wealth right into the ground. And into his own pockets. The feds are building a case against him. His former partner turned against him. Murray, or Michael, or whatever his name is — he decided to gather up as much cash as he could and make a break for it. And he hired Mel here to provide cover."

"So where does Murray the Magnificent come in?" Ellie asked.

"Apparently he rented the guy's identity," Violet said. "He borrowed his website, his bird, the whole deal. Then he replaced the pictures on various websites. Murray the Magnificent is a real guy, but he's mostly retired. Our 'Murray' basically grew a beard, did a tacky photo shoot, and used the guy's passport to get on the ship."

"And you helped him?" Ellie nudged Melanie with one foot. "Why?"

Melanie seemed to shrug off the question. But finally, she spoke. "He told them that the investments were risky. He did! I'm sure it was all a misunderstanding. And we were friends. He tipped me really well when I was having a hard time paying my rent, and he was a good listener." Her voice softened. "I had to help him. It was the right thing to do." She met Ellie's eyes defiantly. "And yes, he paid me for my time. And why not? Michael doesn't take advantage of people, ever. That's not who he is."

"If that's true, why is he running?" Ellie asked.

Worry flickered across Melanie's face. "Well, some of his former clients are not good people. They blamed him for the market crash, and they were going to hurt him if they caught him. Otherwise he would have stayed in town to fight the charges. He would have won too! He had the truth on his side." She shrugged. "But his former clients don't care about the truth. They're just blaming him."

Violet groaned. "I swear, this is so *like you*, Mel. Only this time, you didn't just give some bozo with a sob story all your lunch money. You committed actual crimes for him. Did you even think about that? Did you think about what would happen to you when you got back to LA? He was going to walk, and you were going to go to jail!"

She shook her head. "No, they wouldn't be able to prove anything in the end. All I did was take a cruise."

"All you did was assist in the commission of a felony," Violet snapped. "But your 'friend' glossed right over that part, didn't he?"

Two soft knocks on the door announced Paul's arrival. When the door swung open, Junior stood beside him.

PAUL PUT THE DOOR AT his back. Junior stood next to Ellie, and he leaned over, speaking quietly. "Ma. I'm sorry—"

She put a hand on his arm, silencing him. "It's okay," she said softly. "We'll be fine. I promise. Just explain everything to Marcie."

He blinked rapidly, "It's just..."

Ellie squeezed his hand. "I understand."

Violet was telling Paul what they'd learned so far. Before long, Paul raised his hand to interrupt. "I know. We located the couple that you confronted outside the theater. Apparently, the gentleman was a client of one Mr. Michael Bilsack, a wealth manager currently under investigation for running a Ponzi scheme. Mr. Bilsack reportedly ran off with fifty million dollars that don't belong to him." Paul's expression darkened. "It seems our magician is hiding more than business cards up his sleeve. He must have been alarmed to see one of his former clients here aboard the ship. But 'Murray' offered Robert hush money in the form of jewelry and a high-value poker chip."

"And the guy took them?" Ellie asked.

Paul nodded. "Robert said that a conviction was unlikely to get his investment back, so he agreed to accept payment here, aboard the ship, and let the matter drop." His nostrils flared. "Apparently Robert's wife hadn't realized the extent of her husband's losses. Kameron is finding her a new place to stay. It was either that or hold her for an assault charge."

"She hit him with her purse? Again?" Ellie asked.

"A high-heeled shoe," Junior said, wincing.

Ellie felt a flutter of pride. "Well, we suspected Murray was faking the theft! Now we have proof. He must have stowed the bird away to add credence to the lie." She gestured at Melanie. "And we have an eyewitness to the conspiracy." She grinned. "You got him, Paul!"

"Unfortunately, I don't. I've got a ship-wide search going. No one has seen 'Murray' in hours. And don't forget, we still don't know who killed Samantha. It may have been the same guy, but—"

"Michael didn't hurt anyone!" Melanie bit her lip. "He's not like that."

"Do you know where he went?" Paul asked.

"No," Melanie's voice was salt and acid.

"Mel, you *have* to tell," Violet said. "Besides, I'm sure Paul would be *happy* to tell the feds how you helped us catch the guy. Maybe it will keep you out of prison." She stared daggers at Paul. "That's right, isn't it, Officer Gumbs?"

"I'm sure that could be arranged."

Melanie looked miserable. "I'm serious. I don't know where he is. He left in the afternoon and he said he was going up on the deck to get some air. I haven't seen him since." Catching Violet's skeptical expression, she added, "I don't know why you won't believe me."

"Your stint as pathological liar might have something to do with it," Violet snapped.

"I was *acting*. It was a *job*."

Paul pulled out his radio and instructed his team to check all the bars and restaurants for their missing person. "We'll find him," he said. "We found the parrot, and we'll find him too. It's just a matter of time."

"We may have a bigger problem," Ellie said. She told him what Melanie had said about 'Murray's' former clients. "If our victim was chasing Murray, and if *she* was murdered, maybe it's because someone else was after Murray too. If his former clients were as dangerous as he implied, perhaps they were willing to mow down anyone in their way."

"Or he could have killed the girl himself," Violet said. "Let's not let him off the hook so easily."

"Michael made mistakes," Melanie said. "And maybe he is *technically* a criminal. But we were together the whole time. There's no way he killed that woman. And after it happened, he was totally freaked. At first, he didn't want to leave the room at all, but then later he said he was safer when he was out with other people. I didn't understand at the time, I thought he was just trying to convince everyone he was Murray, but...."

"But maybe he knew someone wanted him dead," Violet finished.

"I'm going to help with the search," Paul said. "Violet, I want you to keep Melanie with you. Ron, stay with Ellie. I—" The radio in Paul's hand flared to life.

"Officer Gumbs come back. This is the bridge."

Paul's face flashed in surprise. But he immediately responded. "Gumbs here."

"Um. I'm not sure what to make of this, but we've spotted a small craft starboard. It's one of ours." As he spoke, the low thrum of the engines, almost always present, increased in vibration. The ship was slowing down.

"What does he mean?" Ellie asked.

"Bridge, this is Officer Achebe. Confirmed. We're missing a lifeboat. Number sixteen, starboard forward. Hold on." There was a crackle and a long silence. "I have a visual. There are two men in the craft. One appears to be bound. Speed, approximately ten knots."

"Acknowledged," the man from the bridge replied. "Officer Gumbs, please advise."

"Officer Achebe here," Kameron's voice sounded eager now. "Requesting permission to deploy the silver shark."

Paul stood for a moment, the radio hanging in his hand, his eyes focused far away. She imagined him flipping through all the clipboards on his office wall. Ellie held her breath. What was the silver shark? And why did Kameron sound like she was ready to open her presents on Christmas morning? She wanted to ask, but she couldn't risk interrupting his concentration.

"Officer Gumbs? Come back." Kameron's voice was steady.

When Paul spoke, his voice had a new urgency. "All available security personnel. We have a code *diamond.* I repeat: we have a code diamond. This is not a drill. Man your stations and await further instructions. I want flood lights, now." His mouth compressed. "Silver shark authorized. But I want you in constant radio contact." He depressed the button one more time. "Bridge. I recommend you call the local authorities. Backup is appreciated. Code diamond confirmed."

He glanced at the group. "I need to run. Tappets, you keep our witness *safe*. Do you hear me?" And then he was out the door, bounding down the hall like a horse on the gallop, his radio crackling and spitting out information as he went.

"Oh my God," Violet said, turning to Ellie, her eyes bright with excitement. She got up off the mattress and gestured that Melanie should do the same. "We *have* to see this. Come on."

"But Paul said—" Junior began.

"It's fine. We'll keep her close." Violet nodded. "Come on, Mel. Ellie, do you have binoculars?"

Chapter Thirty-One

THEY POUNDED UP THE WIDE, blue-carpeted stairs like a herd of small elephants. The plastic strap of the binoculars bit into Ellie's wrist. She'd found them in the Lost and Found box in the kitchen, and they looked like they'd been purchased during the Carter administration, but they would have to do. Julian and the rest of the television watchers were gone, or she might have asked to borrow his. Her quad muscles burned as she took step after step.

Junior was keeping pace with her, walking at her side, even though his long legs could have propelled him faster. He glanced back at Violet and Melanie. "Violet, what's a code diamond?"

She was right at his heels. "Piracy."

"Piracy!" Junior boomed. A young couple holding hands was headed down the stairs to their right, and their heads snapped over to stare. Junior lowered his voice as they continued up, turning on the carpeted platform between landings. "Okay. I know you guys do things differently here. But why are we moving *toward* the piracy. Shouldn't we be moving away? Like far, far, away?"

Violet grinned at him. "Oh, don't worry. Piracy means that valuables or personnel have been taken from the ship by force. It's not like we're facing off against Bluebeard, or the Pirates of Peking, or even a bunch of kidnappers with semi-automatic machine guns. Whoever those two are, they stole a *lifeboat*. And have you ever ridden in one?"

"No."

"I have. And stealing a lifeboat – Well, it's like..." Violet was breathing hard with the effort of the climb, "it's like fleeing the scene of a crime in a golf cart. Yes, lifeboats are secure and full of emergency equipment. But they're super slow." She paused on the promenade level, one hand on her back, taking deeper breaths. "Come on. If Paul let Kameron take the silver shark out, she's probably having the best day of her life."

The promenade deck circled the ship like a wide wooden belt. Cool sea air slapped their faces as soon as they went outside, and Ellie brushed back the hair whipping around her face. It was windy! All around the ship, the sea was black. Tiny white-capped waves made the surface distinct from the night sky. Flood lights blared outward onto the water, creating a pool of light. The engines idled, but the enormous cruise ship was motionless in the water. They went to the wooden rail and looked out toward the horizon. Ellie scanned the water. Next to her, she heard Junior's sharp intake of breath. He pointed. "I see them!"

Further down, the couple they'd passed on the stairs was at the railing too. They must have doubled back. The man pointed. "There! I see the pirates!" Around him, a small crowd was gathering. The mass of people began flattening toward the railing. Ellie took Junior's hand and edged down the rail, looking for a better view of the small white boat in the distance. It bobbed in the water just past the edge of the floodlit circle like a child's toy. She could see two tiny figures, both with dark hair. She lifted the binoculars and shifted her head back and forth, trying to settle the viewfinder on the small craft. She turned the dial to make the image clearer. Only the right side offered a sharper view.

"I think I see the magician!" she said. "He's sitting in the middle, and he's not moving." She squinted. "He might have his hands tied behind his back."

"Who is driving the boat?" Junior asked. "He's bigger. But that's not saying much."

"I know, right?" Violet said. "He's such a tiny wart of a man."

"Stop it," Melanie said, her voice thick like she might cry. "Is Michael okay? Is he hurt?" She leaned over the railing, gripping it hard, struggling to see. Ellie repositioned the binoculars and focused on the man in the back of the lifeboat. The center of his body was dark, and his shirtsleeves were a lighter color. A vest? When she saw a small white circle, surrounded by a halo of red, her heart skipped a beat. "I can't believe it. It's Dick!" she called out, turning to Violet. "He was one of mine. Such a nice guy too."

Junior said, "Let me see." He took the binoculars and looked closely. "Seriously, Ma? Is there *anyone* you won't make friends with? Those symbols on his vest? That man belongs to The Hollywood Reapers. They're a gang. A gang with ties to organized crime. And you've been *hanging out* with him?"

Ellie felt her face getting hot. "Hey! You met him too. At lunch, on Saint John. And where was this valuable intelligence then, huh? But no. Blame your mother for not knowing every motorcycle gang in the world."

"I didn't see his vest, Ma. He was far away."

"Uh-huh." She smiled at him. Then a fresh flood of worry raced through her body, and she reached for the radio at her waist. In all the excitement, she'd forgotten to turn the volume up. "Paul, the other man on the boat is Dick Salvo. He was staying in *The Lofts*. Junior says he might be in a gang."

"Acknowledged." Paul's voice sounded tight. Just then, a small silver speedboat made a wide arc through the water around the back of the cruise ship, throwing up spray.

"Oh, now she's just showing off," Violet said, grinning. Ellie took the binoculars back. There were three people in the silver shark. She spotted a driver, someone in a security uniform, and someone in head to toe black, crouched down. The ship was moving so fast that they were hard to see. The speedboat reached the lifeboat in no time and did a wide circle all the way around it, throwing up spray as it went. For a moment, it was hard to see the lifeboat.

"Deployed," an unfamiliar voice said over the radio.

"See?" Violet said. "It's like watching a cheetah catch a slug. They're fine. They'll—" Her eyes went wide. "Oh!"

Even at a distance, Dick's body language was clear. He held one hand out in front of himself. *It must be a weapon*, Ellie thought. And the two occupants of the speedboat were standing now, their hands held high, not moving.

Ellie's heart leapt into her throat. To her left and right, she heard gasps and bursts of anxious voices. The deck was chock full of passengers now. The railing was loaded, and the audience was five layers deep. Women stood on tiptoe. A young couple dressed for dinner had just stepped out onto the deck, holding hands. A darling little black girl sat high on her father's shoulders, trying to get a better look. Out on the choppy water, the occupants of the boat stood motionless like they were frozen in time. Dick held his arm out, unwavering despite the rocking motion of the boat. She lowered her hand from her mouth. "Are they negotiating?" She whispered. The silver shark had come to rest near the lifeboat, and the man in the officer's uniform was standing tall with his arms at his sides.

Junior nodded. "I assume so. Wait. Do you see that?"

Behind Dick, moving very slowly, a dark figure was climbing up the opposite side of the lifeboat. *They're wearing a wetsuit,* Ellie thought. The figure was slender. Feminine, even from a distance. Ellie's heart did a triple jump inside her chest. "Kameron," she whispered, her left hand tightening on the slippery wooden rail. She squeezed her eyes shut and dropped the binoculars to her chest. "Please, Lord. Keep her safe."

On her left, Violet gripped her hand. Melanie was at Violet's side, her expression anxious. Junior's presence was comforting. He pointed at the tiny figure, speaking quietly. "It's okay. She's got this, Ma. Look! The boat isn't even rocking. And I don't think that's a gun. If it were, he'd have fired already."

At the center of the boat, Murray was wiggling like a landed fish, jerking his body from side to side. The motion caught Dick's attention, and he swung around. As he moved his outstretched arm swung with him, traveling perpendicularly like the boom at the bottom of a sail.

Violet's hand gripped Ellie's harder. "No! He can't."

But fast — almost too fast to see — Kameron's arm swept upward, forcing his weapon-hand high. At the same time, her other hand went up to grasp his wrist, and she torqued her whole body to the side, twisting her hips. Dick's body rotated, and now his weapon hand was behind him, pinioned. Something jutted upward from his hand. Kameron's knee came up, hard, slamming into the big man's chin.

"Ow!" Someone shouted from the left. "That had to hurt."

"You go girl!" A woman was shouting high up on the lido deck. "You beat that pirate down!" Scattered applause followed.

Ellie lifted the binoculars again. *Oh my.* Kameron's face was serene as she dropped her leg and used an additional twist of her upper body to jerk the knife (it was a knife!) free from Dick's hand. She flung the knife into the water and put her knee square on his back, dropping him onto the floor of the boat. The two men from the speedboat came over, and they swarmed over top of the man, bending down to add their strength to hers. Murray was still wiggling. He looked like he was working his way toward the back of the lifeboat. "He'd better not jump in the ocean with his hands tied behind his back." Ellie said, almost to herself. "He's no Houdini."

Melanie huffed. "You'd get out of the way too, if you were nearly murdered."

Murray managed to get to his feet. One of his arms waved up in the air – he'd managed to get it loose. But just then, the captive on the floor of the boat struggled, and the lifeboat tilted. Murray fell into the water with a splash.

Ellie grabbed her radio, but before she could talk, Kameron had dived back into the water. She treaded water nearby while Murray splashed and spluttered and tried to swim away. As he began to sink, she swam forward. Before long, she was dragging him back to the boat, her arm cradled around his head, swimming backward with easy strokes, Murray's head resting on her chest like he was a big baby. Her companions reached down to pull both of them back into the silver shark.

Ellie's radio flared back to life. "Officer Achebe here. Mission success. Advise Doctor Strunk we have a detainee with a broken wrist. Lifeboat sixteen is ready for retrieval. Achebe out." A few moments later, the silver shark swept past the starboard side of the ship, and Kameron looked up, noticing her audience for the first time. She waved and smiled. Someone hooted. Someone was clapping, and before long the sounds of hundreds of people cheering rose like a happy wave, drowning out the sounds of the sea and the thrum of an approaching helicopter. The helicopter's bright light shone like an eye in the darkness, sweeping the water and the now-empty lifeboat.

Two chimes sounded over the ship's intercom. Ben's voice was calm and self-assured. "Good evening. This is your captain speaking. You may have noticed we've come to a stop, but we'll be back on the move shortly. If you look to our left, you'll see some lights in the distance. We're approaching The Commonwealth of the Bahamas, seven hundred beautiful islands full of spectacular sightseeing and entertainment. And if you look out to our right, you'll see our security team raising a lifeboat as part of a late-night safety drill."

Violet and Ellie exchanged an amused look.

"If you're in the mood for something sweet," Ben continued, "the kitchen staff tells me they're preparing their famous midnight dessert buffet. They're serving twenty kinds of chocolate tonight! And don't forget to try our signature drink: the coconut crocodile. Enjoy your evening, my friends, and we'll have you all safe and sound in Nassau by sunrise."

Chapter Thirty-Two

THE NEXT NIGHT, A JAZZ quartet played a slow song on the stage at the Moonlight lounge. The lights were dim, and the low murmur of conversation was a comforting accompaniment to the music and the movements of the dancers. According to *Cruise News You Can Use*, this event was called 'Grooving after Dark' and it was nothing more than slow dance music and a wonderful atmosphere to relax in after the end of a long and active day. Junior and Marcie had spent the day on Nassau while she and Clara had hung out in Roberta's office, making phone calls and being goofy. And then had come several episodes of The Bossy Bee, and more sweets than Marcie was likely to approve of.

Junior and Marcie were dancing near the stage, talking animatedly about something or another. Violet and Melanie were closer, swaying to the music, their eyes closed. After the song ended, they broke apart and Violet clapped, waving at the players with a big smile. The saxophonist smiled back and leaned over to whisper something in the cello player's ear.

Ellie pulled away from Ben's embrace as Violet came over. Ben was a good dancer; and after a bit of practice she'd managed to avoid stepping on his toes. It had been a long time since she'd danced!

"How are you two this fine evening?" Violet asked.

"I'm good," Ben said, stifling a yawn. "But I'll sleep like a champ tonight. It turns out that conducting a boat chase in international waters creates a lot of paperwork. I gave Paul and Kameron the day off. They were *so* exhausted."

"Well, they've had a busy week," Ellie said. "Although Kameron insisted on watching Clara for us this evening. She said that Marcie and Junior needed the evening to themselves. But I think she just loves kids. We need to find Kameron a good guy, stat. She needs some babies of her own."

"Are you back to matchmaking?" Violet grinned. "I thought you only did that for the guests. Please tell us you're not going to start matching the crew up, willy-nilly. If they break up, there's going to be way too much drama."

"So I've seen," Ellie said, pretending to glare at Violet. "But yes, I apply my talents wherever they're needed. And speaking of matchmaking, what's going on with you and Melanie? Did you make up?"

"I guess that depends upon what you mean." She looked over at Melanie, who was at the bar, talking to the bartender. "I said what I needed to say. So did she. What happened between us wasn't just her fault. It was mine too."

"That doesn't mean it was right for her to—"

Violet shook her head. "Oh, I know. She was cruel in the end. But she had her reasons. She's headed back to Los Angeles to testify. She spoke to the D.A.'s assistant, and if she cooperates, she may get away with just probation. She's moving on. And so am I." Violet sighed and looked down at her toes. When she looked up, she said. "You can be sad about a good decision, right?"

Ben nodded. "Yes. You can be happy and sad at the same time. Just like Ellie's kids are glad she's happy, but they're sad to see her with someone who isn't their dad." He squeezed Ellie's hand, and she squeezed back.

After a bit, Violet went over to chat with the kids, and Ellie rested her chin on Ben's shoulder as the music started up again. He was a good dancer. Sometimes it was hard to tell which one of them was leading, but did it matter, so long as they were both in sync? "I forgot to tell you that Madame Tiffany wants you come by her store the next chance you have. She said she's getting some stuff into stock that you'll like."

"Is that so?" Ben remarked.

"Oh, she was full of helpful suggestions. Apparently, she told Junior that she had a vision that there was a dangerous person aboard the *Spirit* and that he needed to keep a close eye on me. My son, being the practical man that he is, immediately dismissed her warning as nonsense. But that didn't stop him from bossing me around all week to make sure I wasn't in any danger." She chuckled. "It reminded me of something Marcie said when we were at the beach. She said we Tappets have a very bossy form of love. And I think she's right." She looked up at Ben. "I ever get too bossy, I want you to tell me. Right away."

"Are you *telling me* what to do?" Ben pulled back.

"Ah, no. I just..."

He smiled down at her with those deep blue eyes of his. "El, if we ever have a problem, I'll let you know. I promise."

"I know." She sighed. "It's just that I've been stressed, watching Marcie and Junior fight, and I don't want *us* to fight."

Ben looked over at Junior and Marcie. They were sitting at a booth talking to Violet. Violet was gesturing with expansive gestures of her hands and Marcie was laughing. "They look like they're doing fine to me."

"I know. But—"

"How's this," Ben said. "Someday, you and I are going to fight. I'll hurt your feelings. And you'll hurt mine. Let's just agree right now that we're going to work through it."

"Oh, it's that simple huh?" She smiled at him.

He shrugged. “Storms come and go. All that matters is that we’re in the same ship, right?” He leaned in close and put his arms around her, turning her gently in time with the music.

She closed her eyes. “Next time I go home for a visit, will you come with me?”

He held her tighter. “Next time.”

Chapter Thirty-Three

ELLIE'S EYES FLEW OPEN BEFORE her alarm went off the next morning. She turned off the alarm with a slap of her hand and jumped out of bed. It was time to go home! To see Cole, and to spend whole weeks with the family, and to catch up with her friends back in Florida. She put on her traveling clothes: comfortable pants and a long pink tunic with an embroidered edge. Her turquoise-blue suitcase stood packed and ready by the door. In the hallway outside her room, she tucked her crew badge into her purse. She stepped into the lounge, made sure it was tidy, and looked around the big room. *I'll be back*, she thought. Why feel sad about one home or the other when you were fortunate enough to have two? Until she came back, this one would keep.

Junior was waiting at *Cuppa* when she arrived. He handed her a paper cup. It was warm in her hands, and she looked down at it dubiously. "Coffee?"

"Earl Grey," he said, stifling a yawn. "Where are we headed?"

"Paul wanted us to meet him downstairs," she said.

He took a long drink from his cup and nodded. "Well, whatever this thing is that he wanted to show us, I hope it was worth getting up in the dark." His eyes were sleepy, and she looped her arm through his. "I'll show you the way."

Paul stood outside the captain's dining room in his formal uniform. And he had his arms behind his back like a soldier in formation. But he relaxed when he saw them. "I'm glad you made it," he said. "Here, I thought you two would want to see this." He opened the door to the dining room and let them inside. Then he beckoned them over to the panoramic window, standing on the port side. At the moment, the view was of the front of another cruise ship. Hydraulic lifts were raised up alongside it, loading pallets of material for resupply. Paul pointed down at the concrete dock between the two ships. "There. That's where it's going to happen."

Before long two men in dark suits emerged from a small van parked alongside the dock. "They're FBI," he said proudly. "And they flew here from the LA Field office." Five people marched toward the men in a V-formation. Kameron was in the center. On her right and left were Michael Bilsack and Dick Salvo. Each of the men were escorted by a security guard. Michael and Dick were both handcuffed with their hands in front of them. Kameron shook the hands of both agents, handed them something to sign, and then waited while the two men were loaded into the van.

"Why aren't you down there?" Ellie asked.

Paul was watching Kameron with a small, proud smile. "It was her arrest. She should be the one to bring them in."

Kameron beckoned to someone behind her. Melanie walked up, her spine stiff, her hands at her sides. She was wearing one of her magician's assistant dresses and pulling her luggage behind her. Kameron spoke to the FBI agents for several minutes. She gestured at Melanie, at the ship, and at the van. The agents spoke to Melanie at length, and then at last they seemed to come to an agreement. One of them signaled the van, and it drove off. Melanie followed the agents toward the parking lot in the distance.

"There you go! One fugitive and one murderer, safely in federal custody," Paul said, tearing his eyes away from the dock reluctantly. He smiled at Ellie. "And I couldn't have done it without you interfering Tappets."

"Did you just quote Scooby-Doo?" Junior asked, laughing a little.

Paul flicked his eyes in Junior's direction. "I've studied the classics. But seriously, thank you. Both of you."

Ellie smiled up at him. "That's nice of you to say, but I didn't solve this mystery. Dick was right in front of me, and I had *no* idea he was involved."

"Your questions led us to Sal," Paul reminded her. "You knew that birdnapping note was bogus. And you found the man with the pearls, didn't you?"

"Yes, but..." She thought for a moment. "Wait. If Dick killed Samantha, those pearls didn't have anything to do with the crime, did they?"

Paul tipped his hand back and forth like a teeter totter. "Well, they *were* used in the commission of a crime. A bribe, specifically. And they did lead us in the right direction. Your suspicion about 'Murray'? It was spot on. He faked the theft of the bird to send us on a wild goose chase. When you asked about the pearls, he'd already given them to Robert as a bribe, so he improvised and claimed they were all stolen together. He was afraid we'd figure out who he really was before he disembarked in Nassau."

"Then what happened to Samantha?" Ellie asked.

"Dick used his wallet chain to strangle her," Paul said. "Strunk matched it to the marks on her neck. He probably intercepted her in the gangway. Maybe he saw her pick up Melanie's luggage tag before she checked in at the terminal. Or perhaps he'd been following her for longer. I'm not sure."

"How did her body end up outside the stateroom?" Ellie asked.

"Well, luggage is X-rayed at the terminal, so I figure Dick wheeled her body right on the ship like she was luggage. And he probably put the suitcase outside the room to intimidate Murray into going along with him. We found Samantha's brand-new crew badge in Dick's possession. He nabbed Murray at some point yesterday and stashed him in a utility closet downstairs. When Violet said she knew Murray's real identity, Dick decided to make a break for it. We were closing in. Thankfully, he didn't know the first thing about lifeboats."

"You keep calling him Murray," Ellie said.

Paul grinned. "He'll always be Murray the moron to me. He claims that Dick demanded two hundred grand, or else he'd end up just like the bounty hunter. When Murray hesitated, Dick knocked him out and tied him up. Murray probably wasn't worth anything to him dead. Dick was taking him back to collect the reward."

"Either that or he was going to turn him into one of his former clients," Junior said, clearly disturbed by the thought. "That gang is notorious."

"And where's Sal?" Ellie asked anxiously. "Did the FBI want him too?"

Paul smirked. "They agreed to let a local parrot rescue group take custody of him. They've got two dozen parrots at the sanctuary, and they say Sal will fit right in."

"That's wonderful!" Ellie felt a surge of joy. "I'll email Julian to let him know. He's going to be *so* happy."

Junior looked at Paul. "Tell Mom the best part. I haven't; I figured you'd want to break the news."

Paul grinned. "Do you remember that long number you found on the notepad in Murray room? It's a *bank account* number. As in, offshore banking! As in, you found the money he stole from his customers."

Ellie's heart lifted. At least some of the victims were going to get their savings back! "That's wonderful! When did you figure that out?"

"Last night, after we questioned Robert. As soon as we knew there was missing money involved, it clicked." Paul tapped his temple. "And your son was immensely helpful during the interrogation. Robert swore he wouldn't talk without a lawyer, but Ron calmed him right down and got the information from him." He glanced at Junior. "Are you sure you don't want to be a cop? Because you've got your mother's instincts. Your father's too, I expect."

Junior ducked his head. "I know. It's just, after my Dad died, I realized that I had been doing it for him all along. And now that he's gone it's not the same. Can I be a good cop? Sure. But is it going to make me happy? No. Maybe it's selfish of me, but I can't spend the rest of my life in a job I don't want."

"That's not selfish," Paul said. "That's common sense. What will you do next?"

"I have no idea! Maybe I'll finish up my bachelor's degree. I'll need to work, but that's fine. Marcie suggested that we swap. She'll do full time and I'll work part time for a while. She seemed pretty happy about that, actually. She's been wanting to work more hours without feeling bad about leaving Clara in daycare." He reached out to shake Paul's hand. "Thanks for looking out for my Mom. She'll never admit it, but she needs someone to watch her back. She gets all revved up and then there's no slowing her down."

"I'm standing right here," Ellie said. She wanted to hug them both, but she had the sense it might spoil the moment, so she waited.

Paul glanced at her as if he knew what she'd been thinking. "Can you stick around for one more hour? I know you have a long drive home, but I think you'll want to be here for this. Bring Marcie and Clara too."

THE CEREMONY TOOK PLACE ON the starboard side of the upper deck. The blue waters of PortMiami sparkled beneath the cheerful yellow sun in the distance. Someone had set out a dozen chairs and a podium. Tall arrangements of orange tiger lilies rustled gently in the breeze. Ellie sat in the back row with Marcie, Junior, and Clara.

The chairs filled up quickly. Most attendees were from the security team, but Elie spotted two housekeepers in their uniforms and a young woman she'd seen working as a host in the steakhouse. Paul stood at the front, waiting, his hands resting together in front of his body. At the last minute, Violet dropped into the seat next to Ellie. She was wearing her formal officer's uniform, the one with the corded epaulets on her shoulders, and she'd pinned up her hair.

Ben arrived last, walking down the center aisle with his back straight like an arrow. He stood behind the podium and beamed at the audience like they were the most beautiful thing he'd ever seen. "Welcome, everyone. As you all know, our security team works hard every day to keep our guests and crew safe from harm. When a guest joins us for a cruise, we invite them to stow their worries away. For a week or longer, they get to set their cares aside and enjoy time with friends and family, knowing that we'll keep them safe. But threats exist. Now, not all security issues are as thrilling as the ones we've recently experienced," Ben raised an eyebrow and laughter rang out from the group, "and sometimes we worry that we'll lose our best people to a more — how shall I put it? — high-adrenaline life. None of you are here on the *Spirit* because you have to be, you're here because you choose to be. And you work hard to keep your skills sharp, even though you may not need those skills on every sailing, but the work pays off. Lives are saved. Threats are neutralized. And dangerous criminals are brought to justice."

A murmur of agreement ran through the group.

"Today," Ben said, "I'm pleased to recognize one of the finest officers I've ever had the pleasure of working with. She holds black belts in Aikido, Tae Kwon Do, and Krav Maga. She's endlessly calm under pressure, which is something we senior officers could learn from, I think." His eyes flicked toward the back of the group, almost too quick to catch. Ellie turned her head slightly and caught sight of Violet's pink cheeks and downward glance. She nodded at the captain and sat up taller.

"Kameron Achebe has many talents, but her talents are borne out of hard work. She runs our crew fitness program, she mentors aspiring officers, and she even takes the time to do a little babysitting now and again." Ben waved with his fingers at Clara, and everyone turned to look. Clara, blushing, turned her head away. "But yesterday we all saw something new. Something frightening. A guest was taken off our ship by force, and Kameron, along with her rapid response team, neutralized the threat. Those responsible are now in custody, thanks to her." Ben glanced at Paul and he nodded.

"Officer Achebe. Please step forward," Paul said.

Kameron must have been waiting nearby! She walked up the aisle and stood in front of Paul. She'd loosened her braids, and her natural dark hair hung loose and beautiful down her back. Her nails were freshly painted and shaped, and she'd put on makeup. Ellie thought she recognized Violet's touch, and she glanced over. Violet beamed at her, and Ellie knew exactly what she was thinking. Wasn't Kameron beautiful?

Kameron saluted Paul, and he returned the gesture. From his jacket pocket, he produced two dark rectangles of fabric, adorned with strips of golden cord. He deftly removed the rank from Kameron's shoulders and attached the new one, which carried a diamond shape. He seemed to be taking care not to look into her eyes, and his mouth compressed slightly in concentration. From her position near the edge of the audience, Ellie thought she spotted Kameron's mouth quirk up in a smile.

"Kameron Achebe," the captain continued, "Today we are pleased to confer upon you the rank of Master of Arms, which symbolizes your honor, your courage, and the responsibilities you've taken on."

Paul stepped back and shouted, "Three cheers for Officer Achebe!"

The audience rose to their feet and cheered. Kameron turned to face them, and she smiled, a rare blush crossing her cheeks. She waved them off, and they cheered even louder. "I thank you," she said simply. "And I promise to always do my best."

"Well," Ben said, once the cheering had subsided, "I hate to be the buzzkill, but I'm afraid we all have duties to attend to."

Kameron nodded and took a step toward the door. Paul grabbed her shoulder. "No. Not *you*," he said in his Jamaican-accented English. "You will stay for ten minutes and allow people to compliment you."

He whispered something in her ear, and she looked surprised. She looked up at him and smiled. Ellie watched, holding her breath, as Paul smiled back. That was *not* the smile of a boss proud of his employee. It was something else entirely! Did Paul even know how he was coming across? Probably not, but Kameron certainly caught it.

But the moment passed as quickly as it had come, and Kameron went to stand next to the captain. Paul stepped back, his expression all business now.

Well, that's promising, Ellie thought. *As soon as I get back, we'll need to see what can be done about those two!*

When she reached Kameron, Ellie skipped the handshake and reached out, giving her a firm hug. Kameron laughed a little. "I'm overwhelmed," Kameron said. "I'm glad I didn't notice half the ship watching me during the rescue, or I think I would have lost my nerve."

"Everyone likes a hero, hon. Enjoy your moment! And on behalf of the owners, thank you." She sensed that Kameron was becoming increasingly uncomfortable with the attention, so she turned and beckoned Marcie over. Marcie leaned down and whispered something in Clara's ear, and the little girl ran over, her legs fast beneath her pale blue dress.

"Hi," Clara said.

Kameron crouched down immediately. "Hello Clara."

"Did you want to say something?" Ellie prompted.

"Con-gat-yoo-lations!" Clara shouted, slurring the syllables but making her meaning clear with her bright smile and upthrust arms. She looked back at Marcie, then forward again. "I'll meese you."

Kameron swept her up in a hug. "And I'll miss you, little one. Come see us again, okay?"

Marcie came up to retrieve her daughter. "Thank you, Kameron, for everything. You're always welcome at our home in Gainesville. You can stay in Mom's room."

"Oh, I see," Ellie teased. "I'm gone for less than a year and you're already turning my room into a hotel." She smiled at Kameron. "She means it, too."

Marcie said goodbye to Kameron and carried Clara off, bouncing her a little in the way that made the girl laugh. Ellie stepped away to make room for a fresh group of admirers. "We do keep things interesting, don't we?" Violet said, coming up alongside her.

"I saw Melanie go off with the FBI this morning," Ellie said. "It looked like it went okay. They didn't cuff her, anyway. Paul says she's a witness, not a suspect."

"That's good. I hope it turns out okay for her," Violet said. "And how are you doing? Are you ready for a proper vacation?"

Ellie laughed. "Oh my, yes! Speaking of which, this is for you." She reached into her handbag and pulled out a portable radio. "Roberta will be boarding soon. Please give her my regards, along with her radio, and ask her never to leave us again, for any reason! As of this exact moment, I am officially off the clock."

"Enjoy your time away. But do hurry back! We're headed to the Mexican Riviera, and you're going to love it." Her green eyes sparkled with mischief. "Think about all the fun we'll have! Golden sunsets. New beaches! Thirty different kinds of margaritas. Salsa music! While you're gone, I'm going to rework my act." She held her arms up and danced forward and back. "In fact, I'm thinking—" Violet's eye caught on something in the back of the room and Ellie turned to see. Junior had his car keys in his hand, and he was twirling them around in a circle.

Ellie smiled at Violet. "Don't get into too much trouble while I'm gone," she said. Ben was over by the podium, watching them talk. He blew her a kiss, and she caught it before spinning around and walking up to the kids, putting her arm around Junior's shoulder. "What do you say we get out of here? Fast? Before something else happens?"

They pulled their luggage through the ship, zig-zagging through the crowd. Guests formed a snaking line through the atrium as they waited for their turn to disembark. Ellie led her family to an unmarked elevator and took them downstairs to the crew level. As they exited the carriage, they saw a flock of housekeepers waiting, their freshly pressed uniforms as neat as pins, chattering companionably as they waited for the signal bell. The moment the last of the guests had departed, the crew would zoom into action. Literal tons of laundry would head down to the industrial machines on the lower decks for a wash and tumble. Sheets and blankets would be tossed over a thousand beds, vegetables would be chopped up for soups, garnishes, and delicacies to make even the most jaded eater swoon. Wynona would implore her actors to sing louder and emote even harder. And Ben would find the love letter she'd stuck under his stateroom door, telling him how much she couldn't wait to be back on board and in his arms.

The horn blasted outside, just once, and Ellie closed her eyes for a moment, feeling the atmosphere of the ship pressing inward on her like an enveloping hug. *I'll be back*, she thought.

"What are you thinking, Ma?" Junior asked.

She looped her arm through his. "Just that I'm ready to go home."

"Me too," he said. "How about you, Clara? Are you ready to go?"

But the little girl wasn't listening. She was looking back at the *Adventurous Spirit* as her mother walked her forward, holding her hand. They stepped across the gangplank and onto the concrete deck. All the while Clara was calling, "Bye, ship! Byeeeeee!"

What's Next for Ellie Tappet?

Thanks for joining me for another Ellie Tappet adventure. I want to offer special thanks to my wonderful beta readers, Micha, Miraz, and Sara for helping me make this story even better. You're the best!

Are You Ready for Ellie's Spookiest Case Yet?

Next up, Ellie and her friends face their most puzzling mystery yet in The Case of the Red Phantom. When a contestant in the Sweetie Pie Baking Competition goes overboard inside their locked stateroom rumors float through the air like vapor. Did a vengeful spirit known as the Red Phantom push the victim into the churning waters below?

Let's Stay in Touch!

Sign up for my list to receive fun and nerdy notes, travelogues, and a FREE starter library. Visit **cheribaker.com/News** to get started.

More from this Series

For a complete list of books in this series and the latest Ellie Tappet news, visit **cheribaker.com/Ellie**

Find Your Next Series

Want more cozy mysteries that celebrate friendship and fun? Check out the **Butterfly Island Mysteries**.

Do you love snarky sleuths, office mysteries, and workplace drama? You'll enjoy the **Kat Voyzey Mysteries**.

How about a world of corporate espionage and betrayal? Meet Jessica Warne in the **Emerald City Spies Trilogy**.

Excited for more Ellie Tappet? See what's available and what's coming next at **CheriBaker.com/Ellie**

More from Cheri Baker

The Kat Voyzey Mysteries

Involuntary Turnover
Orientation to Murder
Death by Team Building
Cutting the Track

The Ellie Tappet Cruise Ship Mysteries

The Case of the Missing Finger
The Case of the Karaoke Killer
The Case of the Floating Funeral
The Case of the Lady in the Luggage
The Case of the Red Phantom
The Case of the Fond Farewell

Emerald City Spies

The Assistant
Power Play
Hostile Takeover

The Butterfly Island Mysteries

A View to Die For
Death at Dagger Cove
Shadow of a Doubt

About The Author

Hey there. My name is Cheri, and I'm a writer from Seattle, Washington.

I've been a book lover my entire life, and for many years writing was my hobby, something I did on the weekends or in the early morning before work. My first novel, *Involuntary Turnover*, was loosely based on my experiences working in human resources. Not the murder part; just the setting! It took me ten years to write my first two novels, working around the demands of a busy job, but eventually I traded my business suits for jeans and began writing full time. Now, I'm lucky enough to have wonderful readers all around the globe.

When I'm not writing I spend my time reading, hanging out with my husband, watching terrible monster movies, drinking coffee, having movie nights with friends, playing Dungeons and Dragons, walking through the city, and thinking up twisty murder plots. Rainy weather makes me happy, and so does the fact that you read one of my books! Thanks so much for supporting my work.

www.ingramcontent.com/pod-product-compliance
Ingram Content Group UK Ltd.
Pitfield, Milton Keynes, MK11 3LW, UK
UKHW020224250726
13967UKWH00001B/176

9 781952 200083